THE
UNFORGETTABLE
Miss Baldwin

GAIL INGIS

GAIL INGIS
THE UNFORGETTABLE MISS BALDWIN

Copyright © 2023 by Gail Ingis
gailingis.com
Revised Edition
Cover Image and Design: Jun Ares Cover Design.
Interior Book Design/Formatting: Jennipher Tripp
Copy Editor: Deborah Dove

Published in the United States of America Published by Ingis Design Ideas
ISBN (Print) 978-0-578-54647-6
ISBN (eBook) 978-0-578-54604-9

Ingis

ACKNOWLEDGMENTS

Enormous thanks to my special team for turning the original book into a better one.

Joanna D'Angelo, my amazing editor, publicist, friend, and confidant, for her enthusiastic support, plotting, creativity, wisdom, and guidance. She pushes me to reach higher with every word, every line, and every page. Special thanks for finding my talented cover artist.

Jean Largis, copy editor, and Sue Connelly, reader. Tireless readers and friends, they offer their opinions of my work with a smile.

Jennipher Tripp, formatter, a force to reckon with, figures out the best way to display my books and turns them into works of art. She is a fabulous formatter and is always there.

Barbara Gerber, my fantastic sister-in-law, never stops supporting my writing, my art and has been there through the years. She reads my writing, applauds me, hugs me, and tells all her friends about my books and artwork.

My children and my fifteen grandchildren never stop giving me the greatest greetings, support, and warm hugs. They keep me on my toes with their texts. I love each one of them!

Tom Claus, my hero hubby, crops my wild prose into something resembling a botanical garden and makes sure my books have the polish our readers appreciate.

Last, dear reader, for choosing to spend time with this book, writing to me, giving me your thoughts about my books, and making me your friend.

Dear Reader,

Thank you for choosing *The Unforgettable Miss Baldwin* and spending time with Allie and Peter. I hope you find a good laugh and a good cry as you follow their adventure. For me, there's nothing better.

This tale is a historical romance set in the Gilded Age in New York City. I created the settings to reflect nineteenth-century New York City and Connecticut, with research and a sprinkle of imagination, as I love to do. My heroine, Allie, a forward-thinking reporter and supporter of women's right to vote, has no time to fall in love—until she meets Peter, the owner of a successful detective agency. But he's all business. Romance will not distract him until he's good and ready.

Allie and Peter travel together to investigate a fire in Fairfield, Connecticut, when she receives a mysterious music box with a thinly veiled menacing note. Her well-meaning family does what they usually do—meddle. Allie's sweet dog, a black-and-white Great Dane, causes rounds of ruckuses. My secondary characters offer fun, mystery, and more than a few challenges. But hey, is fiction less strange than the truth?

At present, I'm working on my next book, my memoirs of growing up in blue-collar neighborhoods, my family, career, school, and life lessons I've learned.

I'd love to hear from you anytime—visit my website at gailingis.com.

All the best,
    Gail

DEDICATION

End-to-end thanks to my amazing husband, Thomas Harrison Claus, who acted as an editor on my behalf, tirelessly supporting me and my writing. He has shown me what happily ever after means. For that, and a million other reasons, this book is dedicated to you, Tom

CHAPTER 1

NEW YORK CITY ~ MONDAY, NOVEMBER 1, 1886

*J*oseph Baldwin slammed his hand on the desk and waved a stack of complaint letters in his daughter's face. "These are evidence of our readers' objections to your presence at a dance hall and your support for women's suffrage."

Allie Baldwin wiped her sweaty hands on her dress, her stomach dropping with nauseating abruptness. "This is impossible, Papa, to stand here and listen to your tirade."

"You are dabbling in dangerous waters. There's no place for women in politics. They will never earn the right to vote," he said, pointing to Allie with his inking pen.

Allie clamped her hand to her throat and waited for a moment, gathering her thoughts. "Papa, not that long ago, the authorities arrested women in Rochester, New York, after they illegally tried to vote in the presidential election. I am sure they will try to vote again. These women will starve and sacrifice their lives for their rights."

"I'm aware, but they disobeyed the law. Jailing them is just punishment."

Allie gasped and slammed her hand against her mouth, then lowered it as she spoke. "It's shameful. The women did not deserve jail."

"No daughter of mine would ever be so bold. Your disagreement shows me you do not understand the seriousness of these issues."

"I'm sorry, Papa, but you are wrong. There's a law stating that single women can vote if they own property. That's ridiculous since the law stops them from owning property. It's demoralizing. How dare men think women cannot handle voting. We must change the law. At the moment, my concern is today's rally and why you forbid me to go."

"Stop this stubbornness. The fight is going nowhere, and it's dangerous."

Allie's face felt flushed. "This is my opportunity to write about women's rights, voting, and freedom. Assign another reporter to society issues, please, Papa."

The banjo clock's *tick, tick, tick* evoked memories of Mama's lessons to mind her manners. The steady rhythm usually calmed Allie. But not today. A daughter should not defy her father, much less her superior.

"Papa, remember your promise?"

He stroked the edge of his thick mustache. "My promise?"

She gripped the edge of his desk. "Yes, you promised after graduation, my writing could include public issues like this suffrage rally."

"Maybe you had better talk to your mother."

"Why? Does Mama disapprove?"

"Our concern is your safety."

"What? That's absurd." She grabbed the side chair by the window, rolled it to his desk, and sat, her spine straight as Mama's knitting needle. She smoothed the peacock-blue, high-collared dress billowing over her knees and stared into her father's face. "I do not see what could be harmful. I am wearing my tattered coat and hat. No one will bother with an old lady in rags."

"Once again, you're putting yourself in . . ." Allie's father hesitated and cleared his throat. "This is an unsubstantial argument. You cannot create subterfuge with a coat and hat." He pointed to the stack of letters. "These letters are not jesting. Serious readers wrote disparaging remarks about you."

She clasped her hands to her chest. "About me?"

"I'm afraid so. Our readers question your visit to a dance hall. It might well have been a brothel."

"Brothel? It was not. I saved a young girl from being accosted. What are the objections?"

His forehead furrowed. "Aside from several whining about this vote, that you—a sophisticated, young woman—frequented a questionable place. Good deeds do not always reflect wise decision-making."

She bent over in her chair. Bile bubbled up from her throat. "Were all the readers upset?"

"Not all the letters were damning. I will admit a few indicated your bravery was commendable."

She straightened up and placed her hands together under her chin. "That is a small victory, don't you think so?"

"You cannot keep writing about controversial subjects. Our readers will stop buying our paper and pick up the *City Sun Times*."

"We have scores of women readers. Why would you not think they will remain loyal?"

"Do you believe your support of the vote has captured our women readers?"

"I do. The ladies I have spoken to at society luncheons also want the vote."

Her father shook his head. "I don't know. It's a gamble."

Her heart pounded in her ears. "Please, Papa, how can I convince you to approve? I will not be in danger in those old clothes."

"Listen to me, my ambitious daughter. Today's rally is not fresh news. The fight for the vote is half a century old, and nothing has changed. Do you understand?"

"Women keep fighting despite the failures. Don't you find that worthwhile?"

He stood and crossed his arms over his chest. "No. Women's rights are a hopeless cause to pursue."

"It's a problem, Papa. Women have no choice. They stay home—raise the children, crochet, and gossip. They should be able to choose, even if they prefer to stay home and gossip."

"If they don't run the house and raise the children, who will?"

"Voting and freedom of choice are the requests. Do you think women will forego their responsibilities?"

Allie refused to back down. Disobedience to her father crushed her spirit. The fight was not with her father but with her father's obligation, as publisher of his newspaper, *The New York Sentinel,* to inform and support women. She had to convince him to agree. The excitement and enthusiasm for her column could increase the readership, but his worry about losing readers pushed him into a corner. He worried more about money than women's rights. Her heart cried out. She had a voice. But it was her voice he wanted to silence.

"The women will continue to raise the children and keep house." Allie bit her lip, trying to hold back the tears and keep her lips from trembling.

Joseph shook his head. "I cannot give you permission to write about these sensitive political issues."

"You have inspired me to be a writer, to tell the truth, to be diverse. Why not give me the freedom to write this column? My column offers women respect and acknowledges their intelligence."

He leaned forward and twisted his lips. "Your safety is vital."

"It's a public event. There will be patrolmen there."

"Your writing will bring unrest."

"Why?"

"Enough!" Her father's hand came down hard on his desk, the letters fluttering to the floor.

Allie jerked to her feet, sending her chair flying backward. It hit the wall across from his desk with a satisfying bang. "If Adam were sitting here instead of me, this would not be a discussion." Her voice was loud enough to wake the family. She fixed her hand over her mouth. A tear escaped. She always enjoyed her father's library, but not today. Now the deep wine colors seemed morbid, and the touches of green and gold from his porcelain collection felt gauche and pretentious.

"For heaven's sake, your brother has nothing to do with this. Maybe it will be different in fifty years, but right now, I don't want another caper, and I don't want another stack of letters complaining about you." He hesitated for a long moment. "I don't want you putting yourself at risk. I will not publish your rally articles. We'll see about going to this event. I'll talk it over with your mother. Maybe take Mia along to keep you out of trouble."

Allie should not have to get consent for anything, especially not attending the rally. After all, at twenty-three and not a child, she wanted to be a serious journalist, at a serious paper, covering serious news. Instead, she was still writing about another wedding, another birth, another engagement, and wasting time answering readers' inquiries to the "Dear Miss Demeanor's" advice column.

Why must I ask for permission?

She plucked at her dress, her muscles quivering. Her father

pulled a handkerchief from his coat pocket and handed it to her. She dried her tears.

She put her arms around him and planted a kiss on his cheek. "I'm sure you know that you have taught me to be courageous and stand up for what I believe."

He gave her a kiss that tickled and made her giggle. "And you know that I only want the best for you. I'm proud of you despite your antics."

Darn him.

"Regardless, Papa, I will get those interviews . . ." she said, turning away with "today" on her lips. She closed the door, leaving the harsh words behind her, and marched down the hallway to get some breakfast.

It was late, and she had to get to the rally. Allie stopped in the kitchen for a cup of coffee and one of Mrs. Bigelow's baked muffins cooling on the counter. She wrapped one in a napkin, took a few sips of coffee, and ran past the library. The carpeted stairs silenced her footsteps as she ran to her bedroom.

Allie took a bite of the soft cinnamon muffin topped with crunchy, buttery crumbs. Captyn, her black-and-white Great Dane, sidled up to her. She patted his smooth, furry head. "This is too sugary for you, and I can't play now. I'm off to do my duty. Shhh. No barking."

She pulled her carpetbag out from the back of her wardrobe and changed into a long, brown day dress and a bulky, tattered coat that hid her slender frame. She tucked her curls under a floppy hat, stuffed her feet into scruffy boots, and tied the laces while Captyn licked the back of her hand.

"Captyn, stop that." She wiped the back of her hand on the old coat, picked up the bag with its three bocce balls sewed into the lining for protection, and hefted it over her shoulder. Taking her unfinished muffin and closing the door behind her, she ran past her sister's bedroom and down the back stairs to the hallway. She darted into the courtyard where the gardener worked with the fall plantings, filling the garden with the warm colors of orange and yellow chrysanthemums. "Morning, Miss Allie."

"Good morning," Allie said in a cheery tone. *Uh-oh. He recognized me hiding under this hat.*

She opened the gate, ran to the line of carriages waiting for a fare, and beckoned the nearest buggy.

CHAPTER 2

On a sunny, brisk autumn day, hundreds of people surrounded New York City Hall, where Presidents Lincoln and Grant lay in state the year before. The building became a symbol for Peter—the touchstone to life as a boy of eleven when he went to work with his father. The flags and the thousands with their tears viewing the past presidents remained in his heart.

This day, the crowds stood shoulder to shoulder, filling the streets and gardens across the way. Hundreds of women and men assembled for the women's rally. Many carried signs with the word *VOTE*. A few eggs thrown at the display signs by those who opposed the rally partially obliterated the inked letters.

In his spiffy checked trousers, Peter Harrison did not see the missile coming as he stood guard on the hall's steps. Raw, rotten egg coated his forehead and dripped down his face onto his high-buttoned, grey sack coat, perfectly clean and tailored not too many minutes ago. His stomach retched at the awful smell he would have to tolerate all day. He yanked a handkerchief out of his pocket and wiped off the dirty, sticky mess.

"Where are you, you sneaky bastards?" Peter mumbled.

The culprits blended in with the spectators. Peter spotted more eggs hurtling over the crowd, splattering on the steps and knocking off hats. When the miscreants moved closer, Peter's six-foot-four frame allowed him to observe two youths battling a woman. Zigzagging his way past clusters of listeners, his face tight and his eyes keen, he prepared to confront the criminals.

"Stand back, stand back. Let me through." Peter, now stuck in the thick of the crowd, spied the two stocky youths reaching for eggs piled high in two buckets on the cobblestone street. A woman, engulfed in a tattered coat, shouted, "Stop it!" Her dark blue hat flopped as she grunted, hefting an oversized carpetbag and swinging it at the head of the taller youth.

The Women's Social Reform Society had hired the Harrison Detective Agency to keep order at the rally. Damned if he'd let a cantankerous old woman and two oversized youths ruin the peace at one of his events. Peter pushed through the crowd to get to the troublesome trio. He grinned at the sight of the old woman. Who was this person trying to be an enforcer for the beleaguered ladies on the podium?

The old woman swung her bag at the youths again. "How dare you bully those women!"

The boys leaned back, avoiding the swing, and snorted with laughter. She gawked and wound up for another go. After another swing and a miss, the bag made a strange thumping sound, like a croquet mallet hitting a ball through a wicket, as it moved through the air.

"Lady, you look funny," the taller of the two crowed.

"You find me funny? I'll give you funny." She took a deep breath and tightened her hold on the handles, then whirled the bag in a wide arc, missing the shorter youth by a hair's breadth.

"Look out, Jeb," he shouted.

She clipped the older one on the shoulder.

"Ouch! Ya could've given me more warning, Ed." Jeb rubbed the sore spot and glared at the woman.

The woman stood with her feet shoulder-width apart, sporting a pair of brown galoshes that looked like they'd slogged across Ireland and back.

"What's your problem? We ain't got no beef with you," Ed echoed.

Jeb lobbed two more eggs at the stage and knocked off a speaker's plumed hat.

Before the woman could swing her flowered bag again, Jeb grabbed ahold of it, but her steely grip on the handle triggered a tug-of-war. People came alongside to help. A sturdy woman in a baker's apron reached for the purse to help while an older man sporting a porkpie hat joined Jeb's side. A football cheer went up for their favorite, the boys or the woman. "Rah, Rah, S-s-s-t! Boom! Ah-hh!"

With no other choice, Peter dug into his pants' pocket for his whistle and blew it three times to signal his men stationed around the perimeter. Everyone froze. The bag thumped on the cobblestones and lay there. Two of Peter's best men, O'Malley and Spencer, arrived from opposite directions and grabbed the brothers by their collars.

"Dang," Ed said. "Let go. We ain't done nothin' wrong. Just tryin' to get those wacky women to shut up."

"Throwing eggs and shouting insults is wrong!" Peter thundered as he reached the boys, grabbing the bucket of eggs at their feet.

Jeb shook his fist at Peter. "You ain't got no right to steal 'r eggs."

They both earned a slap on their ears from his men.

"Take these young men to the station. Captain O'Sullivan can remind them about proper behavior and notify their parents," Peter ordered.

Ed and Jeb continued to squawk as Peter's men dragged them away.

"Hey, why did you take those boys away?" the porkpie-hat

man yelled.

"Having some harmless fun," another joined in.

"Throwing eggs at women is not harmless fun," the apron lady declared.

"Trash is what they are," a man bellowed from the crowd.

"The boys belong in jail!" hollered another.

Peter's hackles rose as the people traded angry barbs.

He addressed the woman with the carpetbag. "Ma'am, there's trouble brewing from your interference. I cannot trust you. You are going to have to come with me to the guest tent to calm down."

"I will do no such thing." The old woman yanked her hat downward. "If you don't mind, I will stay right here and listen to the rest of the speeches."

Her voice sounded loud for an old woman.

"Ma'am." Peter offered the crook of his arm. "Permit me to escort you to the tent where you can have a cup of tea and collect yourself. Then you may return to hear the women speakers."

"I am not moving."

A screech of wagon wheels sounded down the street. Peter's eyes narrowed. A mob of men and women climbed down from a wagon and rushed into the excited crowd. "Stop the vote! Stop the vote!"

"Damn! Rabble-rousers," Peter projected.

Three short whistles from Peter and his men launched into action again. The old woman could be trouble in the burgeoning melee. Scooping her into his arms, he strode to the tent, taking her out of the commotion.

"Unhand me!" she yelled.

"Just keeping you from making more trouble, ma'am."

She pointed at him. "I am not the troublemaker here."

He moved straight away, not paying attention to her or her

squirming. "Must you shriek in my ear?" he asked in a stern tone.

"I wanted to be sure you heard me."

"I heard you fine, and I'm not unhanding you."

She sucked in a big breath. "Put me down, or I'll scream in your ear again."

"Ma'am, I'm sure you had good intentions to stop those boys, but your actions added to the commotion."

Peter tightened his hold and hauled her to a tented area on the side of the building. The woman squirmed like a monkey in a barrel of eels.

"You have nerve. Who do you think you are, anyway? Put me down this instant."

Peter tried to keep his balance and maintain his hold.

"I can't do that, ma'am. You can either calm down here or in a jail cell," Peter said in a biting tone while looking straight ahead. He leaned his head left and then right, trying to see around the woman's confounded hat, realizing too late when his booted foot tripped on one of the thick ropes on the ground securing the tent.

"My hat!"

"Oomph!" Peter toppled over, twisting his large frame to cushion the woman's body. Unfortunately, it also meant taking the brunt of the fall. His bowler went flying.

They landed with a bone-jarring thud.

The old woman yelped.

Peter groaned and shifted on the hard-packed earth. Still clutching the woman, he winced and shook his head to clear his vision.

His breath caught at the sight in his arms. He stared at an oval face with high cheekbones, a sprinkling of freckles decorating a pert nose, and a tumble of enchanting red curls.

Peter straightened the spectacles on her nose. With the

magnificent, impish creature sprawled atop him, the commotion behind him faded away.

He knitted his brows. "You are no old lady."

"I never said I was," she said, her words clipped.

"Miss, I believe we need to alter our positions." Peter smoothly lifted her off his body, scrambled to his feet, and helped her up.

"Heavens." The young woman wobbled in her clunky galoshes, and her hands flew to her wild curls.

"My hat," she whined in a loud voice.

Spotting the monstrosity dangling from a tent pole, Peter reached up and unhooked it. He turned it over as if seeking an identifying mark and regarded her with a teasing gaze.

The woman stared back at him. A rueful smile curved her lips. She cocked her head. "Sir, will you please return my hat?" she asked in a sweet voice while her eyes shot daggers at him.

He almost grinned. Almost. There was something irresistible about the woman, a coquettish feminism he'd never encountered before. The women he'd met were anything but flirty. They were rather serious ladies with an unrelenting passion for seeing this rally succeed. How he ever mistook her for an elderly matron was beyond him. Her youthfulness was apparent not only in her actions but in her beauty. It was the old, tattered clothing that made him assume her age matched her appearance.

"My hat if you please."

"Not until you answer my question," he said, his voice mellow. "Why did you wear these unlikely clothes?" he asked, trying to ignore how the lady's freckles made her look like a naughty imp.

She planted both hands squarely on her hips. At least he thought they were her hips under that bulky coat.

"Did no one teach you it's rude to be blunt?"

"You were engaged in a public altercation, placing yourself and others at risk."

Her smirk changed into a regal smile. "I did no such thing."

Peter waved the hat in front of her pert nose. "Then explain."

She shrugged. "I dressed for inclement weather. Besides, what I am wearing is none of your business. Those thugs needed a lesson. I did well on my own, thank you."

"You think so, do you?" He cracked a smile at her antics.

"I will take my hat if you don't mind." She snatched it from his hands, yanked it down on her head, and tied the strings under her stubborn chin.

Peter could not resist teasing her. "Did you get those boots to muck about in a barn?"

"Harrison," a voice said, booming from down the street.

Allie crossed her arms and glared at the man. "I will have you know these boots are the latest, most fashionable, finest nubuck leather."

He looked down his nose at her, enjoying their banter. "Your fancy boots can't save you, and you could be in a bit of trouble."

She glared at him. "What kind of trouble?"

"Wait in the tent, or I'll arrest you on charges of disorderly conduct and disturbing the peace," Peter said over his shoulder, grabbing his hat from the ground as he rushed away.

CHAPTER 3

"*N*o one is charging me with that...that...whatever he said." Allie grabbed her bag, hooked on the rope securing the tent, and hefted it onto her shoulder. She poked her head inside. "Humph." There was neither a teapot nor a teacup in sight. Not even a lowly biscuit. Just a few tables and chairs. Nothing inviting there. She supposed the organizers hadn't had time to set up refreshments.

You should stay.

Double darn that annoying inner voice. If she stayed, what would that accomplish?

Allie's good friend Frankie Waverly would know what to do. She could've come and probably would've, if only Allie had invited her. Her wisdom would be useful about now. They met at college and became fast friends, with similar interests in books and studies in journalism. Their fathers had both purchased luxury residences in the Sandanko, a new architectural concept for apartment living across from Central Park.

Her inner voice would not button up. Yes, he was handsome, with deep grooves at the sides of his mouth that no doubt made women swoon when he smiled. So what? She was not about to faint at the feet of any man, let alone a tall security agent with dark, wavy hair that tumbled over his forehead.

And do not forget his broad shoulders.

"Good heavens, stop thinking about him."

Allie was not waiting around. No one would toss her in jail for disturbing the peace. She rushed across the street, her mind on the handsome man that kept her from the crushing crowds.

"Watch out, lady!" the driver hollered out, horse and carriage flying past her. She stopped, pressed a delicate hand to her chest, and caught her breath. She cut through the City Hall gardens, running past men in suits, mothers pushing baby carriages, and children playing under the watchful eye of nurse-maids. The colors of fall flowers were a blur, her floppy hat bouncing against her back. She slowed her pace to a scurry, huffing and puffing. After a few more minutes, she shifted the bag to her other shoulder with a grunt. Her smart idea of sewing the balls into the bag's lining was not conducive to making a quick getaway. *When I get home, I'll dispose of it as garden décor.*

"Get hold of yourself, Allie. You just got out of a sticky situa-tion, so stop overthinking." She cast a quick peek over her shoulder and exhaled—no one in sight, thank goodness. She turned the corner and shrieked when she bumped into a hard, broad chest.

"What in the world are you up to now?" asked a deep male voice.

She stumbled and would have toppled over if a pair of masculine hands hadn't grabbed her shoulders.

Allie heaved a sigh and beamed at her foster brother, John MacGregor, looking up at his face.

"I thought for a minute it was someone else. I'm so glad it's you. You can let me go now."

Johnny dropped his hands. "What sticky situation?"

"What do you mean? Nothing is sticky," she said, refusing to feel guilty. "Thank you for running into me," she squeaked in a singsong voice. "What are you doing downtown?"

Good work, Allie. You're doing an excellent job keeping Johnny's suspicions at bay.

Johnny threw his head back and laughed. "I had some business to do in the financial district, but I will not let you turn this into a John MacGregor conversation. You ran into me, Allie, not the other way around."

"Well, it's all a matter of perspective, is it not?"

He looked her over with eyes gleaming with humor. "You're all disheveled."

"Is that so? You came to us a scruffy, messy ten-year-old boy. Look at you now in your striped, gray cutaway and spiffy bowler. Even your trousers have a pressed crease, and it doesn't look like you ever sit down."

"Come on, Allie. You don't fool me." He crossed his arms over his chest. "Now, explain. Why are you dressed like a rag lady?"

She took a deep breath and let it out. "It's a long story. Can we talk about it later?"

"Sure. But have you been raiding Mrs. Bigelow's closet again?"

"Mrs. Bigelow asked me to donate these clothes to charity—"

"And do you intend to wear them to the Sisters of Charity's home?" he interrupted.

Allie grimaced and looked down at her boots.

"Come on, Curly Locks." He tipped up her chin with his finger and grinned. "I know you're up to something. I'll do what I can to help."

"I could never fool you, Johnny."

"Nope."

"If you must know, I tried to blend in with the crowd at the Will of Women Rally. I intended to speak to several of the spectators and speakers. Unfortunately, two louts began throwing eggs at the speakers, and of course, I had to confront them."

"Uh-huh."

"And then I, uh, left and bumped into you."

"You just left."

"Yes, no reason to stay."

Johnny slipped his hands into his pockets. "And when you confronted the louts, did you by chance use that awful sack to punctuate your comments?" He gestured toward the bag with his chin.

"I had no choice. They were aggressive. The bag is more of a threat than a weapon. I've hurt no one. Most of the time, my aim is off."

"Really? You're going to break a shoulder with that thing. Either give it up or stop trying to be what you are not—rude and aggressive. Were the police involved?"

She scuffed her boot. "The police, yikes, thank goodness they were not there. Otherwise, it would have made all the newspapers in town. The planners hired a private detective agency to protect the rally."

"Ah." His brows lifted. "Let me guess, an agent caught you and the hoodlums."

"You figured it all out, did you? Missed your calling, you did, as a splendid detective."

"You ran to escape his clutches, right?" Johnny said, ignoring her jibe.

"I wouldn't call them clutches, exactly. The man asked me to wait for him inside a tent while he settled a riot."

"You did not wait," he said with a wink.

"I could not risk getting arrested, so I bolted."

"You could have avoided all this trouble if you had taken me with you."

She thrust her chin up. "If I were a man, you wouldn't say that."

Johnny blew out a breath. He reached for her hand.

"Papa permitted me to attend the rally but worried for my safety. I mentioned wearing old lady clothes, but he didn't think it important."

Johnny tapped her on the nose. "Let me know next time you want to conduct an inquisition."

"I will." She stood on her tiptoes and kissed him on the cheek.

"C'mon, we'll hire a carriage. I'll ride home with you and help you sneak past Barnes."

He signaled a passing carriage and held her heavy sack while helping her climb in. Allie slid to the far end of the worn leather seat, giving Johnny room to sit. She fussed with her gloves and crossed her ankles.

"I am writing about truth in my column this week. Papa is not happy with my support of woman suffrage. He doesn't want me involved with politics. I am tired of writing about society news." She took a breath. "Today's rally will be big news in my column."

He placed the bag between them and leaned back.

"The truth? Gads, that is a broad topic. Will your column meet with father's approval?"

"Papa will squash any controversial articles. But the women speak truth. I intend to persist and write for all to read. I did not hear the speakers today, but my experience with the naysayers will suffice."

"You are a gifted writer with a determined spirit. Guess father needs some convincing."

Allie smiled. "Thank you, Johnny."

"I will stay around. Maybe I can help."

"Sounds wonderful. Thank you."

"If I am away next time you venture out, remember to take a couple of hulking brutes from the newspaper so you do not end up in jail."

She uncrossed her ankles. "I do not need watchdogs."

Johnny held up a hand. "You must always be cautious. It's sad, but that's life."

"I don't look for trouble; it finds me." Allie glanced out at the passing scenery, disappointed that Johnny, of all people, didn't understand her. No one did.

He tugged her chin.

Her eyes met his.

"You can't keep trying to bend the world to your will, Allie. It doesn't work that way. There are dangers out there that would overwhelm the most intrepid reporter, man or woman. The world beyond Central Park is not safe."

Allie's voice was soft. "I have never asked you this before because I did not think I had to. Where is your vote?"

His face was grim. "Want the truth, Curly Locks?"

"I thought you were always in my corner."

"I am, but I think this fight is for naught. You will never win. Women have their role and men have theirs. It's clear who does what. If the women get what they're asking for, who will raise the children? The men? Never. Women's vote will never happen."

Johnny's answer hit her in the gut. She took a deep breath and fastened her gaze out the window once more, not seeing the stores, not seeing the carriages, not seeing the people.

She swallowed a lump in her throat.

Johnny doesn't believe in me or the fight.

Was this the way it would always be? Would life always be a struggle to make men and women believe in what was right and just? And fair? If she never married, she would not have to answer to a man. Spinsterhood was becoming more and more appealing.

She straightened her shoulders and allowed the words to spill from her mouth. "I do not believe what you said. You are afraid to counter Papa."

"I agree with your father."

"You realize you are against everything I am working toward?"

"I am sorry I have upset you, but taking back what I said will make no difference. I know you work hard, but I agree with Joseph. He is right about your plight being hopeless. But I will help you get your articles published. I believe it is important to inform our readers of the latest."

The carriage rumbled past the stately new buildings, past the fancy dress shops and restaurants that peppered the burgeoning city. So much was changing, but it was all a blur to her.

JOHNNY KEPT BARNES BUSY WHILE ALLIE SAID A QUICK HELLO AND hurried up the stairs to her sanctuary, a place of peace, her pink wallpapered bedroom. Captyn jumped off her bed and darted to her. He sniffed, backed up, and barked while sitting back on his haunches. He cocked his head.

"I smell funny, don't I? Rotten eggs. I'll get these clothes off and scrub my hands."

She put her hat, the carpetbag, and the day's outfit on the bare floor, keeping them off her rug, and got out her laundry basket. Captyn stuck his snout into the middle of the pile and growled.

"I will ask the maid to wash these, and then you can let me know if they are still stinky. A deal, Captyn?" He gave her a soft woof and thumped his tail.

Barefoot, Allie padded over to the washbasin on the dresser and scrubbed her hands and face. She pulled out her blue skirt and white blouse from her wardrobe, donned them, and turned to the cheval mirror to pin up her mass of curls. *Hmm, that tumble I took with the security agent, the tall man with the muscular hands, what was his name? Harrison? Remember, with the stormy gray eyes? Oh hush, I'm never going to see him again, anyway.*

There was a knock on the door. Startled, Allie dropped the hairpins, which scattered on the floor.

The door opened. "I'm so glad you're home. I glimpsed you running past the parlor. What in heaven's name were you wearing?" her mother asked in a soft tone, stepping into the room and closing the door.

"Oh, nothing." Allie hugged her mother and gave her a peck on her cheek. She stepped back. "Mama, does this look all right without my corset?"

"You can put on a shawl, darling. It's only us."

"I can't wait to hear all about your meeting at Baldwin Hospital today and the upcoming fundraiser." Her mother was so caring, always involved in charity work somewhere.

"Cousins Frederick and Louise have been helpful. And by the way, Rork and Leila Millburn have donated to the hospital. Had I mentioned they were home?"

Allie joyfully took her mother's hands and squeezed. "No, Mama, tell me. Where are they living? When can we see them?"

Clara hugged Allie, then stepped back, and looked into her eyes. "It's hard to express how delighted I am. When they arrived yesterday, they sent me a wire telling me they would be guests at Leila's parents' home upstate. Their twenty-three-year-old son Liam and their daughter Victoria, eighteen, will live at home. They planned to purchase an available apartment here on the third floor. Rork's artist friends arranged a place for him at his former Tenth Street studio. I'm thrilled to have them home. Did I ever tell you the story of Leila, Olive, and me as best friends growing up? We protested wearing those strangling corsets and agreed to rebel. Olive and I stopped wearing them before we married, but not Leila. Her mother, your Grannie, forbade her from honoring the agreement."

Allie listened wide-eyed. "With that confession, you can't say anything negative about my fight to gain suffrage for women; you were no goodie-two-shoes in your youth fighting for your rights."

"Of course, my daughter. I understand your passion."

"Thank you."

"Changing the subject, everything is all set for the fundraiser, and of course, you'll be writing about the event, won't you?

Allie paused. "Of course, Mama. Will Aunt Leila be there?"

"I think so."

There she goes, another high society story. At least Allie could write a bit about the posh Angelicus Hotel, how the artist set up the scaffolds, laid on his back, and painted angels, clouds, and birds on the dining hall ceiling. She was sure the Sistine Chapel in Rome must have been his inspiration. Her cousin Frederick built the hotel to appeal to the upper class. He accomplished his goal. Events held there attracted the wealthy.

Allie regarded her mother, Clara Smith Baldwin, the name by which society knew her. After five children and forty-four years, she still maintained her petite, lithe figure. The only sign of her age was the white streak in her bright red hair, adding elegance to her beauty. Her mother had been a writer at the *Sentinel* before she married father. That was the end of her career.

Allie would not follow her mother's path.

"I'll see you in the parlor. Barnes is serving appetizers, and Johnny is staying for dinner."

"All right, Mama. I will be down after I make myself presentable."

Her mother blew her a kiss as she left, closing the door behind her.

Allie applied the finishing touches, tied a blue ribbon that matched her skirt into her hair, smoothed it down, pinched her cheeks, and took her Great Dane by the collar. "Come, Captyn."

Allie approached the parlor entrance and stopped.

"Barnes told me you escorted Allie home, John. Where did you find her?"

"She bumped into me when she was running . . ."

Allie marched up to her father. "Hello, Papa." Her brow scrunched. "Sorry to interrupt. Johnny was just saying I bumped into him leaving the rally today. I had an unexpected experience there and would like to write about it."

CHAPTER 4

She was on her fourth draft.

*In this glorious land, we must be mindful of the brave women
and a few good men fighting for a woman's right to vote. And it
was with great dismay that this lowly reporter observed the abuse
of five such brave women at the Will of Women Rally at City Hall
on the morning of November first. Rotten eggs, the missiles, the
culprits—two miscreant young males, along with a wagon filled
with men and women shouting, "Stop the Vote!"*

Allie crumpled up this latest piece of writing, sure that it
wouldn't meet with her father's approval. She crushed it into a
ball and hurled it across the room. All eighty-three words sailed
through the air, missed the basket, and hit Miss Annette Dover,
Allie's secretary, in the face.

"Oh, my goodness."

The young woman stumbled and sputtered, the glass of
water on her tray splashing down her pristine white blouse. The
weight of the liquid seeped into the starched fabric, making it
wilt like a droopy daisy.

"Miss Allie, I'm sorry. I spilled your water."

Annette resembled an exotic bird in flight, her hands flailing up and down her shirt.

Allie rose from her rolling swivel chair. "You're sorry? I'm sorry. If only I had better aim. Here, let me help." Allie whisked the cloth from her lunch basket and draped it around Annette's shoulders, covering the soaked garment.

"No matter, Miss Allie. I'll make myself presentable in the washroom. But I noticed your basket is full of crumpled paper. I'm worried about you getting your article done."

"Not to worry, Annette. I'll find the way to the words. But my biggest issue is to write the truth and still satisfy my father's harsh critique."

"May I remind you to finish the article by the four o'clock deadline. It's ten thirty now. What are your prospects?"

One corner of Allie's lips quirked up. "Positive."

Annette smiled. "Impressive response. Life offers few choices, yet many obligations. Please excuse me while I reclaim my state of normalcy."

Allie had always encouraged Annette to write. She would make an exceptional essayist. The nineteen-year-old, efficient, organized, and well-educated woman graduated first in her class for women at New York University. Yet she hesitated to dip her quill and put her thoughts on paper.

The breeze drifting through the open window carried more than fresh air. Unpleasant odors of horse waste floated in on a zephyr. A horse and carriage lingered a few stairs down right outside the door. Allie stood and stepped up to the window to close it and spied Johnny coming into work. He had become her father's right-hand man and probably would take over the paper with her brother Adam one day. A few moments later, Johnny stood at her desk.

"Johnny, what are you doing here? Never mind. Thank you for yesterday."

"My pleasure. It's nice to see you dressed in something other than Mrs. Bigelow's clothes. Did they find a new home at the Sisters of Charity?"

Allie gave a good-natured laugh. "Never you mind."

"Just stopping for a minute. I have a meeting upstairs with your father."

She gave Johnny a brief wave. "All right."

"Miss Allie, excuse me. This letter came for you earlier."

"Thank you, Miss Annette. Have you read it?"

"No. They marked it personal." Annette laid it on the desk.

Allie sat back at her desk and studied the cluttered office blooming with sunlight and activity. Reporters, men and a few women, hunched over their desks, immersed in the art of storytelling. Some used their pens, while others clacked on their typewriters, an ingenious contraption for creating words on the page. Allie's ears had become attuned to the mechanical symphony produced by buzzing electric lights, the flush of indoor plumbing, and the tapping of the type-writers.

Still holding the letter, she put aside her work and dreamt about the man at the rally, the man who told her to wait for him. With all the men right here in the office, why dwell on the stranger?

A few minutes later, Allie tossed another balled paper into the bin with enthusiasm. She placed her nimble fingers back on the keyboard. The security agent's face kept sneaking into her vision.

The letter had no identifying return address, only the "personal" marking in black and bold ink. She slid her pearl-handled letter opener into the seal of the envelope.

Miss Baldwin, warning, watch your step, watch what you write, or watch out!

A chill skittered up Allie's spine. She folded the note and picked up the envelope, turning it over and around.

She turned to Annette, whose desk was close to Allie's, and asked, "Annette, do you know who delivered this letter?"

"A young boy handed it to me. I grabbed his collar and asked where he got it. He said he'd tell if I'd let him go. Some old woman paid him a nickel and told him to deliver it to this newspaper office for a lady named Allie. I let go of the squirming boy and he ran off."

Allie nodded. She placed the envelope in her reticule. After all, it could just be another letter of complaint. Only this time, whoever sent it made sure it went directly to her rather than to the newspaper. Not wanting to give her father any more reasons to squash her articles, she would keep this threatening letter to herself.

Could there be a jealous reporter, someone who resented her position? After all, she had an advantage as a journalist and the daughter of a leading New York newspaper owner. She did not take her position for granted and had earned the journalist's rank. She pushed her inner voice away and concentrated on her article.

Allie's fingers rested on the keyboard. This innovative method of getting the words onto paper thrilled her.

"Are the rotten egg throwers important to mention?" she asked no one in particular. She had not noticed short and round Albert Brown, a sportswriter, passing by.

"I believe you must mention the confrontation, Allie. Your readers want details, don't you think?"

She held him silent for a moment with a raised hand, "I will think about the details necessary or not. Thank you."

Gritting her teeth, she lifted her right arm and tossed another crumpled paper into the trash. She placed her nimble fingers back on the memorized keyboard. Her hands traveled in time with her thoughts, but still the security agent's face kept sneaking into her vision.

Why do I keep thinking about him?

Before long, her basket was full to the brim.

Albert plopped down in his swivel chair. It was hard to miss the groan of the springs in protest to his stout frame. He leaned forward across his desk, his mouth open and his finger raised.

"Albert, think before you say anything else. I'm mindful of the benefits of details. I'm giving them their due."

In short order, long-legged Annette reappeared with a fresh glass of water, her blouse a bit weathered, her blonde hair coiled in a bun. "Miss Allie, excuse me. Here's your water." She set the glass down on the desk.

"Perfect. My article is half done. I could use that drink now." Allie took a few sips of the refreshing liquid.

"Half done? That's good news," Annette said.

Allie sat back in her swivel chair and observed the reporters' friendly chatter on their morning break. A bugle horn suddenly piped a blast of marching music. She turned toward the window.

"It's a group of women," shouted Billy Cooper, a fair-haired young man who wrote about business and commerce.

The driver helped five women descend from a carriage piled high with baggage. He pulled out five placards from the rear of the conveyance, handing them out while sporting a broad smile.

Hmm. There was something about him. She squinted and tried to recall where she'd seen this tall, muscular man.

He stood behind the women with his arms crossed and his legs braced apart. The ladies hefted the signs, each imprinted with the same words in bold red paint—Women Vote.

"Heavens." Allie rushed out through the arched doorway onto the first floor offices' front steps. One woman held the bugle up to her lips and played a familiar melody that Allie thought she heard at the rally.

Their voices rose in unison. *"Daughters of freedom, the truth marches on. Yield not the battle till ye have won! Heed not the corner, day by day. Clouds of oppression roll away!"*

Passersby gawked, and carriages slowed their pace. Drivers shouted at the women, now walking arm in arm. "You'll never get the vote," one man hooted.

"Go home where you belong," another shouted.

"Equality for all," the women shouted back. "Women deserve the vote."

The group was now circling the sidewalk, their signs bobbing up and down.

Allie descended the stairs of the brownstone and strode toward the women.

"Greetings. I'm Allie Baldwin of the *New York Sentinel*."

The man accompanying the group turned his head. His eyes were unmistakable.

It's him!

CHAPTER 5

The sun rising in the blue sky spotlighted the signs held by the marching women. They stopped their turnabout. A petite, gray-haired lady stepped up to Allie. "Good day, Miss Baldwin. I'm Sarah Anderson of the National Women's Suffrage Association. We were speakers at the Will of Women Rally yesterday." Her bright blue eyes sparkled.

"Hello, Miss Anderson. Thank you for coming."

A short-brimmed, red, square hat perched at a jaunty angle on Miss Anderson's head gave her the presence of a cheery garden gnome. She leaned the sign against her hip and popped her hand out to Allie in greeting.

"Your work has captured my heart," Allie said.

"I'm pleased to hear that, Miss Baldwin."

"My job at the *Sentinel* is writing about important social issues. Supporting your work in my column is my passion, although, at the moment, society news takes precedence. Please, call me Allie."

"You must call me Sarah. We know the newspaper industry disparages our movement."

Allie's lips pressed into a line. "That's true here at the *Sentinel*."

"We need a miracle to change that attitude," Sarah said. She smiled, her spectacles lifting on her rounded nose. "The rally never quite got off the ground. Some rowdy young men threw eggs at us. Then an altercation cut our speeches short. The organizers told us you might attend, and we had hoped to meet you. You were not available."

"Please accept my apology. I lost my opportunity to speak with you. I...um...had to leave."

She heard a stifled snort behind her. She hoped the ladies had not noticed.

"The rally organizers said two young malefactors were behind the rotten-egg-throwing upheaval until a courageous woman intervened."

This time, there was the sound of a throat clearing. The women could not have missed that.

"Despite that brave woman's intervention, a melee broke out. They escorted us to safety, thanks to Mr. Harrison and his courageous men," said a short woman with springy, whitish curls. She turned and waved to the man in question. Allie dared a peek at him standing there. Mr. Harrison and Moses coming down from the mountain had a great deal in common.

"I'm Anna Anderson, Sarah's cousin. Please call me Anna."

Allie offered a polite, momentary nod. "Of course."

"And this man, Mr. Harrison, president of Harrison Detective Agency, saved the day, a brave fellow," Sarah said. "If it weren't for him, we might have had more to contend with than smelly, sticky hair."

Allie turned to face him. Those gleaming eyes regarded her.

"Miss Baldwin, a pleasure," he said, reaching out his hand.

Allie clasped his—warm, strong. His touch tingled up her arm. She detected a familiar woodsy aroma, a scent her father had after shaving. He bent and touched his lips to the back of her hand. She lowered her eyes, her face burning. Her breath caught. "Thank you, sir, for saving these women."

"No thank you is necessary, Miss Baldwin. I hope we can set matters right."

She lowered her eyes for a moment, then regarded him. "Thank you."

"Although Mr. Harrison has a team of drivers, he escorted us here today. Isn't that lovely?" Anna said.

Mr. Harrison's grin shone like the moon at its apex on a clear night.

"Yes . . ." She paused. "I am sure," Allie said.

"Forgive my manners. Meet my other associates, Hannah Covington, Rebecca Davis, and Rachel Williams, our musician," Sarah said.

Each woman greeted Allie with a firm handshake.

Allie cocked her head and smiled. "My goodness, Rachel, you shook up the office staff with your horn. You are quite the talent."

Rachel's lips turned up, puffing out her already perky cheeks. "Thank you."

"Ladies, please come up to our offices. You are welcome to join us, Mr. Harrison," Allie said over her shoulder.

"I appreciate the invitation." He followed the women and Allie up the stairs and into the main office.

Allie looked up to see her father on his way toward them from his upstairs office. She sucked in a deep breath, met him halfway, leaned toward him, and whispered, "Father, I apologize if we disturbed you."

"I heard the commotion and came down to see what's going on. Annette said the women speakers from the rally stopped by for an interview. Is that so?"

"Yes. Let me get the women settled. Then I'll come right back."

"If you must."

Allie ushered the group into a meeting room. "Please make yourselves comfortable around the table."

Sarah took an end seat, Hannah and Rebecca sat side by side, and Anna and Rachel sat opposite. Mr. Harrison leaned against the wall, his feet crossed.

"Sarah, ladies, Mr. Harrison, please excuse me for a moment."

She left, closing the door behind her. "My goodness, Father, what do you want here?"

"I disagree with their agenda, but as visitors here, I think I should hear what they have to say."

"I don't want to patronize the ladies. Can we at least offer some refreshments to have with our conversation?" Allie asked.

"If you are still trying to convince me to publish news about the rally, I will disappoint you."

"I am not sure if the women will be comfortable talking with you."

Her father stared at his daughter for a moment and smoothed his fingers over his mustache. "Since the speakers are here, and I am as well, let's give it a go, shall we?"

Allie picked a piece of lint from her sleeve and peered at her father like he was King Henry VIII and had ordered "Behead her."

"Open the door. Let's get this conversation started," he said.

"Papa, I'm not ready. Please don't embarrass yourself or me. These women are hardworking and sincere. Don't break their hearts."

"I believe these ladies have a strength that goes beyond their delicate and ladylike appearance."

Allie and her father walked into the meeting room arm in arm.

"Ladies, Mr. Harrison, may I introduce Joseph Baldwin, my father, owner of the *Sentinel*."

Her father nodded and put out his hand to Mr. Harrison.

"Welcome, Harrison."

Peter nodded. "Pleasure, sir."

Mr. Baldwin turned to the women. "Ladies, welcome."

Sarah put out her hand and spoke for the group. "Pleased, I'm sure."

He took Sarah's hand and gave her one of his partial smiles.

Allie sat down at the table. Her father stood behind her.

"The women are here to talk about the rally and their aspirations." Allie said. "Sarah, please elaborate."

"Well, we had hoped to talk with Allie at the rally to get her support, but we didn't connect."

"What did you expect the rally to accomplish?" Mr. Baldwin asked.

"All of our activities are to inform the public. We've abolished slavery, but not for women."

Mr. Baldwin's lips thinned. "You don't say. I never thought of my daughters and my wife as slaves."

"Then, please, can you explain what your wife does with her time?" Sarah asked.

"Clara is a wonderful wife and mother. We have servants, and our children are adults, freeing her to raise money for our hospital."

"Is Mrs. Baldwin paid for her fundraising activities?"

"There is no reason to pay her a salary. Clara has whatever she needs and wants for nothing."

"Has Mrs. Baldwin ever thought about being salaried for her services?"

"Not that I know of," Mr. Baldwin said.

"When you met her, was she employed?"

He clutched the edge of his jacket, then released it and straightened the lapels. "Clara wrote for the paper."

"Mr. Baldwin, do you understand what I'm getting at?"

"Are you saying that a paying job and marriage are an acceptable combination for a woman?"

"I am. We want a woman to have the choice to work outside the home, to have a say in politics by voting, and to be a wife and mother too."

Sounds of affirmation came from the other women at the table. "Hear, hear."

A knock at the door brought in Annette pushing a cart filled with pastries. The aroma of cinnamon spiced the air. Annette served the guests their choices. Allie's father chose one of his favorites, a sugarcoated croissant filled with apples drenched in cinnamon. Mr. Harrison picked out a chocolate-filled croissant, and Annette plated the same for Allie. She bit into the crunchy, flaky dough—the sweetness of the chocolate cream filled her mouth. Not to mention the aroma from the steam of hot coffee. Although she preferred tea, Allie filled her cup with the brew and remained quiet while Sarah and her father conversed.

"Mr. Baldwin, I concur. Your readers come first. Liability of the press is critical."

"Do you, Miss Anderson? I thought your mission supersedes everything else."

"Our goal is to build up, not tear down. The priority is to tell the truth, satisfy your readers, and for your paper to enjoy greater financial success. How's that. Want to try it?" Sarah asked.

"Father," Allie interjected, "will you review the story, and if you approve, print it?"

Mr. Baldwin turned up his palm. "Miss Anderson makes it hard to say no. It's worth a try."

"Thank you, Mr. Baldwin," Sarah said, smiling.

"Allie, I'll expect your writing today."

"You will have it by four."

Her father strode to the door and turned. "Ladies, Mr. Harrison, a pleasure. I'm hoping for positive responses from our readers. Good day."

An audible silence filled the air until breathy releases seemed like shouts of joy.

Without a pause, Mr. Harrison asked Allie, "May I have a word in private, Miss Baldwin?"

Uh-oh. Here comes trouble.

"Excuse us, ladies," Allie said. "Please help yourselves to more refreshments."

Mr. Harrison closed the door behind them. "Miss Baldwin, why did you run away yesterday?"

She wrapped her arms wrapped around her waist and rested against the hallway wall. "There were several reasons."

"The truth, Miss Baldwin." He leaned one hand flat against the wall and bent his head toward her.

Allie swallowed. *Goodness, he's positively fearsome.*

"A fine reporter like you understands what that means."

Her heart beat a rapid tattoo against her chest. *My God, he's leaning so close he can probably hear the beats.*

"I'm waiting, Miss Baldwin."

Heavens, it's time to tell all.

"Mr. Harrison, please forgive me for my deception at the rally and running off. I'm an honest person. I could not go to jail because I'd be in trouble with my parents. Please don't tell those women about my transgression. I think I would faint dead away at the shame of it!"

"Stop." Mr. Harrison lifted his hand in front of her mouth, close enough the heat from his palm made her tremble. "Miss Baldwin, calm yourself."

"You won't throw me in jail?"

He threw back his head and laughed. And she forgot to breathe.

Oh my, he's handsome.

"I promise I won't." His laughter settled down to a grin. Allie couldn't decide which she liked more.

"Miss Baldwin, I returned to the tent to find you gone."

He rubbed the side of his face, and his big hand moved along his jawline. It was most disconcerting.

"I did not know where to find you, where you lived, or your name. I knew nothing about you. Can you understand my job was to make certain that no one got hurt?"

"I understand. I apologize."

"Apology accepted, Miss Baldwin. Shall we return to your guests?" Mr. Harrison opened the door and ushered her back into the room with a sweep of his hand.

"Thank you." Allie followed the invitation into the meeting room. Peter pulled out a chair for Allie and sat beside her.

"This is a perfect finale for our New York City visit," Sarah said with glee.

Allie clapped her hands and asked, "Can we discuss the rally?"

Sarah gave Allie a nod. "That's why we're here."

"Superb. I noted a few questions. For one, do rallies help or hinder your work?"

She slid her gaze to Mr. Harrison. He'd leaned back in his chair and was sipping his coffee. He cast a sly glimpse her way, and their eyes met. *Did he like my question?* Then she caught herself and glanced down at her notebook. *Get a grip on yourself, Allie, girl. Remember your job.*

Sarah set her cup down. "Rallies are productive, but they bring out the naysayers."

"That's true," said Anna, "The message gets lost when violence erupts."

"Not that we don't appreciate reporters." Sarah clasped her hands on the table and sat up straight. "It's just that people focus more on rotten eggs than on the rotten system."

The other women mumbled in agreement. Allie's lips turned up at the corners. Mr. Harrison's eyes reflected his smile behind his coffee cup.

"It's a dilemma in the news business. Scandals always sell more sheets, but what about the issues? What do I emphasize, the violence or the speakers? What do you think, Mr. Harrison?" Allie asked.

He shrugged his shoulders. "When good people work to affect positive change, there is always discontent."

"That's why we need you, Mr. Harrison," Sarah said. "To keep the peace."

A gleam flashed in Mr. Harrison's eyes.

A lively discussion ensued, and after an hour, Rachel raised her hand. "I'm sorry to interrupt, but we must be on our way or we will miss our train."

Allie escorted the ladies out to their carriage. "Thank you for your visit. I hope you found the time well spent."

"You are most welcome. Indeed, it was an enjoyable visit," Sara said.

Mr. Harrison handed each lady into the carriage, climbed into the driver's seat, and picked up the reins.

Allie blurted out, "Mr. Harrison."

He raised his eyebrows. "Yes, Miss Baldwin?"

"Umm, I'm curious about your company's operations. May I interview you at your office, for the sake of my column, of course?"

"We are a private company."

"If it's an inconvenience, I can interview you here at the newspaper."

"It will be more convenient at my office. My men would enjoy the visit as well. Does that work?"

"Yes," Allie said.

"An interview then, tomorrow?"

Sarah called out from the carriage, "An interview, wonderful idea."

Mr. Harrison raised his head, squared his shoulders, and gazed at Allie. "I'll pick you up here tomorrow morning at eight sharp," he said, like Mr. Darcy speaking to Elizabeth in Jane Austen's *Pride and Prejudice*.

"I'm looking forward to it, Mr. Harrison."

She waved goodbye and watched Mr. Harrison maneuver the carriage into the traffic.

"Miss Allie, your deadline. It's already two," Annette said from the building entrance.

"Goodness." Allie darted up the stairs and rushed inside. "Thank you, Annette."

Yesterday she ran from the rally, thinking she would never see Mr. Harrison again. But tomorrow she'd spend time with him.

Allie settled at her desk to finish her column. The suffrage issues would be primary, not the salacious tale of violence. She'd mention the egg throwers and protestors but would not whip up their actions to whet the appetite of readers hungry for scandal. Satisfied with her course of action, she completed her article with ten minutes to spare.

New York Sentinel

November 2nd, 1886

Byline: Miss Allie Baldwin

New York City held the Will of Women Rally, a pro-suffrage event, on the steps of City Hall. Egg-throwing hoodlums and protestors prevented the speakers, led by Sarah Anderson and her peers, from presenting their message. For safety reasons, Peter Harrison Security Company led the speakers from the site. The Woman's Suffrage League, formed earlier this year, became the first dedicated to winning the vote and advancing women's equality. The speakers, members of the League, visited the Sentinel *offices to discuss the issues. They proclaimed their equal right to vote on which leaders should run our great country...*

Allie marked the folder "Joseph Baldwin" and placed the report in her out basket. Ever efficient Annette appeared a moment later and plucked the file to deliver the article.

Tomorrow, eight a.m. sharp couldn't come soon enough.

CHAPTER 6

*a*fter a rainy night, the sun squeezed through the gray clouds. Long shadows blanketed the Fifth Avenue mansions belonging to the people Peter had dined with and protected. The mud-spattered conveyance rose and fell in rhythm with the horse's hooves clip-clopping over the cobblestones. Today, he was on his way to pick up Miss Baldwin for their upcoming meeting and to grab a morning paper. Peter flicked open his pocket watch. It was ten minutes before eight. The watch was a gift from his father five years ago to celebrate him becoming president of Harrison Detective Agency.

Passing the torch gave his father, Thomas, the time to become a better husband to his second wife and a better father to Peter's younger half-sisters than he had been to Peter.

He returned the timepiece to the vest pocket of his tailored, gray-striped day coat and fiddled with the knot of his ascot. The driver pulled the carriage up to the Sentinel building—the horses stomping and whinnying their arrival.

Miss Baldwin waved to him from the top of the stairs, tossing her red locks over her shoulder. Her lips lifted at the corners. The surrounding air seemed to glow.

Peter opened the carriage door and stepped down. "Good morning, Miss Baldwin," he said, climbing the stairs. His gaze traveled from the hem of her skirt to the short, buttoned jacket accentuating her tiny waist. She had a morning paper in hand and a smile on her face.

"What's this, Miss Baldwin?"

"Latest news, my article made the early edition."

"Congratulations. Do you mind if I look?"

"Mind? Not at all. I've earmarked the section."

In the distance, the soft rumble of thunder and the sweet fragrance of rain were in the air. The sun slid behind the clouds.

He handed her into the carriage.

"I hope stopping to pick me up was not an inconvenience," she said, settling into the seat.

He sat opposite. "Quite the contrary."

Miss Baldwin's fingers traced over the plush mohair upholstery. "My, my, such a fancy fabric. Have you used this carriage for a wedding? Yours perhaps?" She gave him a cheeky smirk.

"No. You can blame the decorators, the Herter Brothers. They pick everything for all my facilities. Do I look like I'm married?"

She tapped her chin for a moment. "You're dashing. Why would I not think you're married?"

He sat up straight and adjusted his ascot. "Dashing, am I?" He paused for a long minute, acutely aware of her smiling eyes and soft lips. "Miss Baldwin, I'm not married." He beamed. "Would you be interested?"

They burst out laughing. Peter's eyes held hers for a moment before she lowered them and fiddled with her reticule.

"Along with your apology during our brief chat yesterday, your interview of the women impressed me. It must have satisfied your father since the material appeared in your column."

"Thank you, Mr. Harrison. Please call me Allie. Everyone does."

"Great idea. Please call me Peter."

"Peter, that's a strong name. Well then, Peter, I find it gratifying being involved with the suffrage movement."

"I already gathered that. How about that article?"

"I had forgotten," Allie said, handing him the newspaper.

"Excuse me while I take this in." He read the few lines aloud. "It's quite concise yet says much. I would be interested in your readers' reactions."

"I expect controversy from our readers, especially our male audience, not that women may not be offended."

"It's hard to change anyone's mind," Peter said.

The carriage stopped at a building on Twenty-Third and Third.

"We've arrived. It looks like the storm went elsewhere." Peter hopped down from the carriage and offered his hand.

She took his hand, stepped down, and looked up. "This building is a classic with its fretwork and details on the cornices and window moldings.

He escorted Allie into the lobby with her hand on his arm. The warmth from her closeness washed over him like a wave on a sun-drenched shore. Their steps echoed on the pink marble floor.

"I hadn't noticed the details. To me, this is just a place of business."

Allie smiled. "As you know, our newspaper offices are in a simple brownstone. The aesthetics here would inspire me."

"Aesthetics are not my priority. Ask me about security. Then you'll have my attention."

"I know nothing about your business."

"I'll share what I can." His eyes met hers. "Our work is often secretive."

"Secretive? Can you give me an example?"

He wiggled his brows. "It's a secret."

Her nose crinkled when she smiled. "You can't blame a reporter for trying."

He buzzed for the elevator.

"The elevator doors resemble the bronze metal doors at the Sandanko, our family residence."

Peter grinned. "Do they inspire you as well?"

That earned him an eye roll.

He must admit he enjoyed spending time with Allie. She was everything he admired in a woman—smart, stunning, and daring.

"Top o' the morning, Mr. Harrison," said the porter opening the elevator gate.

"Good day, Ralph."

The seventh-floor office door had an engraved gold plaque mounted in the middle with *Harrison Security Est. 1786* on it. Turning the brass doorknob, he ushered her in with a sweep of his hand.

The receptionist greeted them from behind a high desk. "Good morning, Mr. Harrison."

"Good morning, Miss Foote." He turned to Allie. "Miss Foote is our front office receptionist." After further introductions, Peter escorted Allie into his private office. He left the door open in deference to her reputation.

"Please have a seat here beside my desk. I expect you're interested in Harrison Security's history?"

"History fascinates me," she said, opening her notepad, her pencil poised over the page.

"I have to warn you. My family history is not exactly illustrious."

"What do you mean?"

"My great-great-grandfather, Thomas Harrison, was a thief and a gambler. He was a wanted man in England for more than a few shenanigans. America offered him refuge. He booked passage with his winnings, and a short time after arriving, married a young woman named Rose, the only daughter of the local constabulary in New York. After the wedding, he promptly joined the police force."

"My, love certainly altered the course of his life, didn't it?" Allie's eyes sparkled. "Indeed, in his case, it saved his neck from the noose."

"In his country, what was his crime?"

"It's not for a lady's ears."

Allie tilted her head. "But surely you believed he changed, don't you? Look at the evidence."

Peter leaned back in his chair, drumming his fingers on the edge of the desk.

"I think he did. His wife, Rose, kept a diary. She had nothing but glowing things to say about her husband. Although she added a few choice words about him tracking mud through the house."

"I think it's fascinating that she kept a diary. I'd love to read it one day."

"Perhaps you will."

He'd met no woman like her. One moment she was daring and the next thoughtful.

He regarded Allie as the pencil flew across her notepad. He couldn't help but think of her beauty, her ambition, and her mind.

"Your great-great-grandfather founded Harrison Security?"

She lifted her head. There he was, staring at her. Her gaze locked on his. He felt like a boy caught looking in someone's window.

"No, he did not. He eventually moved his family to Fairfield and became a local magistrate. His son, Thomas Harrison, II, fought in the American Revolution and founded Harrison Security in 1786."

"You come from a long line of Thomas Harrisons. Why are you called Peter?"

"That's a good question. My mother's brother died in childhood. His name was Peter. She named me after him."

"That's a noble reason to break with tradition."

O'Malley knocked on Peter's open door. "Boss, we have a problem. I just received this telegram," he said, waving it in the air. "The Halton baby is missing."

CHAPTER 7

*A*llie leaped out of her chair, dropping her pencil and notepad. She bent, scooped them up, and tossed them into her reticule.

"I'm coming with you."

Peter shook his head. "Sorry, this one's not for you or your paper. I'll have my driver return you to your office."

"I will hire a carriage and go without you."

"We are wasting time here—"

"No. You are wasting time, Peter. The Haltons are family."

His brows shot up.

She cursed under her breath. "My mother and Mrs. Halton are sisters. Louise, the baby's mother, is my cousin."

He whistled. "What a coincidence. Come on, let's go. Maybe you can be useful."

Allie gasped and let Peter's sarcastic comment go for now. She gave him her best glower and stomped out the door.

Twenty minutes later, Peter and Allie arrived with O'Malley at the luxurious twelve-story Hotel Angelicus on Forty-Seventh. O'Malley had telegraphed for additional men at their downtown warehouse after conferring with Peter at the office. The plan was to search throughout the hotel and the surrounding area.

"How do you know the Haltons?" Allie asked on the way to the elevator. She stuffed her hands in the pockets of her short jacket to stop fidgeting. *Get hold of your nerves, Allie, girl, or you'll be of no help to Louise and Frederick.*

"Frederick and I are old college chums, having met at Harvard."

"Have you notified the police?"

He gave her a pointed glance. "No police. We can't risk any leaks to the press. Frederick asked to keep it quiet in the telegram. I suspect it's because he is running for mayor."

Allie opened her mouth to speak again. He silenced her with a raised hand. "Uh-uh-uh. Don't defend your kind."

"My kind?"

"The press."

"Well, I never..." she huffed as they got off the elevator. "I can't speak for all reporters, but I have never schemed to get a story."

He looked up to the heavens. "May I remind you that not two days ago, you wore a disguise as an old lady?" He punctuated his statement with a firm thud of the brass knocker on the penthouse door.

Allie placed her hands on her hips. She forgot her anxiety about the Haltons for a moment. "That was different, and you know it—"

Just then, Frederick's butler opened the door. Peter leaned down to Allie and whispered, "Can we talk about this later, please?"

"Good day, Mr. Harrison. And Miss Allie, your cousins will be pleased to see you. May I take your coats?"

"Thank you, Sanders." Allie lowered her voice. "How are they doing?"

Sanders shook his head. "It's been a hard morning, Miss Allie. Mr. and Mrs. Halton are waiting in the parlor."

The Haltons rose from their seat when Peter and Allie entered the room. Louise, her eyes red, held out her arms to Allie. "We are so glad you're here." They embraced. Allie stepped back and shook her head. "Peter will find your baby."

Louise, still sobbing, said, "Allie, I don't understand. How is it you are here with Peter?"

"I was doing an interview with Peter for my column when the telegram arrived."

"Please, have a seat." Frederick motioned to a pair of Greek revival chairs across from their mohair settee.

Peter leaned forward. "Tell us what happened."

"Betty usually arrives at six to feed and dress baby Andrew. By the time she arrived twenty minutes late, I had already fed him. Betty put him down for his nap and did some dusting, made the beds, her usual chores. When Andrew woke up around eleven, she dressed him and took him out in the carriage for a stroll," Louise said in a shaky voice. In her hand, the starched linen handkerchief was damp and crumpled. "She always brings him back at n-noon…" Her voice broke. "Today she did not come back. I thought perhaps she met friends and lost track of time. I was frantic and told Frederick by half past twelve," she sobbed.

"I went out searching with no luck," Frederick said, wrapping his arm around Louise. "That's when I sent you the telegram."

"Has Betty ever been late before?" Allie asked.

"N-never," Louise replied, wiping her eyes with a handkerchief.

Peter's lips thinned. "How did she behave this morning?"

"Now that you ask, she was all flustered and apologetic."

"Did she say anything about it and why?" Allie's voice brimmed with ire.

Louise dabbed at her nose. "Something about her husband taking a train home to Fairfield to see his sick mother."

"Aren't they both from the same town, Croton on Hudson?" Frederick asked.

Louise paused for a moment. "Why yes, they are. Why would Betty say that? She tells me all the time how she and her husband met there and fell in love. Two years ago, they won the queen and king crowns for the Annual Apple Festival in the town."

Allie lost her breath and clasped her hands to her mouth. "My goodness, I think Betty and her husband have kidnapped the baby!"

Louise gasped. "Whatever do you mean?"

"Let us review what happened," Allie said. "Betty was late this morning. She lied about where her husband was going and left with the baby." Allie's gaze met Peter's.

"I never liked that Mickey Boyd." Frederick stood and began pacing. He smashed his fist into his palm. "When I met him, I asked what he did for a living. He gave me a story about some big business deal."

Peter nodded. "No doubt a ransom note is forthcoming." He stood and placed his hand on Frederick's shoulder. "I must inform my men. Excuse me."

Peter gave Allie a brief nod and strode out of the parlor.

Frederick walked back to the settee, sat down, and took Louise into his arms. A solemn silence filled the air as if someone had died.

Allie held back her tears. She hoped Peter's men would be quick in finding baby Andrew.

"Shall I send for my parents?"

"I would rather wait until Andrew is home," Frederick said.

Louise half smiled. "I will send Aunt Clara and Mother a telegram."

If it were Allie, she would do the same.

An hour later, the trilling of the doorbell announced a visitor. Frederick rushed to the door. Everyone hoped it was good news.

A moment later, Frederick strolled into the parlor holding a squalling bundle in his arms, a grinning Peter following behind.

Louise's joyful cry echoed around the room.

"Heavens, my baby, my baby." Louise ran to her husband and gently took Andrew into her arms. He quieted. Allie's eyes filled with tears watching the loving reunion.

Frederick put his arm around Louise's waist. She whispered soft words to her baby.

"Peter, you're a hero. How did you find the baby so fast?" Frederick asked.

Peter cleared his throat. "We found the nursemaid, Betty, huddled in a shed behind the hotel with the infant howling. She sobbed and blurted out that she was waiting for her husband. He planned the kidnapping but he never showed. Do you want to have Betty arrested?"

Frederick blew out a breath. "I don't want the police, if unnecessary. I will speak to Betty for an explanation."

Louise dabbed her eyes. "Why would she kidnap my baby, her charge?"

"Perhaps Mickey coerced the poor dear," Allie said.

The baby looked peaceful in his mother's arms. "Betty cared for the child of a previous family, good friends of mine. They gave her a good reference."

Peter rubbed his chin and nodded. "She's a naïve sixteen-year-old and doesn't seem like a person who could concoct this scheme

"Damn him," Frederick ground out. "The criminal is Boyd. He conned her into the kidnapping."

"Where is he?" Allie asked.

Peter lifted his brow. "Good question. We don't know yet. My men are searching for him in the area."

"Maybe he's still on the grounds," Allie said, holding up her palm.

Peter grinned. "Possible."

"What will happen to Betty?" Louise asked in a singsong voice while gently rocking her baby.

Frederick held up an index finger. "I will send her to the Bismarck Inn. It's out of the way. She can do kitchen duties until we figure out what to do with her."

ALLIE STAYED WITH LOUISE WHILE THE MEN DEALT WITH BETTY and searched for her husband. They whispered while the baby slept in his cradle. An hour later, Andrew awoke with a hearty cry.

"Heavens, he certainly makes himself heard."

"He's due for a bath. Do you want to help?" Louise asked.

"All right, but I never bathed a baby before." Allie held him. "He smells sweet, and he's so soft."

"It's one joy of motherhood. You'll know soon enough when you have children of your own," Louise said while warming the water on the stove.

Allie smiled in bemusement as Louise prepared the bath for her son. Louise tested the water on the inside of her wrist and poured it into the tin tub on the kitchen table.

"Louise, this is a precious gift." She tucked the baby's head under her chin, closing her eyes at the softness, musing at the miracle of life. Was it possible for a woman to have work and family? Not according to her mother and her friends.

Andrew grabbed Allie's finger and held on, bringing her out of her reverie. She giggled.

"You are adorable," Allie cooed.

"Do you want to put him into his bath?" Louise asked.

She held up her palm. "N-no, no, no, I don't think so. You do it."

"All right, you can hold his head up in the tub, and I'll do the washing," Louise said.

Allie held the small blanket up. "What do I do with this?"

"I'll tell you when he's ready, and you can wrap it around him."

After the bath, Louise excused herself and went into the nursery to feed him. Allie remained in the parlor and poured herself a fresh cup of tea. A half hour later, Louise returned, holding a sleeping baby, and laid him in his cradle.

Allie dunked a lemon cookie into her tea. "That was a new life experience."

"You mean hard work, don't you?" Louise asked.

"Do you find it hard?"

"I thought I could do it all by myself, but you can see that it took the two of us to bathe him. Taking care of a baby is exhausting. Even with a cook and nursemaid, there are still wifely duties, and Frederick is a mayoral candidate. There's so much to do."

Allie had second thoughts about working outside the home and having babies. "What about your mother? Can she come and stay for a while?"

"Mother was planning to come back for the holidays. I'll send her that telegram and ask if she would come now. It's surprising Betty hadn't grown into an excellent nursemaid. Now I must find another."

"May I make a suggestion?"

"Yes, please."

"Let me talk to Mama. I'm certain she can find you the perfect person to tend the baby."

"Your mother knows everybody. I'll mention the need in your mother's telegram. I'll ask Frederick to send out the telegrams immediately."

It was just past three in the afternoon when Peter and Frederick returned.

Peter drove Allie back to the *Sentinel*. It didn't appear she would have any quiet time for reflection on the day's activities.

"Will Frederick press charges against Betty?" Allie grasped the leather loop beside the window to keep her balance in the rumbling carriage.

"I don't know. He said nothing to me about it."

"After you drop me off, will you be resuming your search?"

"Yes, it's going to be a late night."

Allie wanted to ask Peter to take her along on the search. Certainly not because she wanted to spend time with him, she told herself. It was only to observe Peter's insight and investigative methods for her report.

Don't lie to yourself, girl. You know you want to spend time with him.

When the carriage pulled up to the building, the horses neighed their arrival. After helping her down from the carriage, he stood facing her.

"We never finished the interview."

Peter took her hand and kissed it, holding it longer than expected. "Can we do that another time?"

Allie swallowed, and they beamed at each other, then she turned away, her face burning and her fingers icy cold.

"It's time for me to leave," he said, clearing his throat.

"Yes." She looked up at him. "I suppose it is." She caught the flicker in his eyes, and the world fell away, drained of all but him.

Don't let him go, you ninny.

Allie chewed her lower lip. *Say something,* "I'm glad you were there for my cousins today."

"So much for coincidences." Peter bowed and grinned.

My, oh my, those dimples.

He escorted her into her office on his arm. "I'll send word when we find Mickey Boyd," he said, walking away.

She watched him get into the carriage from the office window. Her stomach tightened.

"Good afternoon, Miss Allie. Two envelopes arrived earlier by special messenger," Annette, her secretary, said, interrupting her view of Peter riding away.

"Was your day at Harrison Security enlightening?"

Allie emptied her reticule, dropping her notepad and pencil onto her desk, and blew out a breath. "Enlightening? I'm not sure. I must think about that."

"Miss Allie, I have a sneaking suspicion you have a story to tell about your day."

"I will tell you every bit when there's time."

"Yes, please do." Annette nodded firmly and marched to her desk.

Allie settled against her cane-backed chair and contemplated the two missives in front of her. One was marked "PERSONAL" and the other "URGENT." She picked up her sterling silver letter opener and slid it into the envelope marked URGENT.

Scanning the letter, she cried, "Gracious, I must get home now."

CHAPTER 8

*A*llie arrived home after a brisk walk from the *Sentinel.* She hurried to her room, pulled both letters from her reticule, and dropped them on her writing desk. A disgruntled reader sent the personal one. She undressed, ripping off her hated smothering corset, and rummaged through her wardrobe. Her favorite blue gown required no hoop skirt and no corset, thank goodness. Allie bit her lip while fussing with her sleeves, setting them right on her upper arms.

It would be best if you told your parents about the urgent missive.

Her inner voice had a point. But she couldn't take the risk, not yet.

She stuffed the personal note into the drawer, shut it with finality, pocketed the other, and joined her family in the parlor.

Her mother, holding up what appeared to be a telegram, glanced up from the wine-colored velvet settee, the color drained from her face. "Allie, this telegram just arrived from cousins Frederick and Louise. Baby Andrew, home after a kidnapping. My Lord, what happened?"

"Let me reassure you, the baby is fine. We had a few

harrowing hours. All is well now. Cousin Frederick is seeing to their young nursemaid who was coerced by her husband into stealing Andrew."

"We must stop by tomorrow before the fundraiser to ask if they need help."

"Here is a letter for you to read, Mama, marked urgent. I received it in the office today, from Marla Mitchell, my good friend from a suffrage symposium two years ago. Marla's a nurse, and she and her husband David, a doctor, speak to support the woman's vote in Fairfield, Connecticut. I'm afraid it's not good news."

"My gracious, what have we here?" Clara adjusted her reading glasses and unfolded the letter.

Allie fiddled with the button on her collar and paced.

Why did turmoil hover like a dark cloud? First the incident at the rally, then the kidnapping, now this trouble from Marla.

Not to mention those letters to our newspaper.

Allie stopped her pacing at the window and gazed out at the beautiful colors. Her eyes captured the view in Central Park from their tenth-floor apartment. The leaves had begun their colorful autumn dance fluttering from branch to ground.

A confidant. That's what she needed, a strong friend. A trusting friend. A friend who would listen and wouldn't judge.

Peter says what he thinks. He's real, like the American elms across the way. Still, dare she trust him? She turned away from the window.

Barnes wheeled in the tea service and set it on the sideboard. The aroma followed the cart. "Ah, Barnes, thank you. Just what I need, a bracing cup of tea." Allie poured herself a cup, added a generous spoonful of clotted cream, wrapped her fingers around the handle, and inhaled the earthy aroma. Allie's black-and-white Great Dane, Captyn, wandered over and gazed at her with his soulful brown eyes.

"I know what you want."

She plunged the spoon into the cream, put it on her finger, and Captyn licked it off with enthusiasm, looking for more.

After a sip, she set it down and paced again, Captyn keeping up with her.

"Allie, you're making me dizzy," eighteen-year-old Ava, Allie's sister, said from her seat on the settee. Ava had the same red hair and azure eyes as their petite mother.

"Close your eyes," Allie said, waving her hand in the air as though flicking a fly.

"For someone who crusades for justice, you're quite rude to your sister," her other sister Emma declared from the Savonarola chair facing the fireplace. Emma crossed her legs in the chair. It was challenging but comfortable once accomplished. Her creamy complexion flushed defending Ava, her identical twin.

Allie rolled her eyes at her younger sister. Emma may have been born after Ava, but she was bossier.

Papa stood behind Mama, his hand on Clara's delicate shoulder. "Your mother had enough distress today between the kidnapping and this letter from Marla. Please, can you stop this commotion?"

"*Stop the commotion, stop the commotion, bawwk,*" Lord Wilby, Emma's African Grey parrot, squawked from his perch on her shoulder.

"Don't argue, please. I want to hear Mama read the letter," said twenty-one-year-old Mia, seated on a brocade-covered sofa across from the settee. Mia had her father's raven hair, minus the salt, and her mother's creamy coloring and petite stature.

Her mother rustled the letter in her lap. "Allie, please sit. Otherwise, Captyn will throw up all over my Persian rug."

"Oh, all right, Mama." Allie plunked down beside Mia on the sofa. Captyn followed her and rested his snout on her lap. She caressed his ears as her mother read the letter from Marla.

One night a week ago, while three farm girls were asleep in their quarters at the Longdale Dairy Farm, a villain set fire to the cabin. The loud barking of their loyal hound, Horatio, alerted the girls, Anne and Margaret O'Sullivan and Mary Lynn, to the danger. They escaped the burning building unscathed. Sadly, Mary Lynn fell and broke her leg, and one girl, Janie, has disappeared.

Ava laid her head on her mother's shoulder. "What happened to the girls?"

Clara smoothed the letter on her lap and continued reading:

"The girls returned to the farm. Mary is on the mend, safe at our infirmary. Longdales vowed to place additional guards on the property after they found one man drunk behind the barn with a bottle of gin."

Clara glanced up at Joseph. "Good heavens."

He shook his head. "Did they find who set the fire?"

Allie hesitated and bit her lip. "Not yet. Marla would have mentioned it. If I go to Fairfield, I'll get answers."

Joseph tucked his hands in his jacket pocket. A frown replaced his smile. "No, you don't."

"Papa, I must go. Vandals used fire to scare Marla and others who speak up for the vote."

Clara's lips thinned into a hard line. Allie crossed to her mother and knelt at her feet. She took her mother's hands and looked up into her eyes. "Mama, it's important for me to be there to support Marla."

"I fear for your safety."

Allie held her mother's hand to her cheek. "How can I allay your fears?"

"You put yourself in jeopardy—the dancehall, the rally."

Allie's gaze skittered away.

Clara shook her head and kissed Allie's hand. "This trip to Fairfield could be risky with threatened farmworkers."

Allie met her mother's eyes once more. "That's the point. Children must be in school, not working on farms to provide for their families. Marla and David speak to the farm workers about the children getting an education and their right to vote in the future. Someone wants to stop them from learning about their rights."

Clara's eyes shimmered with tears. Allie swallowed a lump in her throat.

Mia intervened. "Isn't it true that you and Papa founded Baldwin Hospital to help women and children?"

"How about this. Why not take Captyn with you?" Emma asked, putting Lord Wilby back in his cage.

"That's perfect," Ava said. "His size alone is scary. Look at him."

Allie sat cross-legged on the floor. Captyn got up from his cozy corner at the sound of his name, trotted over to his mistress, and planted a paw on her knee. Allie patted his side.

She wrapped her arms around Captyn. "You'll take care of me, won't you?"

He barked and wagged his tail. A chorus of laughter resounded.

Joseph had seated himself at his desk by the window. "He is a stalwart companion."

Clara scratched behind Captyn's ear. He did what dogs do—he licked the side of her face. "Oh, my." Clara pulled a handkerchief from her sleeve and dabbed at the drool.

"Captyn cares," Mia said. "I could come along. What do you think?"

Clara's shoulders relaxed. "Good idea."

Allie turned to her sister. "What will you do? I might bore you. You can take along your paints and sketch pad."

Mia looked up at the ceiling and let out a breath. "I will not have time to do my art. I'll be busy making sure you don't behave incautiously."

"I am never incautious."

"Yes, you are," her family shouted in unison.

"Just a moment, Joseph. May I speak to you in the hallway?" Clara asked.

Joseph got up from his desk, offered Clara his arm, and they stepped out of the parlor, closing the door behind them.

"Mama is so clever," Allie said in a timid voice.

"What's your guess, Emma?" Ava asked.

"I'm not sure."

Mia tucked a strand of her hair behind her ear. "Do you think Mama's changing her mind?"

"There's only one way to find out."

Allie tiptoed to the closed door and got down on her hands and knees, putting her ear to the keyhole. Captyn scampered after her and knocked her over.

Emma put her hand over her mouth and giggled. "Captyn wants to spy too."

Allie righted herself and then crouched down. Captyn thumped his tail on the floor and bellowed a playful growl.

"Shh, Captyn, they will hear you. Come on, boy." Allie led Captyn away by the collar. "Mia, take the keyhole."

"They're whispering," Mia said, placing her ear to the door.

"We know." Ava tugged down the sleeve of her dress.

Emma gave Ava a glance—an entire conversation exchanged in their secret twin language that could consist of only a look— and they broke into laughter.

"Shush, I can't hear," Mia whispered.

"*Shush! Shush,*" Lord Wilby mimicked in a perfect stage whisper from his cage.

Allie groaned. "This is not going well."

Just then, the door opened, causing Mia to topple onto her backside. Clara and Joseph gaped at Mia sprawled on the floor, then up at Allie and her sisters, who were staring with mouths wide open. Captyn got away from Allie's grip and tumbled down beside Mia, laying his head on her lap and thumping his tail again.

"Well, Clara, I can see your notion was spot-on."

"I'm sorry, Mama, Papa. Please don't be cross. I am too impatient and—"

"Nonsense, it was my idea," Mia said as she sat up and patted Captyn on the head.

"*Captyn's fault. Captyn's fault.*"

"Be quiet, Lord Wilby," Emma scolded.

"Girls, please let's sit," Clara said in a firm tone. "Your father and I have decided about the trip."

"We haven't changed our minds," Joseph said. "Your mother has a solution."

Clara's forehead creased with concern. "We'll hire a security company that will assure us of your welfare."

Ava raised her hand. "Maybe we could telegram Adam to come home. I miss our brother, and he's due for a visit anyway, isn't he?"

"Or maybe Johnny could go," Emma said.

"Adam is far too busy at the Chicago paper." Joseph cleared his throat. "As is Johnny at the *Sentinel.*"

"I've got the perfect man," Allie said. All heads swiveled toward her at her exclamation.

"I mean, Mr. uh, Mr. Peter Harrison. Papa, you met him when he escorted the women from the rally to the office. He also was the agent who rescued baby Andrew. He's Frederick's friend. That's all I was trying to say."

Clara shot Allie a dubious gleam.

You ninny.

"I will speak with Frederick about him tomorrow," her father said.

Allie dipped her head in a quick nod. "And Mia and Captyn

will come. We'll be fine."

"You, my beautiful daughters, are bright and clever and have hearts as big as the moon," their father said. "However, a watchful eye while you're away from home is critical."

Allie opened her mouth and stopped at the gentle squeeze of Mia's hand. "Hush, Allie. We're going, and you'll have your story."

Allie studied her parents, the two people she loved most, next to her siblings and Captyn. "Yes, Papa, you are right."

"Then it's settled." Joseph slipped his arm around Clara's shoulders. She leaned into his side. "As your employer, I trust you will write the story truthfully."

Is there any other way to write a story? I always write the truth, dreaming that Papa will trust me more readily.

"I'm mindful, Papa, and certain we'll be the most well-guarded ladies in Fairfield."

"Good, your father will sort it out tomorrow, and then we'll plan for you to leave. In the meantime, we have our charitable event. Allie, my darling daughter, from your rather morose expression, I gather you are reluctant to attend the event."

You're in for it now. Allie swallowed hard. "Actually, I would rather sit on a pincushion than spend one moment with the grand dames of New York society."

Clara's hands flew to her cheeks. "Allie, you cannot mean that."

"I mean it." Allie reached for the button on her collar and then stopped herself. "I get a bellyache when I see them. They are forever asking me when they'll be getting an invitation to my wedding or if I would meet their son or nephew. More than one matron has told me often that if I don't marry soon, I'll be a spinster."

Clara's lips turned down. "Allie, we'll speak of this later. First, promise me you and Mia will be at the tea. If not, you'll not be going to Fairfield, with or without a security agent."

CHAPTER 9

*A*fter a long night working on the kidnapping report, Peter stepped into the washroom at seven with his shaving gear and a change of clothes stored in his office for occasions like this. Damp, gray bricks held the cold inside the room as if it were a holding cell in a citadel, a chilling reminder of Peter's five years in the army. He shaved his scruffy beard and changed into his clean clothes. By the time he made his way back to his desk, the floor was humming with activity.

Ah, coffee's unmistakable aroma. Peter didn't know of anything that smelled sweeter at the first of the day. Every morning, the Central Park Café breakfast trolley delivered the brew to the desks of his grateful employees.

"Morning, Mr. Harrison." Gray-haired Miss Foote set down his breakfast croissant and his cup of energy.

"Thank you." He stirred the dissolving sugar cube into the dark depths of his coffee and took a sip. He gave Miss Foote a cursory glance above his cup as she handed him a telegram.

"Sir, this message from Joseph Baldwin requests a meeting with you in his office at nine thirty regarding an urgent matter."

"Not much time, is there? Please alert my driver and have him ready a carriage."

"Right away, Mr. Harrison."

Peter assumed Baldwin wanted details about the kidnapping. He planned to keep the investigation quiet until they captured Boyd. At half past eight, he left the Halton report locked in his desk drawer and made his way down in the elevator. "Be back in a couple of hours, Maxwell," he said to the doorman, whose hulking body reminded Peter of the boxer, John L.

"Yes, sir," the doorman said with a wide grin.

Butch, the doorman's bulldog accomplice, skulked over for a head pat and gave Peter a toothless growl.

"See, he likes you, Mr. Harrison."

Peter agreed, stepped out to the street, and hopped into the waiting carriage.

"Good day, boss," the driver said, tipping his cap.

"It is a good day. I assume Miss Foote gave you the address."

"Yes, sir. Your secretary is efficient. We'll be going across town to Sixty-Fifth and Central Park West."

At twenty-five minutes after nine, the butler ushered Peter into Baldwin's sprawling office. Baldwin greeted him with a firm handshake. "Good to have you here, Harrison."

Peter squared his shoulders. "Thank you, sir. A pleasure."

"Please, have a seat." Baldwin gestured to a brown leather chesterfield, a tufted sofa with a soulful attitude. Baldwin sat in his horned chair flanking the sofa.

"That's quite the chair, sir. Did you hunt the animal?"

Baldwin threw his head back and laughed. "No, no, my wife found the chair in an antique shop on Madison. Popular out West these days." He stood. "Try it."

Peter chuckled and sat. "Not bad, pretty comfortable. Cattle horns, eh? Thanks for the unique experience." He rose.

"Stay there. I'll sit on the sofa, and we can get down to business."

Baldwin's desk, across from the seating, contained a neat stack of folders. Peter liked a tidy desk. Leather-bound volumes of noteworthy news lined the bookshelves behind the desk. Peter only had time to read for work. Once home, he was too tired to read anything. His Eighteenth Street brownstone apartment in Gramercy Park had the less-is-more style. According to his father, once Peter married, a wife would redesign his apartment *and* his life.

"Harrison, thank you for your swift action in finding the Halton baby, my grandnephew. Smart, taking Allie along. Frederick told her she could trust you. He also said you were the best."

"Thank you, sir. My men worked the investigation. They know their business."

"That's why I asked you here to hire your protection for my daughter, Allie. She wants to have a conversation with the girls living on the farm. Allie believes whoever set the mysterious fire was trying to put fear into the farmworkers. The fire might stop them from listening to talks about their rights."

"That's an astute assumption."

"Allie is naturally curious and unpredictable. Trouble brews in her court."

"That's what makes her so charming and mysterious."

Baldwin's lips broadened into a smile. "She's fixed on interviewing those involved and writing a report. Given that she's prone to wrangle up trouble, her younger sister Mia will accompany her. But you can understand a father's concern." He leaned forward. "Can I depend on you as their bodyguard?"

Peter ran his fingers through his hair and cast his eyes downward. He didn't think women would ever get the vote, but a determined Allie Baldwin would see it blossom—somehow, someway, sometime. He admired her tenacity. If she'd been born a man a hundred years ago, she would have led the charge against the Red Coats.

A trip to Fairfield would take some time. Close quarters on the train, accompanying the sisters to the dining room, and escorting them around town and to the hotel. All that time in the volatile redhead's company—those long, luscious curls, those brilliant jade eyes. The last thing he needed right now was a complication in his life. Not when he had it all planned out.

"I'll assign one of my best men."

"I don't want your best man," Baldwin blurted. "I want you," he said, pointing his finger at Peter.

"My regrets. The best I can do is offer—"

A knock sounded on the door.

"Come in," Baldwin said.

A young man entered, pushing a cart laden with pastries and coffee.

"Ah, here's O'Toole, my man Friday. It looks like we're in for a treat." O'Toole poured both men a cup of rich, black coffee and plated two turnovers.

"You're the man for the job. I want you." Baldwin walked to his desk, leaned on the front edge, and crossed his arms over his chest.

Although Peter had his breakfast earlier, he never turned down another coffee and sweet treat. Peter took a sip of his coffee.

Baldwin hesitated for a long moment. "Allie thinks with her heart."

The silence was deafening. This man was not letting go. Peter took a bite of the turnover and another sip of the brew. He pushed himself back on the chair. "She's not practical and puts herself in harm's way?"

Baldwin rubbed his chin and stared at Peter. "Exactly. I'm willing to pay amply for your services. Will you indulge a father?"

"When you put it that way, it's hard to say no. However, my men are every bit as skilled as me."

Joseph Baldwin shot him a look with squinty eyes. "Does it matter that Allie suggested I ask you to accompany them to Fairfield?"

Good God, I impressed her?

"Baldwin. Let it go."

Baldwin eyed him with a strange smile. Harrison could tell more lurked in Baldwin's expression.

"I'll pay you three times your day rate."

"This isn't about money."

It wasn't about money at all. It was about that bewitching redhead with the soft mouth and freckles over her nose.

"Is that so? Then you have me baffled."

I can't tell this man that his daughter is trouble for me.

"Think about it. Join me in a nip of bourbon?" Baldwin asked.

"It's a little early, but why not? I never turn down good whiskey."

Baldwin went to his liquor cabinet, pulled out a couple of shot glasses, filled them, and handed one to Harrison.

He held his glass up toward his drinking partner. "Here's to you, Harrison." He downed his.

"Likewise, sir." Gone in one gulp.

"Look, Harrison, you're not a father, but try to understand the importance of what I'm asking."

"I am not a father, but I'm a big brother," he said with a downward twist of his lips. "It could be close to your situation. My three little sisters make hasty choices, worrying our father and their mother. I understand, sir."

"I need someone I can trust. What do you say, Harrison?"

"Frankly, can I speak honestly?" Harrison asked.

"Haven't you been straight with me?"

"Not exactly."

"Go on."

My God, the man is serious. Can I be forthright and tell him what I think about his daughter?

"Your determined daughter is a handful. She has a mind of her own. In the short time I've known her, she can be unreasonable. This trip with Allie will require my daily attention. What advice can you give me to deal with the likes of Allie Baldwin?"

"Oh, is that all? Why didn't you say so?"

Peter's brows furrowed. "Maybe I should have. What's your secret?"

"Just smile, say thank you, and tell her if she must have her way, you will leave. If it comes to that—walk away. She will not let you do that. You are doing business with her father. She's honorable."

"You must know your daughter. If you think she will be cooperative, I am for hire."

"Deal, my offer still stands for triple your pay. You are a good man, Harrison. Thanks for your honesty. That had to be a tough one."

"Thank you. It's a generous offer, Baldwin, though it's unnecessary."

"If you don't mind, Harrison, I want to keep our financial arrangement between us."

"Fine with me. When am I needed, and for how long?"

Peter had serious concerns. Not the time this job would take, but the beauty was irksome. He must stay out of her persona and remember his duty—to provide protection.

"I don't think it should take more than a few days. The girls want to leave as soon as possible. Today, both Allie and Mia are working a fundraiser for our hospital with their mother."

"Consider your daughters under my care."

They shook hands. "By the way, Allie's dog will go along."

Peter's brows shot up. "Dog?"

"Captyn, her Great Dane. He's friendly and fairly well trained."

"Sounds like a stimulating trip."

More like a wild adventure!

"Would you be available for dinner tonight to meet the family?"

"And the dog?"

Baldwin chortled. "And the dog."

Damn! What have I gotten myself into?

A knock on the door drew their attention. "Gentlemen, I trust all is well?" said a deep, gravelly voice.

"John, come in. Good timing. Johnny MacGregor, meet Peter Harrison of the Harrison Detective Agency. He's Allie and Mia's escort to Fairfield. Harrison, this is my foster son and my right-hand man."

Peter regarded the tall man, dressed impeccably in a day coat and well-pleated gray trousers. He knew him from the boxing emporium where they'd sparred on more than one occasion. Peter offered his hand.

"MacGregor, good to see you again."

MacGregor shook his hand. He glanced at Baldwin. "We know each other from Gentleman Gerry's."

Baldwin tipped his head at John and Peter. "Ah, the perfect place to pass the time except for men of my age. I prefer my morning stroll with my wife, Clara."

The men shared a chuckle.

"Excuse me, am I interrupting?" Allie asked, pushing the door open. "I have some files for you, Papa."

Her father walked over and took her hand. "You got your wish, daughter. Mr. Harrison accepted my offer. He'll escort you and Mia to Fairfield and is coming to dinner tonight to meet the family."

Allie hugged her father, stepped back, and glanced at Peter. "Oh, can we leave in two days? We must get on with this, you know? Let me know when you are ready to travel. I can be ready on short notice."

"I'll be pleased to let you know. I have to tie up some loose ends, pack, and then we are off."

Allie's eyes sparkled. "Wonderful. I'm looking forward to our trip."

"If you wouldn't mind waiting a moment, Miss Baldwin."

Allie nodded.

"MacGregor, you were saying?" Harrison asked.

"Perhaps we should plan on a few rounds."

"Would this afternoon work?"

"Three o'clock?"

"Perfect, MacGregor."

"With that, gentlemen, please excuse me," Peter said in a silvery voice.

He stood tall and extended his hand to Baldwin, then MacGregor, clasping theirs hard. He turned to Allie. "Miss Baldwin." He took her hand and brought it to his lips. "This evening then?" Peter said, gazing into her eyes. "It will be a privilege to meet your family." He bowed ever so slightly and strode out the door.

How difficult could it be to escort two young ladies and a dog to Fairfield?

CHAPTER 10

*B*ack at his apartment, Peter grabbed a quick nap and a bite to eat, then made his way uptown to Gentleman Gerry's Boxing Emporium in the New York Athletic Club. He used the club to maintain the high level of physical fitness his job required. Besides rowing for the club's team, he swam, ran track often, and boxed.

"Good afternoon, Harrison," the coach said.

"Good to see you, Buddy."

Buddy O'Connor was a champion boxer from Ireland, famous for dancing his opponents into a corner and pummeling them with his rugged right cross. When he lost sight in his right eye at the height of his career, Nicholas Quinn, owner of Gentleman Gerry's, hired him as head coach.

Buddy grinned. "MacGregor's here."

"He beat me here, did he?"

"Sure did. I t'ink your match might be a draw."

Peter shot him a look. "No matter, it's a friendly one."

"Dat's not what I hear."

Peter turned away for a moment, then back, his eyes narrowed. "What have you heard?"

"Johnny-boy's been hittin' the bag for the past hour. He looks fit."

"Thanks for the tip." Peter rubbed the back of his aching neck. He hadn't gotten enough sleep.

"I'd be watchin' right side. He learnt pretty good how to t'row a decent punch."

Peter laughed and slapped the former champ on the shoulder. "Tell him when to duck."

Buddy winked with his good eye.

Peter winked back. "I'm looking forward to this one," he said with a broad smile, a lyrical tone in his voice.

Peter strode into the locker room and changed into his custom-tailored, black-banded white shorts. Peter and his agents trained and fought friendly matches with each other and occasionally with patrons who were considering hiring Harrison. He'd sparred with MacGregor a few times, but it had always been genial until someone came out with a flood of red from his nose or a black eye or both. No one kept score, but the smug throng had cheered them on, most of the beer-drinking crowd blatantly betting, the greenbacks floating over the heads of the bettors. Approaching the ring now, it took a minute for Peter to register the strange silence. His instincts told him to treat this match with caution.

"MacGregor." Peter nodded at his opponent.

"Harrison." MacGregor inclined his head. "Shall we?" He climbed between the ropes. Peter followed.

The wiry, redheaded referee was Devil Dan, a retired boxer. "All right, boys," he greeted them. "Keep it clean, or I'll toss yous out."

The crowd gathered around the ring, yakking, mumbling, and cheering like a swarm of bees. The two men nodded and touched gloves.

Peter watched Johnny's eyes to see when a punch was coming. The darkened eyes gave it away. MacGregor threw the first punch, a quick jab followed by a right cross. Peter ducked and hit him with a left hook. MacGregor grunted and shuffled back, each exchanging punches, neither giving an inch. About thirty minutes into the match, they were still sparring and staring each other down. Both had delivered some good blows, and both had suffered. Peter could feel the blood oozing from his split lip, while MacGregor was sporting a shiner the color of his stepmother's pansies.

The crowd was booing. "We want a bloody knockout," the men hollered.

"Shut yer traps, you bunch o' girls," Devil Dan shouted at them. "I'd like to see any of yous try to knock out one of these two."

They danced around each other and exchanged a few more punches and breathy confrontations, adhering to the rules set down for amateur championships.

"Allie isn't like one of your dance hall girls," MacGregor said as he sent a fist into Peter's stomach.

"Oomph." Peter doubled over and danced backward, driven by the unexpected pain. "I've never equated Allie with that low element," he grunted.

"I don't want her getting hurt."

Peter landed a hard uppercut and growled, "She'll never get hurt with me watching out."

MacGregor groaned, countering the uppercut with a quick jab and a hook. "Allie's a fine woman."

"You bet." Peter always enjoyed sparring, especially with MacGregor, but he was running on empty.

"Harrison, had enough?"

Peter propped his hands on his hips. His face hurt, one eye half-closed. "I'm good unless you're not. What do you say?" His words were low and even, but they came out like a hungry lion on the prowl.

The referee blew his whistle. A tall, swarthy giant of a man greeted them from the side of the ring. Nicholas Quinn grinned at them, his forearms hooked over the ropes, his booted foot resting casually on the edge of the platform. "Gentlemen, are you finished?"

MacGregor grinned. "A friendly match between friends."

"We were enjoying ourselves," Peter said through gritted teeth.

Nick barked a laugh. "Let's call it a draw. Clean yourselves up and join me for a steak and a scotch."

Harrison and MacGregor stepped out of the ring, and the spectators dispersed.

"No worries, MacGregor. No harm will touch Miss Baldwin."

MacGregor nodded. "I've watched over her for a long time. She's headstrong. It gets her into trouble."

"Why didn't you offer to go to Fairfield?"

"Baldwin's sending me to Boston to launch another paper. I'm leaving this week. The Baldwins are super. They took me in from the streets, a beggar at thirteen. They're the only family I've known. Allie and I are close friends."

Peter shook MacGregor's hand. "I understand. You can rest easy. I will guard her with my life."

In Peter's early years, he became his mother's caretaker in the last year of her life. Peter's grandfather, William, collapsed and died unexpectedly at fifty-five. His father, Thomas, took over the Harrison Detective Agency and dedicated himself to work. At twenty-one, he married Ellen Covington, a kind young woman. Thomas's work continued to come first, but his wife never uttered an unkind word. Her health declined. She passed away from pneumonia and a broken heart when Peter was fourteen. The loss devastated him.

A short year later, much to Peter's dismay, Thomas married Samantha Blackwell, the energetic daughter of a New York State Senator. Despite Peter's resentment of his father's remarriage, he learned to love his stepmother. After a while, his father worked less and eventually signed the company over to twenty-five-year-old Peter.

Thomas moved to their country estate in Fairfield, Connecticut, with his new wife and three daughters, Peter's half-sisters. Peter hoped to copy his retired, contented father. Now only thirty-one, he would not think about marriage until he retired. In the meantime, Peter would enjoy the life of a single man and continue to grow the agency. This job watching over Allie would be just another challenge.

CHAPTER 11

*A*llie didn't want Peter Harrison at dinner—in her house, of all places. Gracious, how did that happen? Her father invited him, that's how. She wished father had asked her first. She shook her head. What in the world was she thinking? No one ever asked her whom to invite to dinner. And she *had* said to him it delighted her he was the escort to Fairfield. But was she delighted? Anyway. Moot point.

Allie had to admit to herself that she wanted to see him. He was handsome, and when that curl fell over his forehead, her face felt hot. Allie didn't understand what bothered her about Peter. His voice was pleasant enough, but the sound of it tightened her stomach. Besides, no excuse would work to get out of this dinner. Hmm... maybe she could feign sickness. But that would be a lie, and Allie never lied. Maybe she stretched the truth a little sometimes. She'd have to think that through soon.

Her ambivalence made little sense. Was she feeling the torment of confusion like Charlotte Bronte's Jane Eyre? Mr. Rochester kept a terrible secret locked away—his mad wife, hidden in the attic. She worried that Mr. Harrison had a mystery hidden away too, profound and dark, that might threaten her somehow. She didn't want to be right this time.

Allie stood in front of her walnut wardrobe with its mirrored center door, pushing her gowns aside one by one. Allie liked that she could see each dress easily. *Ah, my off-the-shoulder, emerald-green one.* The perfect gown for this dinner that she'd rather not attend. She strode over to the antique highboy chest of drawers between the windows opposite her bed and folded away her corset and woolies. Her mama had agreed if she put away her clothes, her room could be her sanctuary.

Allie brushed her hair back and up, winding it on top of her head. She fastened the roll with her two Japanese hair sticks. She let feathery curls fall where they may. *Do I need a pink ribbon?* She sighed. Dressing was taking too long, so forget the ribbon. Allie pinched her cheeks and donned her long gloves.

"Stay," she said to her sweet, obedient dog. She poked her head into her sister's room next door.

"Mia, are you ready?"

"Come in. I'm just finishing reading *Jane Eyre* for the third time," she said from her slipper chair in the corner of her blue room.

"What are you going to wear?"

"I'll be wearing my white blouse and dark blue skirt." Mia stood, grabbed her clothes she had already laid out at the foot of her bed, and donned her outfit.

"Are you sure you don't want to wear something fancier? We have special company coming."

"Nice, but he's not special. Papa told me about our guest when he got home from work. Who do I have to impress? I'm not wearing my corset—or my crinoline. I want to breathe tonight."

"I'm not either, but we don't look like we are going to the same dinner party, Mia. I hope I'm not overdressed. Let's go, or we'll be deserving of a lecture from Papa about being prompt."

Allie adjusted the skirts of her gown, revealing matching green, satin, pointed slippers. "Now that we have no choice, and we'll be traveling with Mr. Harrison—Peter that is—let's think about how we can be nice to him."

Mia smoothed her hair. "I can't wait to meet this man. His business is unlike that of anyone I've ever met. Learning about it should be informative."

"I think the trip will reveal much about his character, and honestly, I can ask him questions about his work and take notes while we are away." Allie clasped her hands. "I think I might be interested in him."

"Uh-oh, that's a revelation."

"He's got those cute dimples. You'll see. And he's well-spoken and intelligent."

Mia pulled her dark hair back and wound it in a blue ribbon. "I don't want to hear what Mr. Harrison will say when we're all packed. We need at least one enormous trunk, maybe two. We'll have to squeeze our things together. I hope he's a patient man."

Laughter seeped up the hallway as Allie and Mia made their way down the winding stairs to the parlor. The family enjoyed a brief get together before dinner and indulged in an aperitif.

"Papa, are we late?" Allie asked.

Joseph checked his watch dangling from his belt loop. "Perhaps ten minutes, my daughters. Please." He swept his hand toward a settee. "I'm giving the family a brief talk about our Peter."

Hmm, our Peter?

"Our dinner company is Mr. Peter Harrison of the Harrison Detective Agency. You've all heard about your cousin's baby and the kidnapping, haven't you?" The answer came in claps and nods. "Allie first met Peter when he escorted the women from the rally to our office. She was interviewing Peter in his office when the telegram arrived. They went to Cousin Halton's together. He's escorting Allie and Mia to Fairfield, so let's make a good impression. Shall we?"

Emma and Ava's answers rang out. "Yes."

The family stepped into the dining room through an adjacent archway. The high, geometric, hand-painted ceiling and depth of the space were majestic, good enough for a queen of the court. Allie, in her delicate slippers, padded over the patterned Persian rug to the floor-to-ceiling windows. She pulled the Pompeian rich, blue, silk draperies back and slipped them into the brass curtain holders on the wall. It was still light enough to enjoy the views of the trees and gardens of Central Park. Bits of light showered through the dusk onto the leaves dancing from their branches. Children rustled around playing hide-and-seek in the leaves as she had done with her sisters and her dog. Her older brother Adam sneaked in, but he played too rough. The girls always shooed him away. He was nothing but a big tease.

Like it or not, tonight she'd be dining with the security agent. Did she remember to pinch her cheeks? She looked at her image in the silver charger—it would do.

Men expected a well-dressed table. She ran her fingers around the edge of the Aynsley dinnerware and raised a goblet to the candlelight. Facets of color sparkled like fireworks.

Barnes appeared at the dining room entrance. "Please welcome Mr. Peter Harrison."

Joseph, with a pleasant air about him, walked up to Harrison and extended his hand.

"Welcome, Harrison. My family is eager to meet you."

Allie took a deep breath and waited for him to approach.

"My dear Miss Baldwin, we meet again."

She offered Peter her hand. "Mr. Harrison." He held it in a firm, warm grip. Anticipation was more problematic than the event. His wavy, dark hair was neat and not falling over his forehead, making her want to comb through it with her fingers. She hadn't forgotten that he was as tall as Papa and Adam.

"Peter, we don't stand on ceremonies here. I suggest we use our first names," Clara said.

Peter nodded politely. "It would be a pleasure, Mrs. Baldwin, Clara. I'm glad you see Allie and I are already on a first name basis." Peter winked, and Clara laughed.

A glance at her mother revealed "that look," telling her to behave.

Why does everyone think I'm going to misbehave? Because, you ninny, you usually do. She would be at her best this evening. After all, what could go wrong?

"Mama, I arranged the seating earlier. You and Papa are across from each other in the middle, with Peter to your right. I'm beside Papa and the girls."

A clap of thunder shook the apartment as the family was sitting down to dinner. Captyn raced into the dining room in a manner of seconds and tried to jump into Allie's arms, knocking her flat onto her derriere. She looked up, and all she could see was Captyn's tongue aimed at her face. She reached out to grasp Captyn's collar, but he backed up and stumbled into Barnes, who was pouring Burgundy into Peter's wine glass. No matter how valiantly Barnes tried, he could not stop the bottle from flying out of his hand, splashing everything in its path—the tablecloth, the antique Persian rug, the silk curtains, and Peter.

"Oh, my goodness," Allie said, one hand flying to her mouth and the other holding onto Captyn. "I am sorry, Peter."

Papa's exceptional vintage covered Peter from his wavy dark hair to his shiny black boots. Allie should have remembered that her big, brave Great Dane dreaded storms.

Poor Captyn dove for cover under the table. Allie, still on the floor, hurried after him and wrapped her arms around her big, goofy dog. "Captyn, don't worry. We'll get through this.

November in New York rarely has thunderstorms. I'm sure Mother Nature feels bad for scaring you."

Captyn panted as if he'd been chasing down a thief. If another clap of thunder boomed, the frightened dog could very well jump up, hit his big head on the table, and shake off the silver and the crystal goblets. She held onto Captyn just in case.

Rain pounded on the twelve-foot windows with such force that Allie was sure the glass panes would crack.

"Barnes, get some towels for Mr. Harrison," Mama said, untouched by the wine.

Allie heard the exasperation in her voice.

"I apologize, Mr. Harrison," Barnes said, patting the front of Peter's stained jacket with a cloth.

Peter took the towel from the flustered butler's hands.

Allie pushed the tablecloth aside and peeked out. "Peter, are you all right?"

"Yes, Allie, thank you for asking." Peter's lips twitched. "I arrived here without a drop of rain on me, but fate had other plans as I find myself awash in this excellent Burgundy."

Papa laughed, followed by Mia, Ava, and Emma, and even Mama.

Peter crouched down and joined Allie under the table. "How is your dog?"

Allie still held onto Captyn. "Promise me you aren't angry."

"I promise." Peter grinned.

Allie realized the pebbles in her stomach had rolled away, and the butterflies had flown. Those deep dimples bracketed his smile in a most arresting manner. Peter could have been angry, and she wouldn't have blamed him one bit. He could have told her parents about the first time they'd met—at the rally, something her parents didn't know. But he didn't. Perhaps there was hope for him after all.

Joseph had a wide grin on his face. "Harrison, come with me, and we'll find something for you to wear. I would guess we're about the same size."

"I appreciate your indulgence, Baldwin. There was no warning I would run into a wine spillage."

Allie cuddled the panting Great Dane for a few more minutes, making sure he settled down. She stood and noticed her shoes. Instead of the vibrant green when she first arrived, they now looked a sludgy brown, ruined by red wine. "Ugh."

"Barnes, would you mind taking Captyn to my room? Best close my door; we want no more mishaps." The butler bobbed his head, relieved to be exiting the crime scene with a now calm Captyn.

"Mama, sisters," Allie said, backing out. "Please excuse me while I change my shoes and my dress—the bottom got splashed. I won't take long."

"Of course." Her mother seemed to have weathered the incident well.

While rushing to her room, she looked down at her dress, twisting and turning to check the spillage. "Oops." Allie crashed into a firm male torso. She looked up at Peter's face. "Excuse me. I didn't see you."

"Perhaps you mistook me. I'm in a set of clothes from your father. He's gone back to the dining room."

Allie's mouth lifted into a sweet smile, making her eyes crinkle at the corners. "It's funny seeing you in his coat and trousers. You almost look like him. You would need his mustache, though, to make it authentic, that is. I apologize again. Are you hurt?"

His lips twitched. "I don't think so."

"Can I ask you a question?" she asked with hesitation, almost in a whisper.

"Ask away."

Allie frowned. "Can we discuss the upcoming trip?"

"I think that would be a capital idea, but I don't think this evening is the best time."

Allie held up one corner of her dress like a dancer about to make a curtsy, her eyes expressionless. "When then?"

"May I call on you tomorrow afternoon?"

"I would like that, maybe even love you, um, love that," she said with her hands in a prayer-like position.

Peter took her hands and wrapped his fingers around them. "We'll take a stroll in the park and discuss what's on your mind. Is that acceptable?"

She gasped and withdrew her hand—not that she wanted to. "It is. I have another matter of concern."

"Yes?"

"Can I trust you won't mention our run-in at the rally?"

"What difference would it make to mention how we met? Let's discuss that tomorrow as well."

"I will wait if I must." A stray lock of her hair became unpinned. His eyes followed her fingers as she tucked it behind her ear.

"I-I will return to the dining room shortly."

"I'll be waiting, Allie," he said, straightening his ascot.

She bit down on her lip and quickened her pace, her squishy dress slippers making slapping noises on the parquet floor as she raced down the hall. Her heartbeat had quickened, but not because of her pace. It was a particular pair of gray eyes that had caused her heart's rhythm to beat out of time.

CHAPTER 12

*A*llie, in her collared, billowed sleeves, green-and-white gingham day dress, and white slippers, made her way to the parlor where her family and Peter discussed the latest news about labor issues.

Allie opened the *Sentinel* to her column. "The recent railroad strike made it to all the newspapers. Workers demanded higher wages. Company management refused them."

Joseph had his copy open as well. "Allie primarily writes society news for our paper, but she requested to work that story."

Allie nodded her head in agreement. "I interviewed some workers and their wives. The women encouraged their husbands to find supplementary jobs out of necessity."

Peter rubbed his chin. "Did you find the women cooperative, Allie?"

"They were eager to complain about the unfairness of the decision-makers."

"The company hired my agency to provide security after someone burned a railroad bridge. Men were working at the site and got caught in the fire. Several died." He glanced at Allie from his wing chair flanking the fireplace. "Too often, we only read the story from an economic perspective, not a human one. I commend you on your work."

Allie, sitting beside Mia on one of a pair of settees, stared at Peter, whose chair was chair diagonally across from her. Her cheeks were burning from his praise. She took a deep breath. "Thank you, I think."

Now, why did she sound like such a ninny? It must be those eyes.

Emma gestured toward Allie. "Allie is always in the middle of whatever is happening."

"Only because she's passionate about the rights of workers," Mia said on her sister's behalf.

Emma shook her head and looked at Allie. "Allie is a firecracker, Mr. Harrison. I mean, Peter. Are you sure you know what you're getting into?"

"I can assure you"—he glanced at Allie and Mia— "your sisters have nothing to fear under my protection. I'm ready, even if Allie is prone to getting herself into a muddle."

Humph. Muddle indeed. Allie lowered her eyes for a moment, then directed them to Peter. "That's absurd. What do you mean?"

Peter grinned. "I reserve any comment at the moment."

After they retired to the parlor, Barnes served a platter of cinnamon sugar biscuits. Allie placed two on her plate, bit into one, and caught Peter watching her. She shifted in her seat and surreptitiously glanced down the front of her dress, flicking off a few golden crumbs. "I hope the few crumbs dotting my dress don't make me muddled."

"Crumbs are easily done away with; no issues there."

Joseph strolled to the bar in the corner. "Peter, care to join me in a port?"

"I'll say, nothing is better than an excellent port after dinner."

Joseph poured two cordial glasses and handed one to Peter.

"Excellent vintage, sir. Thank you."

"Mama, we could hear you all laughing as Mia and I came down the stairs. What was so funny?"

Clara nodded and looked at Allie. "Peter was telling us about his three young sisters. Their antics reminded me of Ava and Emma when they were younger."

Allie beamed at him.

Emma coaxed her African Grey parrot from his cage onto her shoulder. "This is Lord Wilby." Then she whispered to him, "Peter's a spy."

The bird cocked its head and squawked, *"Peter's a spy."*

Allie's lips turned up at the corners. "Did you hear that, Peter? According to Lord Wilby, you're a spy."

Peter smiled at Allie. "My work has led me down some intriguing paths."

A few moments later, the doorbell rang.

"Bawwk, doorbell, doorbell," Lord Wilby announced.

Barnes entered the room carrying a box wrapped in gold paper and tied with a green ribbon.

"Miss Allie, this just arrived for you."

"Thank you, Barnes." She took the box and sat beside Mia on the settee.

"Perhaps it's an early Christmas gift," Mia said, rubbing her hands together.

"Is there a card?" Clara asked.

"No, that's strange." Allie shook the package. It made a ringing sound.

"Maybe you shouldn't open it," Ava said. "What if there is something alive inside?"

"Humph." Emma scratched her head. "What creature makes a ringing sound?"

"That's silly." Allie raised the box. "If it's alive, it would not have paper wrapped all around it."

Mia pointed at the box. "Maybe it's a man-eating plant. Then it could have wrapping, couldn't it?"

Peter watched the family and smiled. "Carnivorous plants are dangerous, but only to small mammals and insects."

Allie glanced at him and gave Mia a playful poke.

"What about small fingers?" Emma asked.

"I don't think so, but if we open it, we'll know in a minute if it will eat your fingers," Allie said with a wink at her sister.

"Please open it," Clara said, sitting on the matching settee across from Mia and Allie. "Before anyone conjures up any further frights."

Allie shook the box again, and it dinged two more times. "It can't be alive and make a ringing sound like that." She pulled on the bows and ribbons, then ripped off the paper. "Oh, of course, it's a music box."

Mia inhaled. "How lovely."

Ava attempted to take the box from Allie. "Let me see."

Emma banged her hand on the table. "No, me."

"Don't fight." Allie looked at her sisters. "I'll wind it up, put it on Papa's desk, and then we can all listen."

"It's playing 'The 'Blue Danube' waltz,'" Emma said.

This box was more significant than most Allie had seen, almost the size of two of her palms. It was adorable with its miniature toys, a top that spun around to the music, tiny dolls, puppets on strings, and soldiers that went round and round.

Allie clapped her hands. "I love this."

"Who is it from?" Joseph asked.

"I had almost forgotten."

"What does the note say, dear?" her mother asked.

Allie peeled open the envelope. "It's a poem. *Words make you bold. Words make you clever. But words can destroy you forever and ever.*

"Oh, this is no doubt from a joker." Allie handed the note to her father.

Joseph fingered the paper, held it up to the candlelight, and then gave it to Peter. "What do you think?"

Allie noticed Peter get all professional. "I suggest we explore this note. It's hard to determine its meaning without further investigation."

The women gasped in unison.

"Balderdash." Allie glanced at Peter. "Someone is just playing a joke."

"I can assure you this is not a joke," Peter said.

"You'll sort this out, won't you?" Joseph asked in a firm tone.

"Guaranteed I will."

Allie had forgotten about the other note she received at the office. The one marked personal. Could it have been from the same person?

Clara faced her husband. "Do you think the girls should cancel their trip to Fairfield?"

Allie looked beseechingly at Peter. He returned her look with a slight nod. "I will guard your daughters with my life. Allie might be safer away from New York for a few days. I will inquire with a colleague who might find some clues from the note."

Allie managed a brief smile at Peter's remarks.

Mia's eyes darted from Peter to Allie. "My heavens, I don't like the way it sounds."

CHAPTER 13

The morning brought another brisk fall day with an azure-blue sky. Sprays and sprigs of leaves in autumn's oranges and reds blew around, settling in the streets, gardens, and building corners. The season's warm colors made everything beautiful. It was Peter's favorite time of year. He arrived at the Sandanko apartments around eight. Soon after Barnes greeted him, he served strong hot coffee and crumpets. The aromas of his favorite wake-up beverage and freshly baked sweets were undoubtedly the best way to begin the day. Peter wrapped his fingers around his cup and took a sip of the hot liquid.

"Ah, thank you, Barnes. Hot, dark, and delicious. Perfect."

His thoughts drifted to Allie. There had never been a woman that interested him, one that he would welcome into his life —until now.

Barnes refreshed Peter's coffee. "My apology again for that wine incident, sir."

"I have forgotten it. Thanks for the refill. Can you tell me anything about Allie's dog?"

"Pardon, sir. Miss Baldwin will join you shortly. Why not ask her yourself?"

~

ALLIE CLENCHED HER JAW, READING THE MORNING PAPER'S article about Wilbur Drumple running for mayor. *Good Lord, if he won, the entire city would fall apart.* The article quoted him saying that women should not strive beyond their limitations. *Indeed. Imagine saying that in this day and age when women are fighting for the right to vote.*

Drumple called women's suffrage poppycock. He said women were "keepers of the hearth and nurturers of the children." Meanwhile, this drudge of humanity spent his days and money at the horse races. Allie wanted to give him a what-for in her column, but Clara asked her to wait until after the hospital fundraiser. Allie agreed. She didn't want her mother's expansion plans derailed.

Her mass of curls had fallen again. "Grrr, to my hair and Drumple." Allie groaned. A sturdy ribbon and a few well-placed pins worked. Her hair would have to be all right. It was time to meet Peter. Captyn padded to her, put his head on her lap, and looked at her with his big, brown eyes. She was sure her dog approved of her hair. She smiled.

"My hair is the way it is. The man is not here to court me, right?"

Captyn wagged his tail and gave her a soft woof and a happy doggie face.

"Come on, big guy. Let's go meet Peter Harrison." Allie patted her left leg, and Captyn stood. "Good boy." She gave his ear a soft pull, and they strode downstairs to the parlor.

They stopped at the threshold of the parlor. As Peter looked up, a wide smile lit his face, and his eyes crinkled in the corners. Her stomach fluttered.

"Good morning, Peter."

"Good morning, Allie." He stood, put his cup down, and walked toward her. "Won't you join me for coffee and a sweet?" He offered his arm. Before she could accept, Captyn jumped up, knocking Peter down, and stood with two paws on his chest and barked in his face.

"Captyn's never done this before. He's usually friendly."

"Please get your dog off me."

"It's all right, Captyn. Come, boy. Over here." She patted her left thigh.

Captyn hesitated, then barked and growled in Peter's face before getting off him.

"Perhaps it's something you're wearing, Peter?"

"Like what?"

"Hmm. You don't appear to have wheels on your shoes. My dog has a habit of barking and growling and lunging at anything with wheels, or if he thinks I'm in danger. Maybe you're still a stranger to him. Maybe he equates you with the fright he had during the stormy night wine incident."

Once Peter stood, Allie raised her eyes to his.

"Are you upset, Peter?"

"At what, mistaken identity? Nothing is upsetting here. He didn't bite me."

As usual, one of her unruly curls snuck out and fell over her cheek. She pinned it back. "Peter, I'm sorry. I never expected Captyn to do that. Something bothered him or frightened him."

She couldn't have known. Her dog had never misbehaved like that.

"Let's go to the park, Allie. If you haven't eaten, maybe you can take a crumpet with you. We'll find a bench where we can sit, and you can have your breakfast. And we can talk."

"Good idea. How about you hold Captyn's leash on our walk?"

Barnes stood waiting in the foyer with Allie's cloak, wrapped food, and Peter's bowler.

"Thank you, Barnes. We'll be out for a walk should anyone inquire."

Once outside, the cool air and sunshine tickled Allie's face. "Fall in New York is my favorite time."

"Mine too, when it's not raining your father's excellent wine."

Allie gaped at Peter, then saw the teasing glint in his eyes. She couldn't suppress a giggle, and soon they were both laughing at the mishap from the night before.

"The streetcar is getting closer. We should hurry across."

He took Allie's elbow with one hand and kept Captyn on his leash in the other. "Shall we?"

Two children running like the wind passed them on the curved walking path.

"The leash keeps Captyn from chasing moving objects like children," Allie said. "We can take him off leash when they aren't nearby. Believe it or not, the hardest job in the park is finding lost children. They wander away from their nurses looking for the zoo."

"From what I've read, this park offers more than the zoo and a pleasant walk. I've heard about runaway horses. How do you protect yourself from getting run down by a wild horse?"

"You've heard of the whistle system, haven't you?"

"No. That's insane. A horse running wild and you stop it with a whistle?"

"Don't panic, Peter. The officer blows three blasts on a whistle."

"Then what?"

"Will you stop interrupting me and listen?"

"I'm picturing you, a delicate woman, in the path of this runaway beast attached to a carriage, of all things. I'm having trouble."

Allie's eyes were wide. She pressed her lips together and took a deep breath. "The police team up and run down the beast and the carriage."

"You make it sound easy."

"It's difficult. People have gotten hurt. Do you have a better idea?"

"Maybe a supervisor checking the restraints and harnesses every day?"

"Good idea. How can you implement that?"

"That's not my job, Allie. It's just that now that I've met you, I want nothing to happen to you, you hear me?"

Their eyes met. He pulled her to him, still holding her dog's leash, and tilted her head up, his finger under her chin. "Are you listening, Allie?"

They stood there in silence. Captyn growled at Peter.

Peter spoke to the dog. "It's all right, fella. You can stop growling."

"If you touch me again, I think Captyn will get upset."

"Never mind the dog. Do you understand what I'm saying to you?"

"Yes," she breathed. "I hear you."

Despite the fact Allie had listened to Peter, he frowned for no apparent reason. She supposed he worried needlessly about her. No matter; she would not dwell on his issues.

"I haven't had time to enjoy this park. Maybe with you, I'll make the time."

"You're here now."

His lips turned up. "That's true—let's not waste a minute."

"You can take Captyn off his leash."

"Are you sure? I wouldn't appreciate him knocking me down or growling at me again."

"He frolics in the leaves and comes back covered in mud. Sometimes he brings back a big stick, drops it at my feet, and barks at me to play. He's the only goofy friend I have."

"You and your dog are originals."

"I'm ready to have my crumpet."

Peter whisked out his handkerchief to wipe off a seat on the bench.

Allie waved it away. "Thanks, that's unnecessary."

"But I enjoy being Prince Charming."

"Oh, by all means, go ahead."

Peter took off his hat, swiped across the bench with his handkerchief, unhooked Captyn's leash, and patted the dog on the head. He bent close to the dog's ear and whispered something. Captyn licked Peter's face, woofed, and ran off into the bushes. Winding the leash into a loop, Peter sat beside Allie.

"I don't think Captyn liked my hat. He let me come close and whisper in his ear after I removed the darn thing."

"Maybe he believes you are someone else. He doesn't know you with that hat."

"That's ridiculous. Dogs use their noses."

Allie crossed her ankles. "Oh, come on. Captyn gave you a doggie kiss. Whatever did you whisper in his ear?"

"Yes, he licked my face. I suppose that's a doggie kiss. I told him not to come back until he found you the biggest stick and not to bother the children."

"You did not."

"I did." He winked.

"We may never figure out why Captyn attacked and barked at you."

"Allie, it's all right. Let's not worry about that. I must ask this question."

Oh, dear, there it was—the big question.

"Tell me, why did you leave the tent at the rally?"

Allie hesitated. She took the last bite of her crumpet. "My parents know I went to the rally but not about my old lady outfit and what happened to me. If you had arrested me, they would have found out." She said nothing more. Her heart had somersaulted when she fell on him and his arms wrapped around her that day at the tent. Goodness.

"Can we start over?"

Peter furrowed his brow.

She lifted her face to the light. Peter noted her clear, delicate facial structure and her light jade eyes the color of the gemstone.

"I'm not usually argumentative or cowardly."

"In the short time I've known you, you are certainly not a coward, far from it. However, argumentative is a different story." He steepled his fingers. "Let's just say you are passionate."

Allie's cheeks burned. "You are generous with your praise."

"You may not think me so generous when I tell you I find it difficult to comply with your request."

"What request?"

"That you don't want me to tell your parents what happened to you at the rally. By not telling them yourself, you were not honest with them. Your father has entrusted me to protect you. How can I do that if you can't be honest?"

She got up, stood in front of the bench, and peered down at him with darkened eyes.

"I'm not a liar. Well, maybe just a little."

"No such thing."

Allie looked out over the sprawling scenery. The air smelled of the leaves that continued to fall and spread across the grounds. Captyn scampered in and out of piles of leaves, getting muddy while chasing squirrels.

Allie sat back down beside Peter, lowered her head, and peeked at him from under her dampened, glistening lashes. She reached out and placed her hand in his. He didn't pull away. He turned to her, held her face in both hands, and touched his lips to hers. Allie gasped, moved back, and gave Peter a look of disbelief.

CHAPTER 14

The softness of her lips dazzled him, as did the poise she possessed when she moved. He liked the rhythm of her voice and the light in her eyes when she looked at him. He liked her in ways he'd not felt for any woman before. For a moment, she looked as though she would say something.

"Allie, is there a problem?" he asked, lifting his hand as though to halt her.

She tilted her head slightly, her fingers pressed against her lips. "You kissed me!"

"Correct. I kissed your soft and inviting lips, and you touched me despite our disagreement. It is not too soon to say that I find you charming. You've enchanted me with your sass, your delightful spirit, and now with your warm touch." *Stay focused on the job, Harrison.*

"Oh," she said, pushing back, blinking. *That was just a friendly touch, nothing special.* "We will spend the next few days together, let us focus on our mission."

"You are right," he breathed. "We need to clarify a few points before we leave for Fairfield."

They sat in silence for what seemed an eternity. Losing his

patience, he was about to take her in his arms when she folded her hands in her lap and spoke up. "All right, go ahead, I'm listening."

"There's a scoundrel out there bent on frightening you. For your safety and the safety of Mia, I would like to be the one to make any major decisions." His jaw tensed. "What do you say?"

She got up from the bench like she was leaving, then turned back around. "Mr. Harrison," she said with a half-smile that didn't reach her eyes, "I asked a simple favor—that you not tell my parents about the day at the rally—and you refused. Now you want to order me around. Father hired you to protect me, not to control me."

Peter watched Captyn romp around through the leaves for a moment. "Why must you overreact? I'm not trying to control you. Keeping you and your sister secure is my goal."

Captyn's sharp barks reached their ears. The spotted Great Dane gave chase after a young man riding a penny-farthing along the main path. Peter leaped into action and ran after the dog. No sooner had he started than he heard Allie's footsteps fast on his heels. The young man had been shakily riding on the contraption with its oversized front wheel, but the leaf-littered path covered obstacles. He went flying off while the penny-farthing continued on its wobbly way. The bicycle was bearing down on two young ladies in its direct path. Foreseeing the pending accident, Peter lengthened his stride and, with a flying leap, knocked the bicycle over before it plowed into the women. Peter went down along with penny-farthing and landed in a thick forsythia bush.

The two young ladies, who appeared stricken with fear, launched into a screaming duet. Captyn was barking at the spinning wheels, the tree root, and perhaps at the girls too.

Allie froze for a second. "Captyn is so sorry. He saw that confounded bicycle and gave chase. It's what dogs do. They naturally chase after a fast-moving object. I hope you understand my dog was not trying to scare you," she said with a friendly smile.

A shrill whistle pierced through the barking and the screaming. Captyn whipped his head around and, with a guilty-sounding whimper, shuffled his way to his mistress. Police officers came running, no doubt alerted by the sound of Captyn's barking.

Peter stood and watched the unforgettable young woman scold her dog and turn to what seemed like the entire police force. She snapped Captyn's leash onto his collar and apologized on behalf of her dog to the police and the wide-eyed young ladies.

Leaves and small branches covered the young man who had fallen off his bicycle. He righted himself, limped over to Allie, and pointed. "That's my penny-farthing. That dog is a menace. Put him away."

Allie took a deep breath and snapped back. "I beg your pardon? You were the one who was riding along a walking path. Why didn't you watch where you were going? What if there had been children playing? You would have run into them, and then you would be in trouble." She planted her hands on her hips.

"The only one in trouble here is that mangy beast," the bike rider said.

Allie shook her finger at the instigator. "How dare you insult one of God's magnificent creatures? You, sir, are the mangy beast."

The ladies squealed. The police officers stared.

The young man's face turned a red shade that Peter thought was close to a beet, his least favorite vegetable. If Peter did not act now, there was no telling what Allie would do next.

"Stop." Peter pulled the penny-farthing off the tree root and to the side of the path out of the way. Then he marched up to the young man and peered down into his face. The bike rider cowered at Peter's height and stance. "A gentleman never insults or argues with a lady. Apologize at once."

The two young ladies stood gaping. The police officers made grumbling noises of agreement. Captyn stood at attention and gave a low growl aimed directly at the young man. Allie placed her hand on the Great Dane's head. "It's all right, Captyn. The boy is harmless."

Allie stood tall and proud like Athena, the goddess of wisdom. She was magnificent.

The young man blew out a breath. His red cheeks clashed with his white-blonde hair, and he likely was shy of twenty years. Peter understood the young man's dilemma. He was trying to save face and appear manly at the same time.

"I am sorry. I didn't mean to lash out at you, miss. I should not have been riding my penny-farthing along this path."

"Thank you." The pins in Allie's hair had come undone because of her mad dash, and her mass of curls tumbled down. Peter loved her hair down. He must remember to discuss that with her, or maybe not. He wasn't sure.

Peter helped the young man pick up his penny-farthing and place it on the path. "You took quite a flying leap. Are you hurt?"

"My backside, but more so my ego." The young man's lips trembled, and he straightened his shoulders.

Allie introduced herself to the two ladies before they bid their farewell. Allie patted her Great Dane on the head. "Good boy, Captyn. Not the most ideal, but thanks to you, I met some more people of this great city and have another story for my column."

"Allie, we can head home, but first, relative to our discussion interrupted by the penny-farthing, I want to be clear. I will do nothing that will jeopardize your safety."

"How will telling my parents about my idiocy put me in danger?"

"Why are you asking such an obvious question?" he asked, his tone escalating.

"It appears we cannot agree here," she said, her reddish eyebrows coming together in an exasperated expression.

"Permit me to escort you home."

"For heaven's sake, that's unnecessary, thank you. She gritted her teeth, whipped around, and tugged at Captyn's leash. "Come on, boy."

CHAPTER 15

$\mathcal{T}$eary-eyed and fueled by anger, Allie ran home, hurrying over the trolley tracks, dodging the carriages that filled the busy streets. She patted the panting dog's head when they reached the Sandanko lobby. "Good boy, Captyn. You behaved well after all that excitement." She wiped away the tears with the sleeve of her short velvet jacket. Barnes opened the door at her knocking.

"I'm so glad to be home. It's been quite the day."

Barnes took her wrap. "Welcome back, Miss Allie."

She acknowledged him with a mournful smile.

"We had a grand old time at the park this morning. Well, sort of. It could have been a disaster. Two young ladies and their baby carriage almost got run over by a strange contraption. It had a most unusual large front wheel and two small back ones."

"Did you ride it?" Mia asked, striding into the foyer.

"I did not, but I had an adventure. You'll never guess what happened."

"Knowing you, dear sister, something outrageous."

Barnes opened the door again. "Hello, Mr. Harrison."

"Hello, Barnes," Peter said, handing Barnes his bowler.

Allie took her sister's hand. "Come, let's all sit in the parlor."

They settled onto the two settees across from one another, and Peter shot Allie a furious glance.

She skewered him with a constant glare.

"Allie, why did you run off again? Is this how you typically behave when you don't get your way?"

Allie turned her face away, her hands tightening into fists. "Your refusal and arguing tires me. Perhaps Captyn sensed my discontent, and that's why he growled at you."

A strange-sounding snort escaped Peter. Allie threw a suspicious glance his way. Was he laughing at her?

"In that case, I better watch how I treat you if I must keep Captyn in line. Now, can we put aside our disagreements?"

"I don't know how we can put them aside."

"Don't you think that the music box mystery takes priority? I planned to meet with my forensic colleague at two today."

"Were you planning to go without me? It's my music box and my mystery. I am going with you."

"I want to come along too," Mia interjected.

"I don't think it's a good idea. My friend is a little, shall we say, eccentric. I don't think he would appreciate the visit."

"We *are* coming with you," Allie said. "This is business. We aren't visiting."

"All right! All right! But don't blame me when my colleague misbehaves."

Allie rang for Barnes.

"You rang?"

"Captyn needs his lunch and a bath. Will you tend to him, please? You can see by his colorful coat that he got into some mischief."

Captyn cocked his head and peered at his mistress, then Barnes.

"Of course," Barnes said, taking the leash from her hand. "Come on, boy, the cook has some delicious, stewed beef waiting for you in the kitchen." Captyn padded alongside Barnes, his tail bobbing behind him.

"Peter, would you care to join us for luncheon?" Allie asked.

Peter's eyebrows shot up and he spread-eagled his arms. "I'm a mess." Peter glanced down at his mud-and-leaf-stained coat. "I should return home."

"Nonsense," Allie insisted. "You can change here. Something of Papa's will fit again. A quick lunch, and we'll be on our way. Barnes can clean and press your clothes."

"I think Barnes will make an enemy of my valet."

"Why so?" Mia asked.

"It seems whenever I'm in the company of the Baldwin family, something happens to my clothes, and Barnes gets the cleaning job."

Mia and Allie tittered in unison.

Mia gave him a warm smile. "Oh, do join us for lunch. You can share this morning's incident."

Allie knew that smile. Peter would say yes in *three, two, one.*

"Thank you," Peter said.

Allie threw Mia a wink.

THE DOOR FLUNG OPEN. "WHAT IN THE HELL COULD BE SO important that ye bother a man at such an ungodly hour?"

A giant stood there in the afternoon sunlight. Allie caught her breath. Wavy, black hair stood on end as though his fingers had just run through the unruly mass. Heavy-lidded, midnight eyes captured hers for a moment before shifting to Peter. Allie was sure his scruffy beard had grown like he was Rip Van Winkle. A growl emanated from the man's throat. "Did we have a meeting scheduled?"

"Sorry old chap, but I sent you a note that I'd be stopping by this afternoon," Peter said, lifting an eyebrow.

The big man blew out a breath. "Ach, my apologies." This mangy man did not appear to have a genuine apology anywhere in him.

Allie tried to hide the shock on her face. Was *he* the brilliant doctor? He looked more like a bumbling bandit from one of those western novels. Peter had explained on the carriage ride that his friend worked for the police department conducting autopsies, examining murders and evidence. Allie shivered at the thought of cutting open a human corpse to learn their secrets.

"Afternoon?" Robert McDougall asked.

"Yes, it's two in the afternoon."

Robert pulled out a watch from the pocket of his vest and glanced at it. "So it is. My apologies." Robert stepped back and waved. "Please, come in."

"McDougall, this is Miss Allie Baldwin and her sister, Miss Mia Baldwin. Miss Allie received the music box."

"Ah, a pleasure, both." Robert nodded. "Please, follow me."

They walked down a hallway to a crowded room with seating for only four—a couple of hard chairs and a small settee sitting on at least two Persian rugs. A rug also covered a table. Rugs were everywhere. A central globed chandelier lit the room. Candlesticks on the table added light when needed. Allie noticed a door open off the room, the glow of a lamp spilling out. His workroom maybe?

Did the doctor live alone? He did not appear to have a wife or children to shine a light on his dark days, but he had art on his walls. One looked familiar to Allie. She stared at the familiar painting, itching to get a closer look.

"I was working late at the morgue. We had a double homicide, and it took me all night to—"

"Excuse me, Robert, perhaps we can discuss the music box," Peter said. He inclined his head toward Allie and Mia as though reminding the doctor of their presence and the need for discretion.

The doctor concurred. "Please have a seat. I'll fetch my gloves and tools." He stepped into the lamp-lit room and returned with his gear.

Peter pulled out the music box from his satchel. He had rewrapped it at the Baldwin's. "There was a note with the box."

Allie removed the note from her reticule and handed it to Robert.

McDougall's face twisted. "Touch nothing with bare fingers," he said as he took the note with his gloved hands. "Your fingers have natural oils that could contaminate the evidence."

"McDougall, remember yourself."

Robert apologized for his rudeness. He took the proffered note and set it on the rug-covered table alongside the music box. He removed the music box from the wrapping and examined it, turning it this way and that, then opened it and did the same. The sweet elegance of "The Blue Danube" waltz floated through the room, and the toys danced and spin. Robert glanced up only to meet Mia's eyes. She glimpsed a flash of torment cross his features. He cleared his throat, pulled a slim baton from a cloth pouch, and began poking inside the box.

"Doctor McDougall," Allie piped up. "I am fascinated by your work. Would it be possible to tour the morgue and watch you work?"

Robert looked up with a scowl. "Why in the hell would you wanna do that?"

"For my readers. They like to know what's happening in their city."

"Are ye daft, woman?"

"Damn, Doc, keep your head. Miss Baldwin writes for the *New York Sentinel*. She was asking for information to write a story."

Robert paused and caught Allie's smile. "I apologize again,

Miss Baldwin." He turned to Mia then. "I apologize to you as well, Miss Baldwin. I rarely get visitors here, and certainly not lovely ladies like yourselves, and my work is…well, it's not conducive to chitchat in a parlor."

"It's understandable, Doctor McDougall," Mia said. "It must be difficult to separate yourself from what you see and do each day."

Robert held the music box up to the light, and bringing the box to his nose and sniffing. He set the box down and did the same with the wrapping paper. Perhaps this was part of his investigative process.

"Vanilla."

Peter rubbed his chin. "You can detect the scent of vanilla from the wrapping paper?"

"From the wrapping paper and the box, but it's faint. Could be a floral scent. I have to investigate further."

"Are you saying that whoever handled this gift transferred that scent to it?" Allie surmised.

"Perhaps." Robert lifted the note from the table, read it, sniffed it, and held it up to the light. "I cannot say for certain at this point. But if you leave this with me for a few days, I will examine it under a microscope."

"We are leaving for Fairfield tomorrow and won't be back for a few days. If you discover something of importance, can you send word to us via Sheriff Baxter in Fairfield?" Peter asked.

"Aye, you can count on it," Robert said. "I do not want to hazard any guesses at this point."

Peter rubbed his chin. "But you have a theory about something, correct?"

"I do."

Allie scratched her head. "Please, anything you can share with us will be helpful."

Robert sighed. "The handwriting on the note could be that of a woman masquerading as a man."

"What is it about the printing?" Allie asked.

Robert turned to Allie. "This person is attempting to hide their handwriting. Cursive is distinctive to an individual."

Allie's mouth turned up. "Fascinating, Doctor."

Allie addressed her sister. "What do you think, Mia?"

"About what?"

Allie smiled at her. "Daydreaming again, Mia? He thinks perhaps it was a woman."

Mia snickered. "I think anything is possible."

Robert shook his head slightly and pursed his lips. "Do you not think a woman could be so evil as to do this on her own?"

"Allie is not assuming any such thing," Peter interrupted. "She simply agrees that it could be a woman."

Allie and Peter continued to ask the doctor questions, but his responses were short and cryptic. Allie wanted to ask about that familiar-looking painting. Better not. This visit did not include sightseeing. Maybe another time. In any case, the doctor was rude and abrasive. But his eyes told Allie a different story— a painful one. He seemed haunted. Allie wanted to know more. They thanked Robert and left. Once outside, Mia poked Allie and leaned into her, trying not to include Peter.

"Did you notice the painting, Allie?"

"I did. It looked familiar. What about it, Mia?"

"It's my painting! I named it *Music of the Mind*."

CHAPTER 16

$\mathcal{T}$he music box mystery echoed Allie's jumbled thoughts which were centered on one man—Peter Harrison. She only knew him as the competent agent. There were more questions than answers about that man.

The chilly weather called for her favorite shawl that reminded Allie of her Gram's sweet scent. Gram always had crochet needles in her hands, creating soft, warm scarves to remember. Allie imagined any minute Gram would call for the wrap that Allie kept on the arm of her slipper chair.

Allie tucked her white blouse with the ruffled collar and cuffs into the blue and white striped skirt, then laced up her boots and draped the shawl over her shoulders, trailing her fingers over the bumpy crocheted stitches. Allie gazed into the courtyard garden from her window as the last of the foliage fluttered down in the wind. The dull fall colors were in a loose arrangement of dried leaves that looked like mud pies from high above. The brittle, gray blanket of winter would soon fill her view.

She stroked Captyn's head, put her finger under his snout,

and peered into his huge brown eyes. "I'm going to breakfast. Come down whenever."

She strode down the hall, following the coffee aroma like she was riding an ocean wave. The smell of freshly brewed coffee and buttery baked biscuits mingled and hung in the air. Barnes was setting the food on the sideboard before the family arrived. Allie looked in the mirror and pinched her cheeks. "Ah, that's good. A little rosy color." She lifted a plate off the warming tray, scooped up a fried egg and a warm biscuit, and poured herself a cup of coffee. She stirred cream into her coffee, transforming the dark brew into a golden one.

"Good morning," Clara announced herself, stepping into the breakfast room. She came over to her daughter and kissed her on the cheek. "Darling, your eyes are dark, and you look troubled." Clara wrapped her arm around Allie's shoulders and gave her a warm squeeze. "We have a little time this morning to stop at Cousin Louise's to ask how she's doing before working on the tea. But come, sit, and tell me what's on your mind."

Allie set her platter and coffee cup on the round oak pedestal table and pulled he chair next to her mother.

"The old goats at the fundraiser with their busy mouths are bothersome. They make my skin crawl. Why can't they mind their own business?" Allie said in a firm voice.

Barnes appeared in the doorway. "Mrs. Dempsey has arrived," he announced.

Clara stood and embraced her good friend. "Darling, I thought you wouldn't make it today, being so busy with Rork's art."

"Oh, he can do without me for a half a day. I wouldn't miss this visit with you to see Louise after that harrowing kidnapping."

Aunt Leila was Clara's lifelong friend back home from the West where she lived for the last twenty years or so. Clara and

Leila had agreed Clara's daughters respectfully address her friend as Aunt Leila, although she wasn't their aunt.

Allie, smiling, wrapped her arms around her Aunt Leila, who responded in kind. "Mama told us you were back. I can't wait to hear about your life in the West."

Leila nodded. "In short, we lived with the Indians who were the first inhabitants in those mountains. We learned to live well in the wilderness. Our children attended the schoolhouse we built. Teachers came, and the population grew. Now I want to hear about your lives here in the wilderness of New York."

Allie laughed. "No one ever called New York a wilderness, but I guess it is. Even this place where we reside was built on empty land. The land all around us is not yet built."

"Leila, please help yourself to breakfast and join us."

"Thank you, I cannot resist. The aroma is tantalizing. Is Mrs. Bigelow still with you doing food preparation?"

Clara nodded. "Yes, she is an excellent cook and baker. We are spoiled."

Leila put sizzling bacon and scrambled eggs on her plate. She took a cup of tea and a freshly baked, aromatic scone and sat with Clara and Allie.

Clara sprinkled cinnamon on her toast. "We were discussing Allie's disdain for the society women."

"Oh, Aunt Leila, they are always wanting to marry me off and telling me how foolish I am not to be pursuing a husband. I can't tolerate them for one second."

Leila patted Allie's cheek. "You are a lady first. It doesn't matter what they say; just smile at them and excuse yourself. They can learn a thing or two from you."

The rest of the family began trickling in with Captyn by Mia's side. The dog sidled up to Barnes. There was no resisting the dog; he slipped him a piece of ham. Captyn, wagging his tail, greeted Leila, then panted after Barnes until breakfast finished.

"He is so adorable, but he is frightfully big. Does he scare little children?"

Allie laughed. "No, they love him and always try to have a ride on his back."

Mia, Emma, and Ava ran over to hug their Aunt Leila. "It's so good to have you join us today," Mia said.

"Mama, can we sit here with you, Allie, and Aunt Leila?"

"Of course. Let's move the chairs so we can sit together."

"Aunt Leila, I love your indigo skirts. They shimmer in the light from the woven silver running through the fabric. You look so elegant," Ava said.

Emma agreed. "I enjoy your fashion sense. You look beautiful."

After breakfast, Barnes had the carriage waiting in the porte cochère ready to take them to the Hotel Angelicus.

"Clara, girls, I regret I won't have time to attend the fundraiser, but Rork and I have already made a significant donation for the hospital. I'll be leaving after our visit with Louise."

"Understood," Clara said. "Let's plan to have tea another time, perhaps at the French Café in the park."

At the hotel, a smiling elevator operator cheerily greeted the women before taking them up to the penthouse where Peter's guards stood on either side of the Haltons' door.

Allie knocked gently. Louise greeted them in the vestibule with her index finger on her lips.

"Shh. The baby's asleep."

"We stopped by to make sure all is well," Allie whispered.

Each of the Baldwin girls gave their cousin Louise a brief hug and kiss. Clara hugged her niece.

Louise took Leila around and stepped back. "Leila, it is so good to see you. Thank you for coming."

"Thank God the baby is safe," Clara said.

Leila took Louise's hand. "My goodness, isn't that the truth."

"I haven't slept well since the kidnapping last Friday," Louise said.

Clara stroked her niece's face. "Allie told me that my sister would arrive soon. Having your mother here should ease your burden."

Louise clasped her hands to her chest. "I can't wait."

Frederick came out of the library with Peter, both laughing and jolly. Peter wore a black day coat over a white shirt with ruffles at the edge of his shirtsleeve poking out and a white ascot. His striped trousers made Peter appear longer. His dark hair had a curl in front that kept falling over his forehead. The two men stood nearby, Peter in his elegant attire and Frederick in his casuals, discussing what sounded like marriage. Allie knew eavesdropping was rude, but she did it anyway.

Allie frowned. Peter's eyes were bloodshot. He looked like they had shot his best agent. She wanted to say something but caught herself. It would be inappropriate with her family standing by. She hoped she could talk to him soon. Surely there would be another opportunity. Allie found herself watching how the sides of Peter's mouth crinkled when he smiled and how he rubbed his stubbled chin and jaw when he was deep in thought. His lips were inviting, full on the bottom with stubble above the top. What would it feel like to have his lips on hers again, or kisses on her neck, or on her toes, one at a time? She shivered at the thought and wanted to kiss Peter. Oh, so much! It didn't matter. It would not happen. *Stop thinking about kissing him or how adorable he is, idiot.*

She refused to think about how he affected her on some deep level. Her feelings would not rule her. Unlike her friend Frankie, who wanted Allie's unavailable brother Adam, she would not fall into the trap of love. She wanted to work for women's freedom, work for their cause, and write her column. Marriage was the furthest thought from her mind.

The men exchanged goodbyes with Clara, Leila, and the girls

before Frederick escorted Peter to the front door. Frederick excused himself and disappeared into his library.

"Please come into the parlor," Louise said to her cousins. "Can you stay for tea?"

"It's not a good time," Clara said. "We have work to do in the tearoom before the guests arrive for the fundraiser."

"Another time then, Louise?" Mia asked.

"Yes, when Mother is here. I'll let you know."

"Allie will let everyone know when she arrives."

More hugs and kisses followed nods and yeses.

Louise whispered to Allie as they were leaving, "That Mr. Harrison is a handsome sort, isn't he?"

"Yes, I suppose he is," Allie whispered with her hand at the side of her mouth. She hoped her mother and sisters hadn't heard.

Handsome or not, she didn't need a man in her life. He had nothing she wanted. Well, maybe she could ask him to go with her to the opera or something so they could spend some time getting to know one another. *Oh no, there you go again. Stop that.* She'd arranged her life just the way she liked it.

CHAPTER 17

*A*llie drifted to the Hotel Angelicus tearoom windows, drawn by the pattering of the bleak, early November rain against the panes. The weather brought her a head full of frizzy curls and finished the last of the leaves clinging to the trees lining the streets. The streets were an obstacle course of steaming manure swarming with flies. Rain added to the stench.

Fifth Avenue was the vibrant heartbeat of the crowded city, with its ebb and flow of coaches and horses on the cobblestone streets. The horses, driven by their owners, worked long days until they collapsed. Nowadays, it took over an hour to get from Uptown to lower Manhattan due to the increased traffic and population growth in the city. New York was booming.

Women passing on the newly paved sidewalks huddled under umbrellas to shield their wide-brimmed, veiled bonnets. Men in buttoned coats, top hats, and curved bowlers—like Peter's, who carried himself like a soldier, straight and proud, moving with fluidity and...

Distracted again, Allie!

"The New York Lady's Club—one hundred of the wealthiest women of New York—would fill the hotel tearoom at a fundraiser in the early afternoon for the Baldwin's Hospital new wing. Allie closed her eyes. She would rather be anywhere than here.

"Allie, are you daydreaming again?" her mother asked.

"I suppose," Allie said with a drawl.

Stop that. She scolded herself. Allie knew how much this meant to her mother.

"Please stay focused," her mother pleaded.

"I am focused, Mama." *Focused on Peter,* she neglected to voice. The way he walked, the way he talked, and she was sure he would unsettle her the way he rode a horse. They would have to go riding one day. Maybe he would be the father of her children.

Yikes, what am I thinking?

Allie smoothed the pristine white cloths on the dining tables, all dressed with the best sparkling tableware, waiting for the meddling matrons to arrive.

Her mother took Allie's arm. "Are you all right?"

Allie caught the look in her mother's eyes. "I'm not sure, Mama. Look at my hair. It is a mess."

"Silly girl, your hair is fine. Stop this dawdling. The day must go well. Please make certain that you seat Mrs. Templeton and Mrs. Higgins at least two tables apart. Their feuding is a constant threat to everyone around them. Your sisters can help if you need extra hands."

"Mama, I can handle this," Allie said with a twitch of her lips. "I promise to keep them as far apart as a penguin stays from a polar bear."

Clara handed Allie name cards and pointed to the next table. Allie gave her mother a peck on the cheek, musing that her mother's penchant for demands and commands would have made her an excellent army general.

With each blink of Allie's eyes, golden butterflies and dragonflies seemed to flutter off the painted, soaring ceiling of the tearoom. She imagined the winged creatures following her as she moved from place setting to place setting, propping up the cards at each table for six. When sitting beside Central Park's Pond on a warm summer day, she watched these same insects' aerial antics. She discovered from her reading that water was vital to complete the dragonfly's life cycle.

"Sorry, Mama. Right now, I would rather tuck into my favorite chair reading by the fire."

Clara placed her hands on her hips. "My dreamy daughter, I promise when this is over, you can curl up in that battered, old chesterfield with Captyn until Christmas. Now, put this raffle basket on the welcome table and check that the donated items are all in order." Allie ran her hand over the basket wrapped in bows and streamers—a colorful bath set, boudoir delights, a music box, and more—worth well over one hundred dollars, plus a gift certificate to the popular Lord & Taylor department store. Allie's mood lifted. She looked over to her mother, noticing her stance with her hands on her hips, her lips thinned.

Allie, you promised to do this. do not be a bother, she scolded herself while arranging the place settings. *Get it together, girl.*

"Mama, the basket has treats for anyone."

"Does it? Let's get those raffle tickets sold. Finish up while I handle details with the chef."

Clara hurried out. Allie gave the basket a last look and finished the place settings, keeping an eye out for the feuding women. One card slipped out of her hand and fell. She bent to pick it up. Not finding it, she got down on her hands and knees and scooted under the table. Aha. She got the card and, crawling out with her treasure, she spied a pair of shiny, black boots standing beside the table. She peeked out. Her eyes traveled up a familiar masculine form, and she sucked in a deep breath.

It's him.

"Fancy finding you down there, Allie. You seem to have a propensity for being under tables. Shall I join you?" Peter asked with a chuckle. Before she could answer, he leaned down and offered his hand. She placed hers in his. Warmth embraced her, and a strange feeling bounced around in the pit of her stomach. She stood, her hand still in his, all the while peering into his eyes.

"May I ask what the reason is this time?"

Her cheeks burned. They had to be rosy red. "I was just checking something," she said, trying to act calm and confident, as though it wasn't her voice.

"Are you planning to check under every table?"

"Oh, no, no. Just this one." Really, how dare he tease her?

She fumbled the cards in her hand. "Why are you still here, Peter? I thought you left."

"Allie, take a break and have a walk with me." He took her hand. At that moment, Mia came over holding a white rose.

"Peter, it's nice to see you again. Are you taking Allie somewhere?"

"I'd like her to join me for a stroll."

"Sounds lovely. I'll take over your job with the tables."

"You both are acting like I'm not here. I will finish my work. Mother would never approve of me handing off my job."

"Then let's plan on doing it soon. Mia, you can come as our chaperone."

Mia looked at Peter. "You may have to ask Papa's permission."

"I'm sure he won't object since he's hired me."

"True," Mia said with a quick nod. "Maybe when we go on our trip."

"That would make sense." He held up his hands in surrender. "Ladies, I will leave you to your work. Please excuse me."

Allie chewed her bottom lip and held up her hand. "Wait."

He turned and smiled. "Do you have questions?"

Allie blinked and pursed her lips. "I…um." With her finger pointed in the air, she said, "Fairfield."

"Fairfield?" Peter reiterated.

Allie picked up a rose and sniffed. "Yes, Fairfield." Goodness, why could she not get a sentence out around this man? "Let's leave for Fairfield tomorrow, early."

"What time are we leaving tomorrow?" Mia asked.

The corner of Peter's mouth slipped upward. "I don't have an answer right at the moment. Sorry ladies, I will let you know when I know."

Allis's heart for Peter had to be on hold, maybe forever. This trip was for business, nothing more. Her schedule at the hospital, the fight for suffrage, and her job at the *Sentinel* held great importance. There was no room for a husband.

No male relationships.

No commitment to marriage.

Men didn't favor working women. No matter, she had no future with Peter. If she made it clear to him what her life plans were, he would find someone else. Her heartbeat quickened. She had drifted away again. Mother was right. She was a dreamer.

FOR THE NEXT TWO WEEKS OR MORE, HE'D BE FACE TO FACE WITH Allie, but he couldn't dwell on her beauty and soft voice or on her strength and passion for those she loved. Spending time with her might prove he needed her in his life. She knew what she wanted. Although it wasn't him, he was sure. But she captured his attention, and somehow, he could not let that go. Filling his life with an ambitious woman could mean trouble. Allie Baldwin in particular. Could he make it work? Then there was his job. He didn't appreciate Halton's remark that Peter would be an old man when he retired. Humph. He could do worse than give in to a commitment to marriage now.

Peter had to concentrate on the issues at hand. A few cases

plagued him that he needed answers to before they left for Fairfield—not the least of them the kidnapper and the music box culprit. His forensic doctor friend was on the hunt and would be in touch with his findings. In the meantime, Peter would keep Allie safe.

On his way into his office building, Maxwell, the doorman, in his army-type uniform, tipped his hat to Peter with two fingers of his white-gloved hand.

Peter gave a brief salute to Maxwell, petted his sleeping guard dog, and continued to walk, then stopped short and faced him to ask a nagging question.

"Maxwell, I hope this does not offend you, but I want to ask you something about marriage. You all right with that?"

"Let's hear it, sir."

"You spend a good deal of time here away from home. Do you have a wife?"

The hefty man cupped his ear. "What's that, Mr. Harrison, sir?"

"Are you married?" Peter repeated louder.

The droopy-jowled massive doorman resembled his bulldog. "I'm married all right, sir. Why you askin'?"

"What do you think about your wife?"

Maxwell looked at him from the corner of his eye. "You gettin' personal, sir?"

Peter took in a deep breath. "When did you know, Maxwell?"

Max gave Peter a blank stare. "When did I know what, sir?"

"When did you know you loved her?"

"Love? I don't even like her."

"I figured it was a wife making you happy—your smiling face when you open your lunch pail. It's that chocolate cake every time, isn't it?"

"Now ya got me, sir. Guess I love her. Maybe I knew at the first bite."

"I thought so. Enjoy your lunch today."

"That I will, sir. That I will."

Peter rode up the elevator to his office. He shook off thoughts of chocolate cake and girls peeking out from under tables. *I have a job to do.*

He put the key in the lock on the door to his office. With *Harrison Detective Agency* written in red cursive lettering on the translucent-glass upper section, the heavy door opened with a push. In his after-hours office, no shoes shuffled, and there was no fresh coffee or hum of pens on paper, only emptiness reminding him of his empty life. There must be a better way. His gut growled. He sat at his desk and turned up the gas lamp, resting his chin in his hand, and reviewed his work papers. Why choose work? The opportunity for marriage or a relationship was evident. Frederick had a point. Why wait until he retired to find a wife?

Allie was not the woman he had dreamed of. Her independence and work made it unlikely she would dedicate herself as a wife and mother like Frederick's wife had done. Allie had good instincts as well as a passion for good works. He loved her kindness and compassion to make the world a better place. This virtuous woman tirelessly fought for women's rights and abolition. Perhaps he *would* pursue the idea of marrying before he retired.

His conversation earlier with Frederick ended up focusing on Peter's single life and Frederick's married one. Frederick said that women had a sixth sense. His wife always knew how things would turn out, so she encouraged him to run for mayor and ignore his opponent Wilbur Drumple's puffery noise. At the time, Peter ignored Frederick's advice. He said he would marry after retirement, and that was that. Frederick laughed at Peter and remarked that women of all sizes—young, old, and almost dead—would pick at his bones.

Peter's feelings were mixed, but he didn't appreciate Halton's remarks.

I'll get married when I damn well please, whether or not I'm an old man.

On his way out, he grabbed his briefcase and carefully slipped in the papers.

With no dog to walk and no wife to come home to, his Gramercy Park residence was too quiet. He dropped off his briefcase, hopped back in his carriage, and headed for the hotel to keep his eye on Allie at the fundraiser.

CHAPTER 18

"*H*ello, Allie. You look lovely today." Mrs. Zinnia Templeton eyed Allie's forest-green silk gown. "A Templeton original, is it not?"

"Yes, Mrs. Templeton." Allie's smile didn't reach her eyes, but she knew Mrs. Templeton would never notice. Unlike her sisters, Allie did not fancy the latest styles. This gown, with its elegant lines, was one of Mrs. Templeton's older designs. It was one of Allie's favorites, although she could not tolerate Mrs. Templeton.

"Your mother's choice of the Angelicus for the fundraiser is extraordinary."

"Thank you, Mrs. Templeton. We appreciate the compliment."

"Did you know I attended my niece's wedding here?" Mrs. Templeton continued, fluffing the bright purple plumage in her broad-brimmed hat. "They raved about her wedding in all the society pages." The older woman leaned closer and whispered, "Elizabeth married the Earl of Everton, you know, from *England*."

"I wrote about their wedding in my column," Allie said. "You must be proud of your niece."

"I am," Mrs. Templeton said with a sniff. "I would think your parents are keeping watch for you, my dear girl. You don't want anyone to declare you on the shelf, do you?"

"My goodness, who would say that?" Allie asked with a lift of her brow.

"Well, society, of course, darling." Mrs. Templeton swept her hand over the women in attendance. "You must be aware how delicate and desperate your situation is at your age."

"Mrs. Templeton, I am certain that my marital status, be it on the shelf or not, is of little concern to anyone."

"I'm shocked, young lady. Of course it is a concern. And your lack of affirmation is a failure," Mrs. Templeton said in a huff.

"You have a concern—but it is my affair."

"Is it, darling? I'm confident your parents wish you to marry before it's too late. You must get married long before anyone would call you a spinster."

"Thank you, Mrs. Templeton. I'll keep my marriage plans private if you don't mind."

"You know that it's far more respectful to be a married woman than an unmarried one. Imagine where you would have to stand at all the balls. It's shameful, my dear, and it's up to you to change that."

"I don't suppose you could understand. I rather enjoy standing in a corner at the balls."

"I don't understand, Allie. You cannot mean that."

"I do. It allows me to admire your company's beautiful and fashionable gowns that are so popular with the ladies," Allie said.

"Thank you for your kind remarks about my designs. My, you go on, don't you, Allie?"

"Also, when I am in the corner at a ball, it allows me to

discuss voting issues with interested women, women who might want to join the fight."

"Suffrage still involves you with its silly business?"

"Yes, I'm active with the women's movement, but thank you for your concern. Tell me more about your niece's grand wedding."

Mrs. Templeton preened under the praise and rambled on about her niece's wedding. She appeared self-engrossed and did not notice her lifelong enemy, Mrs. Forsythia Higgins, had arrived.

Uh-oh, here comes trouble.

Allie held her breath, hoping there would not be an altercation between the two rival queens of fashion. Thankfully, Clara, who had been at the welcome table, stepped in, looped her arm through Mrs. Higgins, escorted her to her table, and then returned to the welcome table.

Allie excused herself from Mrs. Templeton. She and Mia made their way into the tearoom and stopped by an exuberant Mrs. Franklin standing at the welcome table and waving her name card.

"Oh my, I adore these pretty, pink roses painted on this card. How did you guess they are my favorite flower?"

"Mia is the artist in the family. She deserves the praise," Allie said, beaming.

Mrs. Franklin clasped Mia's hand in both of hers. "My dear, you have a special talent. Please visit me soon to paint my portrait."

"Thank you, Mrs. Franklin. It would be an honor," Mia said.

Mrs. Franklin leaned close to Clara and, from the side of her mouth, whispered, "Goodness, did you see Mrs. Templeton and Mrs. Higgins, darling? If hairpins were daggers, there would be bloodshed on this gorgeous, antique Oriental rug."

"Why, Mrs. Franklin, my dear friend, it is delightful to see you. I agree. The rug is a fabulous collector piece. It reminds me of the Persian in our apartment at the Sandanko."

Allie overheard the quip and coughed to cover her laughter. Clara had made a point of seating her daughters at separate tables. It was vital that they mingle instead of sitting in the corner. Allie's seat assignment was between Mrs. Charles Worthington, the widow of a prominent architect, and Mrs. Portia Drumple, the widow of the late banker Wilbert Drumple. Mrs. Worthington and Mrs. Drumple took command of Allie's unmarried status and made a point of mentioning their eligible sons. Allie had never met them, but supposedly, Mrs. Drumple's son Wilbur was running for Mayor of New York.

Allie had asked her parents if Drumple supported women's suffrage, and her father said, "That buffoon only supports himself by filling his pockets. Good thing Wilbur Senior left his wife a protected allowance. Otherwise, that idiot would have wasted everything by now. He spends most of his time at the racetrack." Allie did not know how Drumple expected to win a mayoral race against Halton.

"A young lady of refinement cannot spend her days gadding about collecting stories about unfortunate people. Especially when fine, young gentlemen like my Wilbur require a proper wife."

"I agree with you, Mrs. Drumple. It's all so true." Mrs. Worthington shook her head. "Allie, my dear, you must set a good example for your younger sisters. If you don't marry, it will be a terrible burden on those poor girls."

Allie felt like a ball in a tennis match. The thought reminded her the tennis courts in the rear of the Sandanko and playing there with her sisters. Perhaps she would ask Peter to play. And beat him, of course. Her belly had those pebbles again. She wished she could stop the society matron's obsession with her marital status. The tea service arrived, and the ladies stopped chattering long enough to munch on the delicate watercress sandwiches and the freshly baked, aromatic cakes and pastries placed on each table.

Later on, Mrs. Templeton doubled her donation to the hospital, her way of thanking Clara for a splendid affair. The ladies applauded her generosity. Mrs. Higgins announced an additional donation to build a park with a carousel and a paddock for ponies behind the new wing.

"Mama, congratulations. Your tea was more than successful, and you're smarter than any politician," Allie said to Clara on the carriage ride home.

"Who knew that Mrs. Templeton and Mrs. Higgins were going to outbid each other and raise the rest of the needed funds for the hospital?" Mia said.

Clara smiled at Allie and her sisters. "Darlings, you must understand human nature before you can affect change."

Allie was happy for her mother but exhausted from the constant marital advice from the witchy matrons. She would have to let it go for now. Her parents had placed no such pressure on her, and she had much to accomplish before she contemplated marriage.

Peter appeared at the fundraiser entrance.

Allie stood and bent down to whisper in her mother's ear. "Excuse me. I will be right back."

She hurried over to Peter. "What are you doing here? This event is only for women."

"I'm doing my job."

"What job?"

"Your father hired me to watch over you. Remember?"

"Yes, I remember, but that begins when we leave for Fairfield."

"Your father and I shook hands. That was when my job began."

Allie slammed her hands on her hips. "That is ridiculous. I'm with friends and family and the women's society. I do not need a watchdog."

Peter crossed his arms over his chest. "Anything can happen, anytime. We can't be too cautious."

"The worst that can happen here is Mrs. Templeton and Mrs. Higgins might get in a food fight."

Allie could not help laughing under her breath at the picture of the two ladies tossing petit fours at each other. Maybe it was good that Peter was present.

"No worries. No one needs to know why I'm here."

"What are you going to do, hide behind a potted fern?"

"No, I am just going to stand here and monitor the situation."

Allie threw up her hands. "I don't believe this. Does Father know you are here?"

"Yes. I have to report what's going on with you every day."

"Does my mother know?"

He cocked his head. "She does."

Allie turned and caught her mother staring at them. Clara, with a raised brow and half-smile, wiggled her fingers.

Allie huffed and wagged her finger at him. "All right then, if you are going to stand here, then make yourself useful. Wait, I'll be right back."

She returned with a roll of raffle tickets. "Here, sell these. Use your charm."

"Oh, you find me charming?" he said. A twinge of laughter laced his voice.

Allie brought her hands up to her hot cheeks. She watched him smile and wink at the ladies as they fussed over him while giving up their money. She got those funny feelings in her belly again. He looked over at her. She rolled her eyes. Allie did not want him there, but she could not help peeking to see what he was doing.

CHAPTER 19

*A*llie made her way down from their apartment on the top floor to the Waverly residence on the first floor to meet Frankie. She enjoyed using the stairs rather than the vertical lift; exercise helped her keep her figure.

"Good morning, Mrs. Waverly. How are you this fine morning?"

"And what's so fine about this morning?" Olivia Waverly frowned, glancing up at Allie, then back down at her needlepoint. Mrs. Waverly sat in their sparse parlor in a stiff-backed chair. All the household chairs were stiff-backed, like Mrs. Waverly.

Allie's face lit up. "Why, it's a beautiful day. The sun is shining, and the birds are chirping. There isn't a cloud in the sky. A perfect day for a stroll."

"Humph, it's too humid if you ask me." She looped the delicate blue thread through the hoop of the silk square of her needlepoint.

The woman never failed to mention that idle hands are the devil's playground. It seemed to Allie that needlepoint was an excuse for Mrs. Waverly to gather with her friends and gossip. *Her* mother never had time for needlework. Hospital visits and fundraising overflowed her schedule.

"And it is going to rain. I can feel it in my bones," Mrs. Waverly went on. "Do not stay out too long with Francesca. If she gets wet, she will most likely catch pneumonia."

"Mother, that's absurd," the young woman announced from the doorway, shaking her cane at her. "This is all I need."

Allie tittered at her friend and glanced at Mrs. Waverley from the corner of her eye. "Good morning, Frankie." She and Frankie had been friends from their school days.

Mrs. Waverly *harrumphed* at Allie's use of the nickname, one that Allie invented. The name fit her better than Francesca.

Frankie had a pronounced limp from a fall out of a first-floor window years ago. Mrs. Waverly had kept her daughter in a wheelchair until she rebelled.

"Allie, before you take my daughter for her daily walk—"

"Mother, Allie doesn't take me for my daily anything. She's my friend. We take walks and shop together."

"I was merely going to ask Allie to make sure you don't overtax yourself. The strength in your legs doesn't match your strength of will, and I know they pain you in the evenings."

"I can make my own decisions. I'm not a child."

"Well, I never said you were. I'm concerned about your welfare."

"Thank you for your concern, but I can take care of myself."

"Frankie, shall we?" Allie said, sandwiching her lips together and being careful not to step into the fray of a complicated mother-daughter relationship.

Mrs. Waverly laid her needlework on the side table beside her chair and poured herself a cup of tea. The gold-plated box on the table caught Allie's attention.

"Mrs. Waverly, may I open this, please?"

"Yes, carefully. It's quite old."

When she lifted the lid, a ballerina in a white tutu with

flowers in her hair twirled to the melody of Tchaikovsky's "Waltz of the Flowers."

"Ah, it's a music box. How charming."

"Thank you, Allie. It's my treasure," Mrs. Waverly said, clearing her throat.

"I love it. Did you buy it on one of your trips to Europe?"

"Mr. Waverly gave it to me before we married."

Allie couldn't believe that the taciturn Mrs. Waverly could be sentimental enough to keep a gift from her late husband, especially a whimsical music box. She wasn't sociable and rarely ventured out except to attend Sunday church services.

Frankie slipped on her gloves and tied her poppy-red woolen scarf around her neck. The bright color enhanced her velvet-brown eyes and long, sable hair.

"Enjoy your needlework, Mother. I shall return in a few hours."

Mrs. Waverly sipped her tea and muttered something about young women spending far too much time strolling about the city rather than in genteel pastimes like reading.

Frankie linked her arm with Allie's and whispered, "Is Captyn waiting in the hall?"

"He can't wait to see you," Allie said in a murmur.

Frankie smiled when Captyn trotted over to her and nuzzled her hip with a gentle nudge. "No jumping."

"Good boy, Captyn," Allie commended the Great Dane and rewarded him with one of Mrs. Bigelow's special doggie treats. The Baldwin cook used leftover meat scraps from dinner and baked them in a hearty dough. One day, Allie's father snatched a few cooling on the counter and declared them the best biscuits he'd ever tasted.

Allie looped Captyn's leash onto Frankie's hand before they crossed the trolley-tracked street into Central Park.

"He's staying close to me. You've been training him well."

"That's the first thing I taught him."

"Forget Captyn. You promised to tell me everything about your time with the mysterious Mr. Harrison."

"The unusual day has left me puzzled."

"Out with it, Allie."

Allie told her friend the events that had happened from the moment Mr. Harrison picked her up at the *Sentinel* to the moment of the kidnapping alert and how she insisted on going along to the Haltons. Then she explained about the two letters she'd received at the office. Frankie listened with widened eyes and frequent exclamations.

"What a relief the baby is home with his parents," Frankie said, placing her hand over her heart.

"My mother is with them now."

"Of course, she's Clara Baldwin after all. Sometimes she commands a salute. What about the two letters?"

"We're going to Fairfield to investigate the incident at the Longdale Farm. Papa hired Mr. Harrison to escort us. Imagine that."

"What about the other letter, the threatening one?"

"It was not threatening. Readers think they have a right to dictate to reporters what to write. I think it was just a prankster."

"I hope you're right."

CHAPTER 20

"*D*on't forget this fine fellow." Allie patted Captyn's head. "Let's sit here on the bench for a bit. Captyn can romp around in the leaves."

Allie took off his leash. "Captyn, go play."

Captyn burrowed into a pile of crinkly leaves until his spots all but disappeared. Then a moment later, he popped up and ran to Allie, tugging on her skirt.

"Oh, all right."

She skipped to the pile with him, crouched down, dug her hands into the leaves, and threw them up in the air. Captyn gave a soft woof, and in his exuberance, ended up knocking Allie into the pile.

"You silly dog." She laughed. "Look at me. I am a scarecrow all covered in leaves."

Captyn bowed down on his front paws and offered a couple of playful barks. Frankie came to her rescue. She braced herself on her cane, leaned down, and helped Allie up.

"Thanks." The leaves stuck to her wine-colored wool coat. "Look at this mess."

"Oh, you love it."

Allie brushed off her coat. "Of course I do. I want my big puppy just like this forever."

"My father loved this time of year," Frankie said.

"You think of him often, don't you?"

"I miss him."

Simon Waverly had a cheerful nature that was the joining force between his wife, Olivia, and Frankie. Since his passing, mother and daughter had retreated into their separate spheres.

Allie touched her forehead to her friend's in silent communication. She held her palm up toward her friend. "Have I told you what's been going on in my life lately?"

Frankie's eyes widened, and she shook her finger at Allie. "You are naughty. What more have you not told me?"

"This Mr. Harrison, I mean Peter—"

Frankie interrupted and sucked in a breath. "Oh, my goodness. First names already? He isn't just any man your father hired, is he?"

"All right, I'll tell all. Give me a chance."

Frankie raised both arms. "Come on. Tell me, tell me."

"He's handsome."

"What else? Come on, Allie, you are taking forever."

Allie placed her hands on her hips. "If you can be quiet, I'll give you all the details."

"I'll try."

"We met at the recent suffrage rally." Allie raised her hands in the air. "He threatened to arrest me for disturbing the peace."

"Were you pretending to be someone else—again?"

"Sort of. My old lady outfit revealed the real me when . . ." She covered her mouth, but the words slipped out between her fingers. "I fell on top of him."

"You did not!"

Allie tapped her fingers against her lips. "I did. I felt his body beneath mine, all muscle and perfect."

"Ooh, you have all the fun. Besides the two of you, did you notice anyone else there?"

"No, I think we were alone. Is there anything more mortifying if we were not?"

"I agree, if anyone saw you, it would be extremely embarrassing. Have you seen Peter since?"

"A few times since the event. I expect I will get to know him better on this trip."

Frankie furrowed her brow. "Why get to know him?"

"I get warm all over looking at him, hearing his voice, his laughter, you know? I get this urge to hug him."

"And maybe kiss him?" Frankie asked.

Allie took a deep breath. "Oh, stop it. You are groping."

"I am not. You want Peter to kiss you, don't you?"

"Of course, I want him to kiss me like he did the first time, but I think he'll be all business."

"True, if he's a good detective. But his expertise is a comfort, right?"

"I think so."

"Are we finished talking about kissing?"

Allie laughed. "For now."

Frankie reached out and tugged at Allie's curls. "Oh, pooh, if we must."

"We have important work to do. The farm owners want the women workers to hear the suffrage speakers, but deliberate treachery is a concern."

"I wish I could go along. It gets dull around here."

"I will have lots to share when I get back."

"Let's go to the Esplanade," Frankie said, changing the subject.

"Good idea. I have not seen the fountain in a while."

Frankie slipped her left arm through Allie's and held her cane in her right hand. Captyn loped beside them up the staircase. At the top, Captyn plopped down, his head on his paws, and watched squirrels chattering on a tree branch.

"You know," Allie said, "this is the best view in the park. I could stay here forever and enjoy the fountain."

They strolled to a bench and sat, catching their breath.

Two nannies with their charges bundled up in buggies strolled by, catching Captyn's eye. He leaped up and trotted after them. Allie whistled. He stopped and sauntered back and flopped down at their feet.

Two attractive young couples sashayed past. Allie noted Frankie's intense gaze.

Frankie sighed. "How is Adam doing these days?"

"Adam is courting a young lady in Chicago." Allie caught dismay pass over Frankie's face. "Do you want to know more?"

"No." Frankie sounded sad. She hung her head for a moment. "Oh, fiddlesticks, tell me everything."

"She's the daughter of a duke from England."

"So?"

"Her father lost his money. The duke and duchess came here to find a husband for their daughter, one with deep pockets."

"Adam knows and doesn't care?" She lifted her scarf higher on her neck as the sun slid behind a cloud.

"Papa told Mama when he came home from Chicago the other day . . ." Allie's voice trailed away. She dared not say anything more.

Frankie lifted a brow. "What are you leaving out?"

"Besotted is the word Papa used to describe him. Mama had no choice but to invite them to Baldwin House for Christmas."

Frankie reached down and laid her head atop Captyn's head. She stayed that way for a moment. "The Waverlys will not join the Baldwins this Christmas."

"Whyever not?"

"I believe this holiday Mother and I will remain at our Greenwich mansion and celebrate alone."

Both families had their country homes in Greenwich, Connecticut, and usually spent Christmas together.

"It's a quick ride away if you change your mind."

"I will not."

"Well, if you do, you know you are always welcome."

"Forgive me." She sniffed and retrieved a handkerchief from her pocket, dabbing at her nose. "I seem to be rather sensitive today."

"You never have to apologize to me." Allie gave her friend a warm, sideward hug.

"*Ruff, ruff, ruff.*" Captyn took off after a squirrel.

"Oh, dear." Allie shot up and chased after him. "Captyn, stop." She caught up with him and took hold of his collar. "Heel." He trotted by her side as they returned to the bench.

Allie considered Frankie's reaction. Honestly, men could be so dense. Her brother failed to see the remarkable Frankie. An image of Peter flashed in her mind. He did not seem thickheaded like her brother, thank goodness. Of course, she could not contemplate a courtship now, let alone marriage. Besides, Allie believed Peter thought of her as nothing more than a nosy reporter.

After their return from Fairfield, she would never see him again, except perhaps in polite company.

Yes, that would be just fine.

CHAPTER 21

*H*urried feet and voices passed in the train's corridor. A knock on the door of their private car resounded. Allie's stomach stirred, believing Peter had knocked. She pinched her cheeks and smoothed her upswept hair, exposing her swan-like neck above her bare-shouldered, dark crimson dress.

"I'll get it," Allie said to Mia.

Allie greeted a white-jacketed porter, tall like Peter. Captyn stood by her side. "Ma'am, we are now serving dinner in the dining car forward."

"May I escort you," came a familiar voice from behind the porter.

A smiling Peter stood at the doorway and whistled. "Allie, you look lovely. Your dress is more than elegant—the color enhances your eyes to a deep jade. It's hard to take my eyes away."

"You may escort me, and thank you for the lovely compliment. You flatter me," Allie said in a sugary voice, looping her arm into his. She reached up and kissed his cheek. "Do you mind if Mia joins us?"

He stopped, put his arms around her, and held her close. "Allie, that kiss . . ." Peter interrupted himself. "Not at all."

Mia put up her hands. "Please excuse me. I need to rest and rid myself of this headache. You two enjoy your evening."

"I'm sorry you feel poorly," Peter said.

Allie hugged her sister and stood back. "I hope your headache clears away soon."

In the dining car, Allie noted flowers on the tables and the red flower in the steward's lapel as they slipped into the green-brocade, high-backed chairs at a small table. Captyn fit himself down at the side of the table. Allie patted her dog's head and signaled him to stay. Moments later, in the dim light of the elegantly paneled dining car, a server in a long, white apron handed them menus. Peter wrote their order of fried oysters, white bread and butter, strawberry cakes, and a pot of coffee and cream on the check provided and gave it to the steward.

Allie looked at him. His shirt collar was loose, and she could see a bit of skin where she knew she should not look.

He cocked his head, took a red rose from the arrangement, and tucked it behind Allie's ear. Her stomach tightened. She moistened her lips.

She took a white carnation from the table arrangement, shortened the stem, and placed the flower in the lapel of Peter's gray-striped day coat.

Peter took her hand and wove his fingers with hers, their hands clasped together on the tabletop. Their eyes locked for a moment before she looked away.

"I find your company enchanting. In the words of Shakespeare, 'M'lady, I doth think my heart grows fonder for you.'"

Allie took a deep breath as a chill spiked up her spine. *Oh my, do I feel that way too?*

She hesitated and gazed into his eyes. "We stole a flower from the vase, even if they never notice. Don't we feel guilty?"

she asked in her usual forward fashion, putting her fingers over her lips to cover a smirk. "Do we?" Allie asked again.

"Not for a minute. Borrowed is more like it," Peter said with a smile.

"Or mishap perhaps?"

Peter shook his head. "Nope. Just borrowed."

Allie tilted her head slightly and smiled. "Hmm, borrowed makes sense. That's a pleasant way to enjoy the flower—we borrowed it.

"Yup. Now that's settled, if you don't mind, I'll have Mia's food delivered and be right back."

She stared through the glare of the window into the moonless night, sparks flying up from the train wheels, and noticed the reflection of a familiar figure.

"Allie Baldwin, is that you?"

"Penelope Baines. Heavens, of all places to see you. What are you doing here? Where are you going?"

Allie stood and wrapped her arms around her college roommate and hugged her hard. Penelope returned the embrace.

"How wonderful to see you, Allie. You are forever a feast for the eyes."

Allie was all smiles. "Thank you, Penelope. It's good to . . ."

Peter's return interrupted Allie. "Forgive the interruption. I spoke with the attendant. He's taken care of Mia's dinner. Our food will be here shortly. Please excuse me. Am I interrupting?"

"Peter, this is Penelope Baines, my roommate at Vassar. Peter Harrison here is in charge of my Great Dane, Captyn," Allie said, pointing to her pet.

Peter bowed and kissed Penelope's outstretched hand.

"Why, Allie, he's quite the charmer, isn't he?"

Allie's color blossomed red, like the rose behind her ear. "He tries," she laughed.

"Please join us, won't you?" Peter pulled out the vacant chair and sat beside her. "Our dinner will come soon—a variety of hors d'oeuvres and petite sandwiches—more than enough for three."

"Wonderful, thank you." Captyn nuzzled Penelope's other hand. She scratched behind the dog's ear. "You big, sweet dog. Want to come home with me?" She kissed the top of Captyn's head.

"It's good to meet one of Miss Baldwin's close friends. *Miss...* Baines, I'm assuming?"

"It is. Suffrage speaker, rally, festival planner, and school-teacher, if you will, and I'm traveling alone. I'm delighted for the company."

The attendant set down an assortment of hot and cold platters and finger sandwiches.

"Well, then, I think it'd be best for me to sit across the aisle. I'm sure you want to talk about old times. I'll take Captyn along and a couple of those bite-size finger snacks," Peter said.

"Please excuse me for a moment, Penelope." Allie followed him.

She walked behind Peter, stood on tippy-toes, and whispered in his ear. "I don't know what Penelope is doing or where she's going, but I don't think it's necessary to tell her about your duties with Mia and me. I'd rather wait for an appropriate time. Agreed?"

Peter held his palm up. "Don't put me on the spot like that, Allie. If the lady asks me why I am here with you, I'll be honest."

"You're treating me like a child." She folded her arms across her chest and glared at him.

Peter mimicked her pose. "You're acting like one."

"Now, let me tell you a thing or two. I will not stand for that. Never."

Allie stood by, waiting. Peter's silence sounded like a banging drum. "Oh, go on and dine alone."

She turned, stormed across the aisle, and slipped into her

chair next to Penelope. "Let's catch up. What have you been doing these last three years?"

Penelope took two petite tea sandwiches and put them on her platter. "You know, Peter looks familiar."

"Does he now?"

Penelope shrugged. "I'm trying to figure out why. Perhaps from one of my speaking engagements. What did you say he did? Dog watcher?"

Allie squirmed in her chair. "Well, it's what he is doing for me while I'm traveling."

"What exactly does he do?"

"He runs the Harrison Detective agency."

CHAPTER 22

enelope spread her napkin on her lap and looked up at Allie. "My work has taken me from city to countryside, summers to winters. Peter's work and mine would connect us at some point."

Allie's nose wrinkled. "Heavens. You have stories to tell, right?"

"I suppose. It's difficult for a woman alone," Penelope said.

"Perhaps it's a blessing you have independence. I am never alone. My darling Papa thinks he owns me. Adam, my bratty brother, thinks he knows me better than I do, and he's arrogant. The old bitties at the Ladies Club badger me to marry. Peter also thinks he owns me, and he's bossy. I'm not sure I know what I want."

"Excuse me, ladies. Which one of you is Allie Baldwin?" the porter asked.

Allie raised her hand. "That would be me."

"First, I must apologize for the tardiness of this letter." He handed it to Allie. "A boy, maybe around ten in fine clothes, gave it to me at the station. He pointed to your name on the envelope and said that I should deliver it to you. I'd been taking care of passengers and forgot. I discovered it in my pocket a while ago."

"Thank you. Did you notice anything special about the boy?"

"His fine clothes, perhaps. I paid little attention to him—except he had a letter for you."

Allie reached into her reticule for a token tip for the porter. He thanked her and bowed, backed away, and left.

"Aren't you going to open it?" Penelope asked.

"First, I want to . . ."

A streak of black and white passed Allie, crashing into food and drink carts and raising a ruckus from passengers until someone, cornered at the end of the car, someone grabbed Captyn's leash. Allie caught up to her dog, thanked the brave soul that captured him, and walked Captyn back to where Penelope sat. Men in white aprons had begun cleaning up the mess.

"Looks like Captyn got himself freed. Sit, Captyn, stay," Allie said, holding her hand in a stop position. She looked across the aisle. Peter's head hung down, chin on his chest, slumped in the seat, feet stuck out in front of him, fast asleep despite the excitement. "Shhh, let's not wake him. Peter probably needs a rest."

"That dog is fun," Penelope said, laughing.

Allie called the porter over. "Sir, would you mind taking Captyn to my cabin?"

"Certainly."

"Here's his leash. My sister will take him, thank you. Captyn, go with the nice man."

Allie's mouth drooped. "It will upset Peter that Captyn got away from him."

"You wore Peter out, the poor man. He's asleep like he's home. Nothing will wake him."

"Who, me? I'm awake." Peter said. "What's going on?"

Allie shook her head. "Captyn got loose and caused an uproar. It's over now. The porter took him to my cabin."

"That's good. Guess I dozed off and missed some fun, didn't I? I'll check on Mia and Captyn."

"Thank you, Peter."

Peter turned to leave. "I'll return shortly."

Penelope's face matched the butler's white apron. "Why are you so white? Are you all right?" Allie asked.

"I guess I got upset with all the excitement. Doctors tell me I have a weak heart from scarlet fever."

"How do you take care of yourself?"

The color returned to Penelope's face. "Nothing special. I guess I'm not supposed to get too excited."

"You never told me you had scarlet fever as a child."

"It affected me a couple of years ago. I began having breathing issues."

"Wherever you are going, I hope a doctor is available if you have an emergency."

"I'm on my way to a small town outside the city. I'll be in charge of an upcoming festival and arranging rallies for leaders of the suffrage movement. They travel across the country to speak out for equality. It's hard work, and one never knows what will happen, so the town sheriff is hiring security. I heard there's a doctor in town."

Allie, leaning her elbows on the table, rested her chin in her hand and closed her eyes for a moment. "My heart is fine, but Peter is giving me heartache. I don't want these feelings for Peter that keep cropping up."

Penelope raised a brow. "What are you saying?"

"My feelings for Peter are confusing me. I like him, but he doesn't understand my passion for fighting for the women's vote. We met at the recent rally in New York. I ended up in the middle of some turbulence, and he helped me out before the women spoke."

"If you were at the recent rally at City Hall, it's funny we didn't see each other. Fights seem to be pretty common at these events. After the rally closed, I went back to my parent's house and packed to leave New York. At the moment, I'm on my way to Fairfield, Connecticut, to work. My father is active in politics, and he's a friend of the Fairfield mayor. It all came together when the mayor told Papa he needed a festival planner."

Allie leaned toward Penelope. "Honestly? How strange."

"Why is that?"

Allie put her hand on her chest. "I am on my way there too."

"That's unusual, both of us going to the same place. A wire came to me before I left, alerting me there was a threat at the farm," Penelope said.

"Is it the Longdale Farm?"

"Why yes, it is. I'm hoping the threat isn't serious. Have you heard anything?"

"That's the reason we're going to Fairfield. We're investigating a fire in a cabin where young female farmworkers were asleep. Their dog awakened them, and they skedaddled out of there," Allie said. "One girl broke her leg in a fall."

"Gracious, I hope she'll heal quickly."

At Vassar, Penelope and Allie worked for woman suffrage, abolition, and to support for former slaves. They formed a group to speak at the school about the vote.

"I would like to rest a bit before we get to Fairfield. Would you excuse me?" Penelope asked.

"I'll go to my cabin too. Peter seems to have gotten lost. We'll meet again, I'm sure."

When Allie got to her cabin, Peter and Mia sat chatting. "My goodness, are you all right?"

"All is well," Mia said. "I appreciate Peter coming by, and I'm pleased to have Captyn here too."

"I have a letter to show both of you." Allie pulled it from her reticule and unfolded the envelope. "This arrived earlier. A porter gave it to me. He said a boy about ten gave it to him while at the station. I have not opened it yet."

Peter held out his hand. "The envelope, please."

She handed it to him. Before opening it, Peter smelled it. "I thought so. The same faint aroma of perfume. We need gloves to handle what's inside."

Allie clapped her hands. "My gloves are in my jacket."

CHAPTER 23

The train arrived in Fairfield early in the afternoon. Allie bid Penelope farewell. She suggested they meet up again soon and watched her friend's carriage disappear from view. Allie waved, tears brushing her cheeks.

Captyn sniffed the air laced with diesel fumes and danced around the bouncing light reflecting off the hot, shiny steel wheels. He snapped at the clouds of puffing smoke mixed with dust and oil stench. A south wind brought whiffs of sweating humanity, horse dung, and the audible, nervous din of people coming and going. Allie held onto Captyn's leash while he pulled her into the crowd. She brushed the street dust off her skirt and laughed at her Great Dane's playful curiosity.

Allie glanced at her sister. "I must take Captyn to do his business."

"Go ahead," Mia said. "I'll wait by the station."

Allie took her dog off the footpath. "We will be right back."

Peter approached Allie. "Do you mind if I come along?"

"If you wish. I'm still having trouble with your attitude from our earlier confrontation. However, I will forgive you for your insufferable behavior."

"Is that so? Let's not settle our differences now, and I don't need forgiveness."

Allie hissed a sharp breath. "That's pretty nasty, don't you think?"

Peter gave her a wry smile. "Can we stop bickering?"

"Come on, Captyn. Let's get about your business." Allie stuck her head up in the air and prodded the dog to the shrubbery area, leaving Peter behind. Peter caught up and walked beside them. He ignored their previous disagreement. "I noticed you looking out the train, unless you had your eyes closed."

Allie's lips tightened. "You were watching me?"

"Keeping my eye on you is my job."

She stopped short, pulling Captyn's leash, and faced Peter. "Regardless, my father keeps a watch on me, not you."

"I have an agreement with your father. He's not here, but I am."

"Do you know the wonder watching the view from a moving train?"

"If I'm traveling, I'm working. No, I don't believe I've had that experience. Am I missing a pleasurable pastime?"

"You are missing a special treat. Alone and sipping my tea, I filled the time enjoying the moving train blurring cows, calves, and trees into a pasture of many colors. Penelope came along. I had not seen her since graduation."

Peter had a slight smile on his face. "Surprise?"

"That it was."

"Listen, Allie, can I apologize for our spats? Let's stop tearing at each other's throat."

Her heart beat so hard, her teeth rattled. "I'll think about it."

"We'll be together for some time. You can't stay cross with me. Think about how it will affect your sister."

"Mia is not a problem. She always agrees with me."

"She's fair," you say. "I'm counting on her objectivity."

"You best focus, mister. She will not agree with you and disagree with me. She is loyal."

"Really? I wager you are incorrect. A fair person is always so. They don't pick."

Allie shook her head and grinned. "Let's make a wager she will stick with me."

"How's two dollars?"

"Captyn, come here." He meandered over to Allie. "Sit."

Peter patted Captyn's head. "Asking your dog will not help."

Allie ignored Peter's allegation and continued. "Captyn, we're making a bet with Peter. What shall I wager? All right, Peter, how about upping one over your two that Mia will be a faithful sister, no matter what."

"Agreed."

Peter had wired ahead to arrange for a carriage for their ride into town. The day's sunshine had not kept away the fall chill in the air.

Peter and the driver secured their baggage on top of the coach. Allie beckoned Mia to come. They sat on the cushioned seat in the coach and left the seat opposite for Captyn. The dog took up the entire bench and floor space, leaving little room for Allie's and Mia's feet, let alone another passenger. Good thing they didn't have to share with anyone.

"I will ride on top with the driver," Peter said.

"Mia, do you remember Mrs. Franklin's suggestion about this town?"

"What? Remind me."

Allie kept her fingers crossed Mia would want to make this stop. "At the tea, Mrs. Franklin told us to visit her sister's two-hundred-year-old church, Greenfield Congregational, on Old Academy Road."

Mia stared at her sister. "Now I remember. She said not to miss the graveyard. Sounds spooky. I get scared at places like that. Do we have to go?"

"We must. You know I love history. It's like finding buried treasures. Discovering where our descendants came from and foreign lands, no doubt."

Mia put her hand on Allie's shoulder. "Tombstones offer a peek into the past, don't they?"

Allie imagined the hardships, the lives, the loves, and the losses. "I can't wait to read some of them. Maybe we will unlock secrets of the past."

Mia held her finger in the air. "Hmm, maybe we'll find some of our family there, perhaps a revolutionary soldier who died in battle."

Allie leaned out the window. "Hello," she shouted, her voice shaky from the bumps in the road. "Can we stop at Greenfield Congregational Church?"

The driver hollered out, "It's out of the way. It ain't a passer-by. If you don't mind takin' the time, I'll stop."

Allie sat. "The church is out of the way."

Mia pouted.

"Don't pout. He said he would." Allie said, peering out the carriage window. "Please stop at the church," she yelled to the driver.

"Mia, can you imagine the fighting, the soldiers in their British uniforms burning the village, destroying everything in their path?" Allie shuttered. "It doesn't seem so long ago."

Mia sucked in a breath. "It's dreadful. How can you think those things? An actual war in this beautiful little town. I can't even imagine."

"Oh, Mia, you are such a bore. I'm sure that someone living here might have stories to tell. You know, from grandparents. Folks love to talk about the war and the brave soldiers they had in their family."

"Not me. I don't like to talk about war. Maybe Peter does."

"You are silly. Of course, you are Miss Mia Happiness."

"Good things. Let's talk about good things."

"We might learn about the Revolutionary War from the tombstones. There could be Civil War soldiers buried there too," Allie said. "I think Peter would enjoy the history. Let's invite him to stroll with us in the graveyard."

Along the road to the church, Allie couldn't help noticing places to shop lining the street. "Mia, we must come into town to visit these shops. Wouldn't it be wonderful to explore them?"

"I would love to go shopping here."

"Look at that milliner's front window. It has an assortment of fashionable hats rivaling any in the city. I must buy a hat there." Allie inhaled the heady aroma floating out of a coffeehouse, like the ones in England. She visited one there on a break during her senior year at college. She preferred tea, but she loved the aroma of roasted coffee.

Mia grasped Allie's hand. "Oh my goodness." Mia pointed. "That red and yellow canopy, it's so pretty. What kind of store would that be? Can we stop?"

"Stopping wouldn't be wise, the driver will get impatient. Let's come another time."

Mia sort of smiled. "Good idea. I can wait. We will do a shopping trip."

The driver pulled the coach to a stop. Peter jumped down and assisted the women. "Ladies." He held out his hand. "Your church and graveyard."

With the coach door open, Captyn jumped down, went directly to the nearest tree, and made his mark.

"Heavens, I didn't expect that. Captyn, come." Captyn returned to his mistress, his head hanging. "Sit," Allie said, picking up his leash.

"Join us, please, Peter."

"All right, I would enjoy a brief history lesson."

The driver asked Peter if he should wait.

"Yes, wait."

"If I get itchy, ya can catch me at the local bar. Ya'll has to trek a little to get me."

They walked single file on the narrow, graveled path into the graveyard. Allie stopped short. "Before we get busy reading tombstones, do you mind taking a walk through the church? There might be some helpful information."

Peter turned the door handle, and the front door opened. Allie stepped inside with Peter and Mia behind. A musty odor filled the empty spaces. The late afternoon light penetrated the stained-glass windows and cast colors on the walls and shadows along the wide plank floor. Selected church members had private pews with entry doors imprinted with their family surname. Mia gasped. Allie called out, "Peter, can you come here?"

"Wait, I think I found something. This pew has the name Baines. Isn't that the name of your friend? What was her name?"

"Wait, Mia, I'll be right back." Allie rushed over to double-check the name of the Baines family. "Penelope Baines, yes, that's her surname. My goodness, we'll have to bring Penelope here to see for herself."

Peter appeared. "You called me a few minutes ago before I summoned you. How can I help?"

Allie took Peter's hand and wound her fingers with his. "Over there, where Mia is standing." She pulled him to the pew at the other end of the aisle. In bold letters imprinted on the pew door, it read *Harrison Family.*

"How can that be, Peter?"

Peter raised an eyebrow. "Odd. We've never been to church here. We must have had relatives nearby. I knew we had cousins somewhere around here. Most of the Harrisons lived in Branford."

Allie pressed a hand to her cheek and gazed into his eyes. "Are you excited to discover more family?"

"I have to give that some thought. I suppose it is interesting."

"Will you tell your father of your discovery?" Mia asked.

Peter smiled. "Maybe."

Mia pushed up her sleeves. "Let's go out to the graveyard while it's sunny. Maybe it won't be so dreary and creepy."

Allie took her sister's hand. "Silly girl, why are you scared? Everyone in there is dead. Reading those tombstones will be fun. Maybe we'll find more familiar names."

"It's the dead part I believe Mia is questioning. Is that true?" Peter asked.

Mia squealed and hugged Peter. "You understand how I feel. Thank you."

Allie grinned. "The walking dead, indeed."

Leaving the church, Allie looped her arm through Peter's. Mia, walking behind, caught up, and Peter held his arm for Mia to do the same. The graveyard was shrouded in gloom, and the dogwood's fallen leaves crunched beneath their feet. Leaves wheeled across the yard and banked against the rows of cheerless tombstones.

They spread out to investigate the headstones. Allie yelled out, "Hello, you two. I found one. Come over here."

Mia kept her arm looped in Peter's as they rushed over. The name inscribed on the headstone was Captain Charles Harrison, born 1835, Died in Battle 1862.

Peter's jaw dropped. "Well, a hero at twenty-seven. Maybe he had a wife and children he left behind. So sad."

"Let's keep looking. Maybe there's more of your family here," Mia said. She pulled her arm out of Peter's. "I think I feel less afraid now. Thank you, Peter."

Peter chuckled. "My pleasure. Now you know there's no walking dead."

Mia's laugh reached her eyes.

"Now that we found the Harrison grave, I think I remember my father telling me that my ancestor, Richard Harrison, Senior, founded this cemetery shortly after he arrived here."

"My goodness." Allie anchored her eyes on Peter's.

He returned the gaze, reached for Allie's hand, and put his arm around her shoulders. She snuggled close to him and leaned her head on his chest, while he played with the tendrils of her hair.

"It's creepy in here in the dark. Let's return in daylight," Allie said.

Mia sucked in a breath. "Good idea."

"Can you imagine how beautiful this country must have appeared to your ancestors when they disembarked from the ship?" Allie asked.

"Wait a minute. I don't mean to ignore your question. He founded the cemetery in Branford, not here, a year after he founded the town of Totoket and changed the name to Branford, in the year 1644, according to family discussions. The Harrisons still have a saltbox style house on Main Street. I heard they built the house after the first one burned down. I'd wager part of the family came here to Fairfield."

"And fought in the Revolutionary War right here," Allie surmised. "The history must be fascinating." She looked at Peter from the corner of her eye. "When did the Harrisons come here, and why?"

Peter glanced at Allie. "My father might have a few answers."

"Oh, can I listen in?"

Mia pouted. "What about me? I feel you don't want me around."

Allie put her arm around her sister. "Of course, we want you, don't we, Peter? I wouldn't do anything without you, my darling sister."

Peter took Allie's hand and Mia's. "We are forgetting why we are walking around here, and it's getting dark. We can come back another day."

"For heaven's sake," Allie gasped. "I forgot about the letter. When are we opening the envelope?"

CHAPTER 24

*T*he driver slumped asleep in his seat, with the reins still in his hands.

Peter climbed up and shook him. "Sorry to wake you, old boy. Think you and your coach can get us to our hotel?"

The driver, upon awakening, spit his tobacco out. "I'm ready for you. Let's go."

Allie, Mia, and Peter arrived at the Spring Flower Inn, an elegant hotel that appeared melancholy in the early evening rain. Rumor had it Union soldiers once slept at the inn and left behind spirits. Allie had heard the hotel flourished under an eerie reputation, entertaining a flood of guests seeking a thrill. They passed the entry columns into the main hall of the inn. Allie stood gazing around the large reception area. Guests stood in line to reach the desk clerk. She expected to experience a ghost or two in the smoky, gold, warm light from the gas chandeliers. Allie shuttered; chills crawled up her backbone. The girls took Captyn and settled into their suite, Peter in his adjoining room.

Allie collapsed on the bed and buried her face in the feathery pillow. If only time allowed for sleep. She dared not pull up the covers. Sleep would overtake her. Getting up, she strode to the open casement window and stepped out onto the covered porch. She squinted, trying to see the water. "My heavens. Mia, come out here," Allie said in a loud, high-pitched voice. "I think a storm is brewing, and a visitor is coming from the cemetery."

Mia hurried onto the porch. "If you are trying to scare me, you are doing a good job."

Allie wrapped her arms around herself. "But look, the sky is growing dark, and the empty chairs are rocking." Allie sucked in a breath, grabbed Mia's hand, and pulled her into the room with her.

"Did you hear a knock, Mia?" Allie opened the door to an empty hallway. Another knock. Mia opened the adjoining door. "Peter, please say you knocked just now?"

"I did."

Mia pointed to Peter's door. "Whew. That's a relief."

Peter waved the envelope in the air, "I brought the envelope. Would you like to open it now?"

Allie shook her head. "There's no time. Let's open it later."

Captyn sat by Peter, waiting for attention. He patted the dog's head. "Ladies, can you make yourselves ready for dinner?"

Allie trilled her lips. "I've been busy chasing ghosts. Let's go to dinner. Maybe we will find one in the dining room."

Mia put her arm around her sister. "Don't listen to her. Allie has a wild imagination."

Allie wrapped her shawl around her shoulders, blocking out the chill. "You are blaming the wind that's rocking the chairs, aren't you?"

Mia stopped in the hallway and stared at a painting. "Isn't this beach scene by Chase lovely? In answer to your question, Allie, of course, I blame the wind. I'll be happy if there are no ghosts. We can ask at the desk."

Allie swept up to the attendant at the front desk to discuss the possibility of ghosts.

"No, ma'am, we have never had ghosts, but sometimes our guests imagine they have experienced them when there's stormy weather," the young man in charge said.

"I'm keeping my eye on the situation and will inform you of any sightings."

"Allie, are you seeing things?" Peter asked.

"Not anything solid. Some poor soldier is hanging around here, having promised marriage to a poor soul, but left this world before the wedding, dying in a Civil War battle."

Peter reached out to brush a curl away from her face. "Enough of this ghost game. Let's get dinner done so we can get to bed for an early start in the morning. The Mitchells are expecting us."

THE SUN DID NOT PEEK OVER THE HORIZON. STORMS, SQUALLS, and spirits not yet seen cloaked the day.

"Are you aware we'll be traveling in rainy, windy weather?" Peter asked.

Allie tightened her lips. "I'm not afraid of rain and wind, but ghosts are another thing."

"Why are you still thinking about ghosts? There have been no sightings," Mia said.

"All right, I concede, no more talk about ghosts."

"I can't believe you," Peter said, staring at Allie. "No worries. We'll be free of them at the Mitchell house. Our carriage awaits in the hotel porte cochère."

The threesome climbed aboard under cover of the archway. As they left, rain pounded on the coach roof like pebbles dropping from the heavens. After a short time, the vehicle listed and stopped moving. "We're stuck. I need help," the driver hollered, his voice getting lost in the wind.

By the time Peter jumped out to help, the driver was in the

back trying to push. A thick, muddy groove in the road embedded the wheel.

"I'll pull on the horse's harnesses," the driver said, moving back to the front.

Peter pushed. "Maybe there's too much weight," he shouted.

"Yup. No matter, the rut jammed the wheel," the driver said, spitting out some tobacco.

Peter opened the coach door and stuck his head in. "Allie, we need you to step out to lighten the load," he yelled loud enough to pierce her ears.

"What about me? I can help push," Mia said.

Peter shook his head. "Stay in the coach, Mia. I'll holler if you're needed."

Allie stepped down, holding onto Peter's hand. "My beautiful damsel, would you like to help push us out of the rut?" Allie barely heard him over the wind and rain.

"Push? You said push?" She got behind the rear of the coach on the listing side, with Peter beside her. "One, two, three, push," Peter shouted. Her boots began sinking. Her cape snapped in the wind. Bare Dogwood branches were swinging and bending, threatening to uproot its trunk.

"I don't know if this will work," Allie shrieked. Her dress bottom and cape swirled in the mud. Peter gave the coach a hard push; the coach swayed. Allie's hands slipped off the wagon. She squealed as she fell forward on her knees, her arms keeping her face out of the sloppy, soaked rut. The coach went nowhere, but the brown stuff splattered everywhere, including Allie. Her hat fell into the mud, and water dripped from every curl of her bright red hair that she knew had tightened like a wire braid. Allie was sure she heard a howl pass over Peter's lips. His hat, strangely remaining on his head despite the storm, was now a reservoir for the falling rain.

Allie's stomach churned. Her mother would no doubt give her another lecture on how to have avoided this affair. "Peter, get me unstuck this minute." The coach moved, seemingly by itself. The driver's laughter was louder than the roar of the rain. "The horses are pulling the coach," he shouted. "Are you two all right?"

Peter's silence to the driver's question was palpable. Peter's lips disappeared between his teeth as he bent and offered his hand to Allie. She pointed. "My hat if you please."

She shook the mud from her hands and took Peter's wet ones. She pushed herself up, getting off her knees with Peter's help.

Allie wished she could wash off the mess, but now chills embraced her. Allie imagined Peter doing the embracing. Her mother always told her to dress warm and be careful not to get wet in rainy weather to avoid getting sick. She failed this time.

"This hat isn't happy." Peter couldn't help his steadfast smile. They got into the coach. Mia took the hat. She held it in front of her, keeping herself dry while Peter and Allie sat side by side in drying mud. Once settled, Mia handed Allie the hat.

Allie prided herself on her efficiency. What could she have done to avoid this predicament?

The driver stopped at their destination and hollered they'd arrived and he would return in two hours.

Under a gloomy sky, the gables and two chimneys of the clapboard white house reached the clouds. Allie pictured herself upstairs, sitting by the window, watching the howling winds blow the tree's hanging branches against the window. She loved her visits to the Mitchells. Those rainy smells found only in the country with its fields and cows and horses saturated the air.

"I'll alert your friends," Peter said. He jumped down from the coach and turned to the driver. "Please wait for me to come back for the ladies."

Marla opened the door to Peter's knock. "My goodness, what in the world? Harrison?"

"Aah." Peter let out a breath and covered his drenched coat at his chest with his hand. "Yes, I'm he," Peter said with a slight head bow.

David greeted Peter with an extended hand. He took in the muddy mess. The two men laughed. "First time I shook a muddy hand."

"I didn't give it a thought. Sorry, old man."

"We received your telegram and expected you a little earlier. We were worried. Come in, please."

"Thank you. Perhaps we best get the ladies from the coach. Our vehicle got stuck in the mud. I'm sorry to be in such a condition."

"These things happen," David said.

"Allie, we'll come to get you," Marla hollered above the storm's whipping sounds.

She waved from the carriage door. Growing blackened clouds filled the sky.

Marla and David ran out with umbrellas and escorted Allie and Mia into the vestibule. Allie hung her wet wrap on hooks. The wood floor sported a rug for their footwear.

"Please, come in." Marla gave her guests the once-over and shook her head. "You must be freezing."

Allie opened her palm toward Peter. "You already met Peter, Peter Harrison, that is. He's our security agent and escort. Mia came along to keep me out of trouble."

Marla gave Allie a half-smile. "Uh-oh, I guess your family is on to your shenanigans?"

Allie sucked in a strangled gasp. "Gracious. I thought you were my friend."

Marla slapped her side. "Stop complaining, Allie. You know problems arise when you hide who you are. Wasn't your arrest for impersonating a law officer enough to teach you a lesson?" Marla spoke in a firm, almost unfriendly voice.

Allie's smile wavered. "All right, you can stop preaching."

"I will get a few towels. Excuse me." Marla hurried away.

Silence invaded the room while Mia and Peter smiled at each other and gave a nod to David. Peter tapped his foot on the floor, his hands stuffed in his wet pockets. Allie stood there, twisting one wet curl around her finger.

Peter glanced at Allie. "Are you worried that you disappointed your friend?"

"A little. It's always sad when you let someone down. I have my reasons for covering myself." She let out a breath. "I've been thinking about a different interview approach."

Marla came back with two towels. She handed one to Allie and one to Peter, refraining from hugging her friend in her muddy suit of armor.

The late afternoon light lay heavy and murky. Allie shook her shoulders and tried to brush the mess off.

CHAPTER 25

arla grabbed Allie's hand. "Come on, the mud is almost dry. Let's clean you up."

David, standing by, spoke. "Harrison, how about coming with me? I'm sure I have clothes to fit you."

Allie set her arm on Mia's shoulder and cleared her throat. "Want to come with us?"

"All right. I can help tie any strings or cords and wash out your dress that will be heavy and smelly. I hope you are not wet to the bone."

"I'm chilled, Mia. The rain soaked through my corset. A bath will do me good, or I'll see death waiting round the bend."

The ladies returned, Allie refreshed, to find the men in the parlor, each in an armchair by the roaring fire. The interior had simple and ample seating for visitors. A strong odor of furniture oil filled the air. Allie wriggled her nose. The scent reminded her of oil lamps she used in her childhood bedroom and her schoolroom. She sat on the sofa beside Mia, which appeared to be the softest seat to cushion her bruised body, and laid her embroidered reticule on her lap. She had left it on the coach's bench, and it had survived her adventure.

Marla looked at Peter. "Please don't take this personally. I would like to understand why Allie has a guard, a protector. Is her life in danger?"

Allie twirled the curl closest to her cheek. "Father decided I needed protection, so he hired Peter, umm, Mr. Harrison."

"I didn't miss that slip. First names," Marla said. "Come on, Allie. "I'm sure your father notices your antics, but they are harmless. Why the need for a protector?"

Allie smoothed the creases on the pink, floral day dress Marla exchanged for her muddy one. "I must admit that Papa knows me well. We argued about this, and I tried to fight him. I didn't want a watchdog, but there's a problem. Someone is sending me threatening notes. We don't know who or why yet. The notes threaten me and my column."

"Even I know you play hide-and-seek with trouble," David Mitchell said, his dark eyes focused on Allie. "The overseer, your guardian, is necessary." David faced Harrison, "By the way, I'm the doctor here in town. Everyone calls me Doc."

"Thanks for letting me know. Allie and I met a couple of weeks ago at the recent suffrage rally at City Hall. We met before her father hired me. My name came up as a recommendation from her cousin."

Allie got up from the sofa, went over to the window, and stared out at the dispersing clouds, the setting sun struggling to show itself between them.

"Allie dressed like an old lady and tried to beat up on a couple of hoodlums throwing eggs at the speakers. She caused more of a ruckus than the egg throwers, I might add," Peter said.

Allie faced Peter. "Oh, now the truth ekes out."

"You looked strange don't you think?" Peter asked.

Allie sat back down on the sofa beside Mia opposite Peter. "My appearance was fine, if you don't mind, and don't speak to me like I'm a child. It's not gentlemanly."

Mia took her sister's hand. "Allie, I just remembered that old coat you borrowed from Mrs. Higgins. It was so big you looked like an old lady. All you needed was a hat, and you could fool anyone."

"I finally found a big, floppy hat that was perfect for the outfit," Allie said, holding her hands at the sides of her head, indicating the size of the hat. She hesitated and began laughing along with Mia and Peter. "All right, I guess I'm a little foolish. So what?"

Mia gave her sister the eye. "That conversation with Mama the night before we left—be conscious of our safety and hold back your temper," Mia whispered a little too loud in Allie's ear. "And permit Mr. Harrison to do his job."

Peter rubbed his chin and grinned. "I heard that. Thanks, Mia."

Allie respected her mother's wisdom, even if she disagreed. A woman's opinion is seen as a tantrum, but the opinion of a man was not, her mother pointed out. Allie had never been in the private company of a man outside of her family. Perhaps she could develop a friendship with Peter in time, and then he might consider her opinion valuable.

"Peter, what do you think of the disguises I wear to conduct interviews? Are they a waste of time?" Allie asked.

Marla interrupted. "They are a waste of time, Allie. It's makes sense to be yourself for your interviews. In any case folks always love to talk about themselves. I'm sure they don't care about who is doing the interview."

A smug grin tightened Allie's lips. "This conversation is wearing; can we change the subject?" She pointed to Marla. "You've been to the city. Haven't you seen the way they live in those dreadful tenements?"

Marla nodded. "I have. They live in squalor."

"True. Women need better wages and working conditions. They barely have enough money or time for their families.

"My everyday clothes are too fancy, so I dress down for the interviews, and they welcome me."

"That's ridiculous. You know how to propose a question. What difference do your clothes make? Are you done now?"

Allie twisted her lips and stared at her friend. "Done with what?"

"Done with arguing and done with hiding behind your disguises."

Allie drew her fists up, punching the air like a boxer. "No, I'm not. My fancy fashions make me uncomfortable. Now that I think of it, if you said that honesty is most important, I might consider giving up my old lady disguises."

"Allie is honest. Aren't you?" Mia asked, patting the empty seat next to her on the sofa.

"I think of myself as honest. No? Is my face red? Is it hot? You all have stirred me up. Let's take a vote. Peter, what's yours? For or against wearing clothes that cover my identity?"

He shook his head.

Allie took the spot next to Mia, smoothing her dress under her as she sat. "Mia, what's your vote? For or against?"

Mia shook her head.

"Marla, David, what's yours?" They shook their heads in unison.

"I've lost. Peter, I owe you three dollars for Mia siding with you instead of me."

"There you go for democracy," Marla said.

"Humph, so much for the vote. One last word. I'm not ready to give up on what I believe. But what's more important is working for women like those ladies from Rochester. Maybe I should join them, become one of their speakers. If I can do that openly, my vices will change."

Marla held up her hands and let out a breath. "Can we move on, please? How about some hot cider?"

Allie hugged herself. "Brrrr, this weather goes right through me. Hot cider sounds wonderful."

Marla left the room and came back with a steaming cider vessel, filling the air with an aromatic fragrance of cinnamon, cloves, and oranges.

Allie met Marla a few years ago in New York at a suffrage symposium. They developed a quick connection, realizing a common interest and passion for politics and women's freedom. Letter writing kept up their correspondence and friendship.

They passed the afternoon speaking with Margaret and Anne, two of the three girls who'd escaped the fire two weeks ago. The third girl, Mary Lynn Bower, was resting in the infirmary. Mary Lynn had broken her leg in their mad scramble to escape the smoke-filled cabin. Since the closest hospital was in Bridgeport, the Mitchells set up two separate rooms, one for women and children and the other for male patients. Margaret and Anne slept in the guest room while the men built a new cabin.

Allie promised herself to ask her parents to help the Mitchells build a hospital. She knew her mother would jump at the chance. After all, Papa had built the Baldwin Hospital and should be open to the idea of helping these people.

"Tell us what you did that evening before bed?" Peter asked the girls as they sat in the Mitchells' parlor.

"After supper, we took Horatio for a walk, then went back to our cabin and settled in for the night," Anne said with a soft-spoken Irish lilt in her voice. Horatio, a golden-brown hound dog, sat up when he heard his name, tilted his head, and uttered an inquiring woof. Captyn trotted up to Horatio, sniffed his rear, and set himself down on the rug beside him.

"Margaret, did you notice any strangers lurking about when you went on your walk or after you got back to the cabin?" Peter asked.

"No one, sir."

Margaret was almost the spitting image of her sister, but slightly shorter. Anne squeezed Margaret's hand. Was it a supportive gesture or a warning? Allie would have to ask Mia if she noticed it too.

"We're grateful everyone is all right," Marla said, setting down a plate of a sliced lemon loaf to go with the cider. "I just checked on Mary Lynn, and she's sound asleep. Poor girl."

Allie's shoulders sagged. "How is Mary Lynn's leg? Will it heal?" Allie's most valued friend had a crippling fall from a window at four. Frankie could help Mary Lynn if needed.

"Mary Lynn will be fine," Marla spoke in a warm and reassuring voice. "Her leg is healing."

Allie put her fingers over her half-smiling lips.

Margaret smiled. "When can we see her?"

"Maybe in a day or two. Right now, I want Mary Lynn to get more rest," Doc said.

Margaret's eyes filled with tears. She glanced at her older sister. "We have to tell them, Annie," she whispered.

"Tell us what?" Peter asked.

Margret fidgeted, winding her fingers around each other. "It's about Janie."

"I thought Janie was visiting her aunt in Morgantown?" Marla said. To Allie and Peter, she added, "Jane Thomas works at the farm and bunks with the girls."

Margaret bit her lip.

Allie glanced at Mia.

Mia took a sip of her hot cider and put it down on the small table beside her chair. She leaned forward and patted Margaret's hand. "There, there, Margaret. Don't be afraid. We're here to help."

"Janie is not visiting with her aunt, is she?" Peter asked.

Anne shrugged. "We don't know, sir. That's what worries us."

Peter raised a brow. "Where did Janie go that afternoon—the day of the fire?"

"She left for her aunt's house," Margaret said.

"She may have intended to go there, eventually. Who took her to her aunt's cottage?" Allie asked.

The two girls were shaking. They clasped each other's hands.

Marla crouched down in front of the girls and patted their hands. "It's all right. You can tell us what happened."

"Promise we won't get thrown out by the Longdales?" Anne's lip trembled. "Janie said we would if we told."

"The truth will never get you into trouble," Allie said. "You are both brave. Never forget that."

Mia raised her chin toward Anne, "Allie is right. You saved Mary Lynn's life—you and Horatio."

"I promise you we'll do everything to make this right," Allie said with conviction in her voice.

Margaret pursed her lips and let out a sigh. "Janie went off with George Bellows."

"Janie told us she was old enough to step out with a young man. We thought she had set her cap for George," Annie said.

Marla shook her head. "His family owns Bellows Emporium, the general store in town. And a lazier boy never lived. All he does is brag about himself all around town. He likes to puff himself up so girls will chase him."

"Ah, I see," Allie said. "Where is Janie now?" Allie glanced at both girls.

"She told us George was taking her to her aunt's house, and they were going to have a serious talk about wedding bells, making us assume George and Janie were marrying."

Peter slapped his hand across his knee. "All of this is going to work itself out when Janie returns. I would venture a guess that she ran off with this George fellow or some other guy and eloped. She might be the type to believe George or be swayed by how he looks and overlook his laziness. In any case George boy is no doubt involved somehow.

"If we figure all this out, do you think we'll have the answer to who caused the fire?" Allie asked.

"I believe we will, we must. Janie's safety is essential."

"How can you be so sure, Peter?"

Peter smirked and took Allie's hand. "Experience. I'm sure about those kids. I wager George is not the one Janie is after. It's possible she's off celebrating her newfound freedom with another boy."

At that moment, he kissed the back of her hand in the most provocative way. Allie felt it to the tip of her toes.

"It looks like the storm has passed. It is a good time for us to get back to the hotel. Thank you is not enough. You've been wonderful, Marla, and you as well, David. We'll stop back before we leave for New York to return the borrowed clothes, if that's satisfactory?" Allie asked.

"We'll look forward to your visit," Marla said.

CHAPTER 26

The morning sun swathed the old maple by the inn's porch. Allie and Mia had settled themselves into the rattan rockers, with Captyn by Allie's chair. "Imagine what that old tree could tell us," Allie remarked. "How many kisses do you think that tree has seen?"

Mia giggled. "I'm sure a lot."

Allie hugged herself. "Oh, how romantic. Do you see yourself getting kissed under that tree? I would love it. Wouldn't you?"

Mia looked out over the dewy grass sparkling beneath the tree. "First, I need a boyfriend."

"We'll have to find you one, my dear sister. Let's keep a watch while we're here. But now that I'm thinking about it, maybe Robert, that scientist detective we met back in the city, would be a good one for you."

Mia squirmed in her rocker. "You think so? Those sad, sad eyes touched my heart."

Anxiety tickled Allie's stomach. She needed to be a perky today and pretend she had put aside business—no more mystery and no more unknowns cropping up. She smoothed

183

her blue-flowered full skirt down and fiddled with the bonnet's matching bow under her chin. The wide brim would keep her face from toasting.

"Mia, you look adorable in your straw sunbonnet, and it complements your yellow day dress, making you look sunny. Are you glad you brought the hat along?"

"Thank you, I am glad, and it's comfortable."

Peter came alongside Allie's rocker. "Let's go, ladies. We don't want to keep Baxter waiting."

Captyn stood beside Peter, wagging his tail. Mia wrapped her arms around the dog and gave him a big hug. He turned his head and licked her face with a tongue the size of her cheek.

A driver came with the carriage, giving Peter a break. He helped the ladies up the carriage steps and followed behind. Captyn took much of the floor space, leaving scant foot room.

Allie spoke up. "Next trip, we need a larger carriage if we are all to fit comfortably, or we can leave Captyn at home, which I believe is the better choice."

Mia shook her head. "Captyn is our other bodyguard. We can't leave him behind."

"We don't need two hound dogs. Peter is enough," Allie said.

Peter searched her face. "I beg your pardon. Are you calling me a hound dog?"

Allie giggled. "Yes, I am." She went on, "I know it's not our responsibility, but we must solve Janie's disappearance soon. I'm having trouble moving forward to solve the fire situation with Janie's mysterious departure in the way. I think her disappearance must have something to do with the fire, don't you, Peter?"

"We must establish the facts first," Peter said.

Mia took her sister's hand. "No one disappears for no reason, right, Peter?"

"Right," Peter replied. "I don't intend to leave until we have one."

Allie smoothed her hair. "What if they kidnapped her? What didn't the girls tell us?"

Mia patted Allie's hand. "We'll find out. It's just strange that the fire happened at the same time."

The sheriff was standing on the sidewalk when they arrived. He greeted them, shook Peter's hand, and escorted them into his office.

Allie removed her bonnet, placed it in her lap, and smoothed her hair. She straightened in the hard-backed chair facing Sheriff Baxter's desk. "We think Janie Connors ran away."

Mia nodded in agreement. "Maybe she took a train out West? That seems to be the place people are going these days."

Captyn, curled beside Allie, nudged her hand for an ear rub.

"We haven't established that yet," Baxter said in a firm tone. Allie believed Baxter used that voice when dealing with civilians offering advice. He wouldn't be able to penetrate Allie's rugged interior, though. She was smart and had a nose for solving a mystery, except her own music box one.

"Janie promised the Longdales she would return on Sunday last, but she didn't," Mia said.

Baxter leaned back in his chair and crossed his arms over his chest. "Janie's aunt told my deputies that a young man came to pick Janie up Sunday morning. The old woman assumed it was Bellows from the general store."

Mia raised a brow. "We can't assume she ran away."

"That's right," Allie agreed. "There are unanswered questions here. I think the person we need to talk to is the mysterious young man who picked her up. He's missing as well. I'm sure he is with young Janie. What do you think, Sheriff?"

"We only know what her aunt told my men."

Allie turned to her sister. "We need to talk to those girls again, or maybe George at the Emporium."

Mia nodded. "The girls fidgeted the entire time we were talking with them."

Sheriff Baxter threw a wide-eyed glance and an odd grin at Peter. Peter figured he'd best rescue the man before Allie and Mia took over his entire operation. Peter gave Baxter a subtle nod that Baxter returned.

"Ladies, we'll stop at Doc Mitchell's, and you can speak with Mary Lynn, then I'll take you to the Longdale Farm," Peter said.

Baxter's parting words were, "Talk about Drumple later?"

Peter leaned into Baxter and whispered, "Drumple's up to no good."

Baxter grinned and gave Peter a slight nod.

Allie climbed into the carriage and placed her bonnet on the seat. Peter dropped them off at the Mitchells. "I'll return from Baxter shortly. Go on without me."

"Peter, I'm leaving my bonnet in the coach. We'll be indoors. I won't be needing it."

"That's fine," Peter said.

Marla was in the doorway when they arrived. She escorted Allie and Mia into the infirmary to speak with Mary Lynn.

"I don't understand, ma'am," Mary Lynn said.

"I think you do, Mary Lynn," Allie said in a soft voice. Allie sat beside her bed. Mia reached for Mary Lynn's hand and held it between her own. She was all of fourteen, too young for a beau, but not too young to pine after one.

"Tell us what happened. We promise no one will take you away, and we will make sure you are safe," Marla said. Mary Lynn's dark eyes filled with tears. Her ponytail and pale face gave her an impish look younger than her age. "I didn't do it on purpose, I promise," Mary Lynn said.

Allied coaxed her with a smile. "Didn't do what?"

"I didn't set that fire in the cabin on purpose." Tears streamed down her face. "The letters I wrote to George about my feelings turned out to be bad, so I burned them. I wanted to give them to him, but Janie said he-he . . ." She broke down and sobbed.

Mia tucked a stray wisp of hair behind Mary Lynn's ear. "When Janie told you George was taking her to her aunt's house, you figured they were a couple."

Mary Lynn nodded and burst into more tears.

Allie sighed and stood up. "Well, Marla, that's one mystery solved."

Mia helped Mary Lynn lie back on her pillows. "The poor girl has exhausted herself crying."

"Mary Lynn's heart will mend. One day she'll write letters to a young man deserving of them," Allie said as they walked back to the parlor and sat beside the fireplace.

"I expected these young girls were innocent, didn't you?" Marla asked Allie. "What do you think happened to Janie?"

Allie blew out a breath. "I think we need to visit the Longdale family. They might help."

"At least we know it had nothing to do with violence against the suffrage speech I gave at the farm. That worried me. If there were any violence, I would have to end my speeches," Marla said.

Allie, worried about women and the years to come, faced Marla. "We have hope in your talks—for us, for all women, for our future."

Marla didn't smile. She gave Allie a nod.

Allie blinked. "Despite what could have been a tragedy, we've learned a valuable lesson."

"What's that?" Marla asked.

A smile quirked Allie's lip. "The girls learned a lesson about life and what's important, and maybe I did too—honesty."

"Good. Now let me tell you about the Longdale family," Marla said. "They have three sons, two married, and the youngest teaches the farmworkers how to read and write on his summer break from Harvard. He just left to return to school. It's a shame that you didn't get to meet him. He's a fine young man."

"You say, Marla, he taught the young people working for the family how to read and write?" Allie asked.

"Yes, a few were eager learners. Mary Lynn was one of them."

Allie squirmed in her chair. "What about Janie?"

"She, Anne, and Margaret took lessons. They enjoyed reading. Janie especially loved reading *Jane Eyre*. They started a reading club with Edward."

"Edward?"

"Yes, Edward Longdale, an older boy." Marla stared at Allie. "You know young girls often admire the charm of a college boy."

Allie raised her brows. "I believe we have solved another mystery."

Marla put her hand on her throat. "Oh, my goodness. Do you think that Edward and Janie—?"

"I think Jane Eyre and her love for Edward Rochester have influenced Edward and Janie,"

Mia laughed. "Oh, heavens, how sweet. Really? Now there's a captivating story. They fell in love like Jane and Edward, the characters in the book."

"George Bellows was simply a ruse for their plan to elope," Allie said. "When Peter returns, let's pay a visit to the Longdale family and ask if Edward is back in school."

CHAPTER 27

*P*eter returned to his suite, where he found a note slipped under the door. He picked it up and walked over the bare wood floor and a thick Persian rug to the desk by the window. He read the note from Baxter in the dimming light. The darkened sky reminding Peter of his childhood home on the lake and riding his steed over country roads in stormy weather. He removed his boots to wriggle his toes in the rug like the one in his mother's bedroom. He missed her pleasant voice, her soft manner. She took the only love he knew to her grave. The warmth of the rug calmed him before he visited the sheriff, a visit he wasn't relishing, a visit that brought unwanted work.

With a groan, he knocked on the door connecting his suite with the Baldwin sisters.

Allie opened her side of the door. "Is everything all right?" She beckoned him. "Come in."

His body filled with heat. He wanted Allie in his arms. He needed her.

"Thank you." He stepped into her room and stood at the doorway. "All is well. I'm handling security for an upcoming festival in town. Sheriff Baxter wants to go over the details now."

Allie put a hand over her heart. "Now? Will you never get some rest?"

He chuckled and clutched the front of his jacket. "I may not." He let go and straightened the fabric with long, smooth strokes.

"I'm sorry. Can you sit for a minute?" Allie, sitting on the edge of her chaise lounge, pointed to the desk chair facing her. "Did you say upcoming festival?"

"I did," he said and sat. "Do you think that's the one your friend, Penelope, is doing?"

"How many festivals could Fairfield have? I'm sure it's the same."

Her voice—lyrical, like a songbird—drew him in.

Stop it, Harrison. You're here to do a job. No distractions.

"I'll get the details when I talk to the sheriff."

"This trip to Fairfield is good, isn't it?"

"Yes, I come monthly. This trip is perfect. My family estate is nearby."

"Peter, do you have that envelope the porter delivered? How about we open it before you go? Good thing we left it here. Imagine if we had it with us. Mud would have destroyed it."

Peter shook his head and held his palm up. "I don't have it. I gave the letter back to you when we left the train."

"Uh-oh. I'll bet it's in my muddy clothes at the Michell's. Whatever it said has no doubt been washed away."

Peter lifted a brow. "Maybe not."

Allie beamed at him. "Perhaps. Let's not worry about the letter and change the subject. Could we visit your family estate?"

"I doubt we'll have the time."

Allie's smile wilted. "Maybe we can make time? Anyway, Mia and I hoped to watch the sunset on the beach. Afterwards we will go to dinner, and it's getting late. If we wait any longer, the sun will have set."

"Stay here and enjoy all those sunset colors from your balcony. Keep the door locked and wait for my return. I will escort you and Mia to dinner."

He stood, ready to leave.

Allie gave him a blank stare. "We will do nothing of the sort. We are famished. Mia and I will have dinner in the dining room after sundown."

He underestimated her stubborn streak. "It's not smart to go alone. Danger lurks in the unknown."

"What could harm us here other than a nasty meal?"

"You have had threats. Whoever is responsible could hurt you."

Allie raised one eyebrow and looked down. "Very well."

"There's nothing I would like more than to watch the sunset with you wrapped in my arms. Let's plan another time."

She lifted her head. He gazed into her eyes and at her delicate, full, luscious lips. He wanted to kiss her, but a gentleman rarely bows to such impulses without permission. Although kissing her did not seem like a bad idea. He wrapped his fingers around her hand and pulled her to him. He bent his head to press his lips to hers—she wasn't resisting.

"Hello, you two," Mia said, coming into the suite's sitting room from their bedroom.

Peter stepped away. "Hello. I was just leaving. I'll see you both when I return." He closed the adjoining door.

Allie closed her door and turned the key in the lock.

Peter's carriage waited to take him to Baxter's office. He climbed into the driver's seat. Clusters of shops with dark windows reflected the late afternoon's fall colors, and trees in their early winter guise lined the sidewalks. The clouds had dissipated, and the sky's sunset glowed the same peachy orange of Allie's cheeks when she laughed.

Peter's gut told him that Allie would not heed his warning. She never mentioned waiting for his return. He chuckled to himself. *What a woman.* Allie Baldwin was one of a kind and just right for him. Her beauty was more than skin deep—she was caring and tender. His mother would have loved her.

"Baxter." They shook hands. "Two damsels are waiting impatiently for dinner. I must get back to the inn. Can we make this brief?"

"Yes, of course. It seems the festival invited suffrage speakers."

"You didn't need me yet. I'm busy. It's not a good time. Can't this wait?"

"I want to plan out the security."

"The festival is still some time away. Do you have someone to run it?"

"I have a good worker. She came highly recommended and will run the entire event down to hiring workers and folks to handle the details. She is moving here to start a school for girls when she's not working on our festivals."

"This is a small world, after all. Penelope Baines, is it?"

"Matter of fact, it is. She came directly from the train to meet me. The mayor hired her. She will take directions from the mayor and me. How do you know her?"

"Miss Baines and my client, Allie Baldwin, were schoolmates. The two connected on the train where I met her. She seems confident in her abilities. How about you set up a meeting?"

"I'll send you a messenger with the time and date," Baxter said.

It was past sundown when Peter returned to the inn and found a note under his door.

Since we are not prisoners and we are both hungry, Mia and I

*went to the dining room for dinner. See you there. Yours, Allie
Baldwin.*

Peter blew out air, trilling his lips, shook his head, and
hurried downstairs to the dining room. He stood at the
entrance, searching for his clients. The hum of the diners in the
elegant room distracted him from his disappointment in Allie.
Her decision to leave the protection of their suite could prove
disastrous. He hoped otherwise.

"Good evening, sir. May I seat you?" the maître d' asked.

That intrusion snapped Peter out of his reverie. "Ah, I see the
table I'm looking for. Thank you."

The inn was usually bustling with guests coming and going
during business hours, and in the evening, it came alive with
music and dining. His father and stepmother came into town
occasionally to sample the excellent wines and French cuisine in
the columned room. While making his way to the table, a long,
narrow man cocooned in a black morning coat and trousers
approached the table and hovered over Allie and Mia. If he
wore a crown of acanthus leaves, Peter knew the Romans would
slay him.

The man's hands crept up to his pale, thinning hair and
slicked it back. He leveled a suspicious gawking gaze at the
women like he wanted to kidnap them and cart them away.

Peter stopped within earshot of the table and stared at Allie
—gorgeous in a day dress the same color as her beautiful, green
cat's eyes. *If that skulk lays a hand on her or Mia, I'll put him away.*

"Well, lovely ladies," the man said, "seeing that you're alone
here, I can offer protection from any unwanted attention. You
may have heard of me. I am Wilbert Drumple the Fourth at your
service. Soon to be mayor of the city of New York."

Allie narrowed her eyes and fired back, "First, we are not
alone. I am here with her, and she is here with me."

Peter bit back a laugh when the petite beauty added "Humph" for good measure.

"And second, we know who you are." Allie sucked in her lips like she'd bit into a sour pickle, the ones that come in a barrel. "They plastered your face all over New York City, and you advertise in our father's newspaper. You may have heard of him, Joseph Baldwin the Third, publisher of *The New York Sentinel*?"

Drumple's beady eyes widened at the mention of Baldwin's name. He cleared his throat and puffed up his chest. "I have indeed." His voice boomed around the crowded, noisy dining room. "You do not know the kinds of evil men that dwell in these backwoods towns." The puffed-up peacock leaned in. "As a noble politician and man of honor, allow me to be your escort for the evening and make certain you arrive safely to your room tonight."

Peter, approaching the table, poked his finger at the man's chest. "Keep your voice down, Drumple," Peter said with a deep modulation. He knew of the man's reputation for gambling and cheating from several reliable sources.

Drumple pushed Peter's hand away. "Back off, Harrison. You lookin' for a fight?"

"Not with you, buddy. That would be a waste of my time."

Drumple put up his hands, bent his knees, and shook his fists at Peter. "I'm ready for ya."

Peter had heard rumors of Drumple's latest scheme to pilfer public monies once voted into the mayoral office. Drumple didn't seem to get the message to scoot. He stood by while Peter, chuckling, moved past him to address his charges.

"Allie, Mia, my sincere apologies for my tardiness." Peter sat between them, sliding the only other chair at the table into position. Allie reached out to pick up her water goblet, but Peter stopped her, took her hand, and brought it to his lips. "My darling Allie, you look simply ravishing tonight." He glanced into her eyes that were shooting fire at the moment, aimed directly at him. He turned to Mia and gave her his full attention. "Mia, my stunning future sister-in-law, aren't you joyful I'm going to be your brother-in-law?" Mia grinned and threw both hands around Peter's neck.

"My timing is perfect then. Shall we order? This is a good time to work on our upcoming wedding."

Mia waved her hand in the air with a flourish. She held up the shiny menu. "I shall have the lobster bisque for my first course."

"My choice as well." He turned to his fake fiancée and pretended to fiddle with the menu. "How about you, darling. Are you ready to order?"

Silence sliced the air at the table.

Allie opened her mouth to speak, but Peter touched his finger gently to her lips. "Uh-uh-uh. I have a surprise for you, but first we must bid adieu to Mister Drumple, mustn't we?"

Her lips looked velvety. Damn. She was the most unaffected woman he'd ever met. The sprinkling of freckles over her nose complemented her peaches-and-cream skin. Whoever said freckles were cute had never met Miss Allie Baldwin. She was anything but cute. She was beautiful, vibrant, and desirable.

"Sorry to keep you standing there Drumple. Why are you still here? What brings you to Fairfield?" Peter asked.

"Well, I...uh...I...that is . . ." Drumple cleared his throat. "I am here on official political business, meeting with community leaders." He nodded, "Yes, ah, yes, that's the reason to be in Fairfield."

"Then we won't detain you," Peter said.

Drumple straightened his skinny frame and stalked out of the dining room.

"What an insufferable lout." Mia reached for her water glass. "Thank you, Mr. Harrison, for the rescue."

"Rescue?" Allie exclaimed. "We were doing fine with that buffoon." Her eyes spit fire at Peter. "It was completely unnecessary for that pretense. Fiancée indeed. Drumple's mother is a notorious gossip. She'll have the entire Baldwin Hospital Auxiliary abuzz. Poor Mama will have to deal with the rumors."

Mia shook her head at her sister. "Mr. Harrison is a prince. And Mama has no issues with the likes of Mrs. Portia Drumple. Mr. Harrison, I apologize for Allie's harsh words. She gets cranky when she hasn't eaten."

"No need for an apology. Your sister is forthright and speaks her mind."

Peter didn't want to smile, but it escaped his lips. "May I add that I doubt Mr. Drumple will share his trip to Fairfield with his mama."

A curious expression replaced Allie's frown. "How do you know this?"

"Mr. Drumple is not here on business."

CHAPTER 28

*P*eter glanced at his charges sitting beside him discussing the various dishes on the menu. Based on Allie's blatant defiance of his request to remain in their room until he returned, Miss Allie Baldwin would, at some point, get herself and maybe Mia into trouble.

Mia waved the menu. "Can we order? I'm positively famished."

Allie sipped water from the crystal goblet and glanced at Peter. "How dare you use me to play your silly, make-believe betrothed game."

Peter's jaw tensed. "I am sorry if it offended you." Allie's history, like the recent rally, proved she was impetuous. Peter knew this job would be a challenge given she was convinced she didn't need his protection. Allie reminded him of his younger sisters, always up to mischief.

Throughout dinner, he regaled them with stories of his sisters. "They dubbed me *Peter, the Prince of Peppermint Drops*, always with treats in hand. Little women have surrounded me all my life."

Allie tsked and pointed her finger at Peter. "Well, you may be a prince to your sisters, but not to me."

This woman was spitfire and brimstone, sometimes irritating and often got herself into a pickle. She had a strong sense of right and wrong. Everything was black-and-white to her. With her run-amok red curls, she was always out of sorts. Classically beautiful women had always drawn him in. Allie, with all her nonsense, should put him off. Yet somehow, he found her rather elegant, entertaining, and forthright. She got under his skin.

Peter piped in, "Let's order, shall we?"

"ALLIE, STOP IT RIGHT NOW. THIS COMPLAINING MUST END. What's your problem? You have food in your belly, and your mood has elevated to tolerable," Mia said.

Allie knew that Peter, her knight and savior, only wanted to protect her. But he kept invading her thoughts—his perfectly combed hair, the shadow of stubble showing on his fetching face. He looked tall and handsome in his well-pressed coat and trousers and an ascot that was far more fashionable than the new bowtie look. His gold chain looped on his watch and tucked into his vest pocket. She pushed her hair away from her forehead and straightened the high, tight collar of her uncomfortable dress. Why in heaven's name did she choose that one when she could have stayed in the free-flowing frock she borrowed from Marla? Sometimes she had issues with her choices. Maybe she did need watching. Her mother warned about the importance of excellent decision-making. Did Allie pay heed? Hardly.

"Isn't that so, Allie?" Mia asked.

Allie sat straight as a pencil in her chair. "Isn't what so?" she asked in an inquisitive tone.

"Allie, didn't you hear what I just said?" Mia asked with a blue-eyed stare.

Having finished her dessert, Allie fussed with her empty plate. "No, I'm sorry. I didn't hear you."

Mia thinned her lips and clapped her sister on the shoulder. "You are miles away. What in the world were you thinking about?"

Allie shrugged. "Nothing."

Allie couldn't help sneaking glances at Peter. It was a blessing to be with him. She felt safer. Her father did a good deed hiring him. Allie loved the sound of his voice, and his laugh was attractive enough. Most of all, he cared about her and Mia.

Allie caught herself and faced Mia. "Forgive me. I was thinking about the girls we spoke to this afternoon." She had to cross her fingers under the table for that lie.

"Anne and Margaret were hiding something from us. The question is what?" Peter asked.

Allie nodded. "I believe there is more to their story. My instinct is telling me that there were no vandals involved in that fire. And most likely, nothing to do with suffrage or anyone trying to stop them from speaking to the young women."

Peter gulped his Irish whiskey chaser. "Will you be getting together with the Longdale family?"

Allie held up a finger and hesitated. "We were hoping to do that tomorrow."

"Because of Janie?" Mia asked.

"The girls told us she had gone to visit her aunt. But when pressed, they admitted that the young man, George, whose parents own the general store in town, took her by buggy to her aunt in Morgantown, two hours away."

"We know Janie wasn't with the girls in the cabin when the fire broke out. But she hasn't returned, and it's been almost a week since."

Mia took a sip of her coffee. "This dessert was delicious. Did you like it, Peter?"

"I'm not a big dessert man, but tarts are my favorite."

Allie faced Peter. "Are you talking about desserts or women of the night?"

Peter sucked in a breath. "What do you know about women of the night?"

Allie swallowed. "Not too much. What I know is that when women marry, they give up their rights to be independent. Their husbands get any inheritance from their wife's father's estate."

Peter took Allie's hands. "Does that mean there will be no marriage in your life?"

Allie did not remove her hands from Peter's hold. Her heart beat in her ears as she gazed into his eyes. "While I'm working for women's freedom, I can't think about marriage or any relationship. I want to see results before I commit my life to a man."

Peter held her gaze. "I don't believe you are aware of what you will gain with the right man. Someone who will respect and love you and give you the freedom you desire."

She yanked her hands out of his. "Oh, who might that be?" Allie asked.

Peter raised his brows. "Perhaps me."

Allie slammed her hand against her mouth to conceal a gasp. She bent her head, turning away from Peter, to hide her burning face. *Oh, my God. He really has feelings for me, but can he be supportive of my work?*

"You? I don't think so. You are too know it all, too bossy."

Peter raised a brow. "Look who's calling who bossy."

Allie twirled one of her curls around her finger. "No one is going to win this. Just tell me what happened at Baxter's office. Did he have a reason to request your presence?"

Peter stood. "We best get out of this dining room before everyone forms a circle to watch us fight. Why should I tell you anything? Your behavior is bratty. I can't trust that you know what you're talking about."

Mia excused herself. "Don't think for a minute that I want to be in the middle of your muddle. I suggest you settle your arguments before the night's over. I'm going back to our suite and relax with a book."

Peter and Allie strode out to the balcony. The water beyond the beach sparkled like jewels in the moonlight. November nights were unpredictable—sometimes cold, sometimes warm, sometimes balmy. This night was flawless despite the cold. But her silk, neatly pressed pink dress rustled in the breeze and gently blew her hair off her face.

"Allie, let's enjoy this night." Peter pulled her into his arms and brushed his lips over hers. He held her close and ran his fingers through her hair. It was just what she needed to calm her down and convince her a man could respect her.

"Oh Peter, can we stay like this forever?"

The man tempted her, body and soul. She met his gaze, her eyes snapping to his.

Peter let her go and leaned against the railing. "I'd rather hold you, but my meeting with Baxter was important. May I explain?"

"Of course."

"Turns out it was important to see Baxter. He hired a woman I will work with for the festival."

Allie nodded and grinned with confidence. "I knew it had to be. It's Penelope, isn't it?"

"Yes, it's Penelope." Allie scrunched her nose and put her hand against Peter's cheek to turn his face to hers. "Penelope is a wonderful, dedicated worker, and she's ethical. She'll do more than her share. You have nothing to worry about."

Peter laughed.

"Why are you laughing?" Allie frowned. "Is it strange,

perhaps funny, that you'll be working with a woman who happens to be my good friend?"

"Let me assure you, Penelope's involvement is . . ."

"Aha." Allie's eyes widened, interrupting him at that moment, worried he might say something demeaning about working with Penelope. "Are you confident that you'll have unexpected, supreme support?"

"My job will be less taxing."

"I'm glad you see a woman as supporting.

Allie realized that Peter was like Johnny, her half-brother, and her father both who give her care and respect. Allie had deep feelings for Johnny and her Papa. These men made a difference in her life.

Peter had shown her the same traits. She was more than a job to him.

Peter's words came out delicately, as if he had wrapped them in a cocoon. "I asked Baxter if he needed help to investigate the fire. He said his men had everything under control."

Allie folded her hands in her lap. "What control? I don't believe that, not until we solve the mystery of the missing girl."

Peter rubbed the stubble on his face and laid his hand over hers. "Let's leave it to the sheriff for now and think about tomorrow."

CHAPTER 29

*W*hen Peter returned from meeting Baxter, he drove Allie and Mia to the Longdale farm. Mia sat in the back with Captyn. While Allie sat up front and filled Peter in on their conversation with Mary Lynn and Marla.

Peter clicked his tongue and shook the reins. "You're pretty smart figuring all this out."

Allie clasped her hands in her lap. "Thank you."

The setting sun peeked through scattered clouds. "I can understand two people falling in love. The rest of it is nonsense. Young folk's decisions can be treacherous. Can you imagine? Poor Anne and Margaret were beside themselves with worry. Not to mention Mary Lynn burning her secret letters in the cabin. My goodness, what was she thinking? Love makes people stupid and unreasonably euphoric," Allie said.

Peter held the reins and looked straight ahead. "My mother adored my father."

Allie laid her hand over his. "Did their marriage go awry?"

Peter half smiled. "It did. Mother suffered from consumption and melancholy. Father worked every day and frequently at night. Mother seemed all right in his presence but retreated to her room in his absence."

"You must have suffered after she passed."

"It was hard. I missed her. For the next year, I had a good relationship with my father and treasured his company. But it stopped when he remarried. I knew he wouldn't have time for me, but I didn't know how to fix it. I wanted to escape, but where can a boy of fourteen go? So I stayed. They had babies. Samantha, my stepmother nurtured them. She was tender and loving to me, too, just what I missed when I lost my mother. I softened, and gradually my father noticed. We're good friends now."

"Relationships take on a personality. You can't compare your father and Samantha's relationship to anyone else's."

"What are you saying?" Peter asked.

"I don't think you can base all relationships on theirs. Look how your parents fell apart."

"Father and Samantha seem to be good for each other. I think they have a fine marriage."

Allie squeezed his hand. "You sound unsteady, like you aren't sure you know what a good marriage is."

"Last stop, Longdales." The faded, large sign swinging in the wind with the faded red letters "Longdale" had been hanging for generations.

Peter stopped the coach and turned to Allie. "I know about marriage."

Mia hollered out the window, "Why are we stopping? Have we arrived?"

"Wait a minute, Mia," Allie shouted back.

If a fence didn't separate the pasture from the road, the curious cow meandering to the coach would want a treat. "Uh-oh. It looks like we have a visitor, a friendly cow. What do you know?" Peter said.

"Never mind the cow. What makes you think you figured out their marriage?" Allie asked.

"There's a simple answer. My parent's marriage failed because my father neglected my mother. He is dutiful to his second wife, so theirs is good. It's that simple."

"You are naïve if you believe that."

"Do you know something I don't know?"

"Relationships between two people need more than duty, beginning with respect, understanding, communication, and you must make time for each other and yourself."

"This isn't the time to argue; later, if you must. Mia is waiting in the coach, and it looks like that cow is expecting something we don't have. We need to establish ground rules before we drive through those gates."

"Whatever do you mean?" Allie asked Peter.

He lifted one brow. "We'll inform Edward's parents, being mindful and truthful, and keep our personal feelings to ourselves. Got that?"

Allie nodded.

Peter clicked his tongue, and they drove through the wagon wheel gates. Cows and their calves littered the pasture, grazing on the knee-high grass.

Peter climbed down and assisted Allie down. He strode to the door of the carriage and assisted Mia. They walked together on the worn footpath to the farmhouse. Scents of home cooking filled the air.

The front door, once bright red, now faded and set within a porch, was more than ordinary. It mimicked barn doors with vertical wooden slats punctuated by rusted iron hinges and a worn handle.

As the door opened, Mrs. Longdale's compelling smile warmed Allie. "Please, come in." She led her visitors into the parlor. Nothing in the room looked familiar to Allie—no wallpaper like in houses she visited at home, no tables with detailed carvings, no Oriental rugs piled one on the other. Only an oval, hand-hooked rug of many colors that she had read about in the *Frank Leslie Weekly* lay underfoot. No one she knew had that kind of rug. She must remember to ask Mrs. Longdale if she created this one.

"There's coffee, apple pie, fresh bread, and jam on the server. Help yourselves," Mrs. Longdale said.

Allie smiled. "That's wonderful. Thank you."

A few minutes later, when everyone's plate was full and they had taken a seat, Allie opened the conversation. "I want to reassure you about the fire. Mary Lynn accidentally started it by burning letters she didn't want. She never realized the danger. We have her apology."

The front door burst open. Edward Longdale and Janie, beaming, walked in? "Mama, Papa, I'm glad to find you home."

"Edward!" his father interrupted in a commanding voice. "What happened? Why aren't you in school?"

Allie did what she promised she wouldn't do. "Do you have any idea what you've done?"

"Perhaps we should allow them to explain," Peter suggested in a steady voice.

Allie took a deep breath and closed her mouth.

The Longdales' eyes bulged. Edward's mouth hung open. Janie erupted in tears. Peter scratched the back of his neck, and Captyn was busy scratching something else.

"Excuse me, ma'am. Who are you?" Edward asked.

Allie shifted in her seat. "I'm Allie Baldwin, a reporter from New York. This is Mia Baldwin, my sister, and our security agent, Peter Harrison."

Edward shook Peter's hand. "Pleased to meet you all. I'll be happy to explain. First, can you please tell me why you're here with my parents?"

"That's a reasonable request, young man. You know Mrs. Mitchell, don't you?" Allie said.

A slight grin stole across the young man's lips. "Yes, I do. Why?"

"Mrs. Mitchell sent me a letter asking if I would come to investigate a fire in a cabin here on the farm that almost caused the deaths of the women workers and their dog." Allie said in a firm voice.

"Whose cabin? Which one? The dog, is that Horatio? Is everyone all right?" Janie asked between hiccups.

Allie nodded. "Yes, Janie, your cabin and your dog."

"But we didn't start any fire," Janie cried.

"No, you didn't. The fire was an accident. You told Mary Lynn you were going to get married and asked George to drive you to your aunt in Morgantown. Mary Lynn assumed you were marrying George. That upset her because she was in love with George."

Janie nodded. "I-I needed someone to take me to my aunt's b-because Edward was going to meet me there."

"So you could elope," Allie said.

"Yes." Janie pouted. "But I didn't know that Mary Lynn liked George. Otherwise, I wouldn't have told her anything. Those girls are like my sisters."

"Mia and I are sisters. I would never lie to her. Sisters tell each other the truth, always. That's what sisterhood is all about." Allie crossed her fingers behind her back. Unfortunately, she had not told Mia about going to the suffrage rally in old lady clothes. Her eyes met Peter's stare. He lifted one eyebrow and locked his arms over his chest as if he knew all about sisterhood.

"Heavens, is Mary Lynn all right?" Janie asked.

Mia half smiled. "She's doing much better. She broke her leg running from the cabin."

Allie slowly nodded. "Unfortunately, Sheriff Baxter and his men wasted time investigating a situation full of deceit that got out of control."

Edward took Janie's hand. She smiled at her new husband. "After we married and were on our way home, our carriage wheel broke. The incident delayed us for a couple of days in New Haven. I'm sorry our lateness made the situation more difficult."

"You didn't think to send word to your family?" Peter asked.

"Mr. Harrison, I am sorry. We...we didn't think things through, sir. My family thought I was safe at school. We did not know that everyone thought Janie was missing when she was not at her aunt's." Edward stood close to his parents. His mother's face was wet with tears, his father grim and taciturn.

Edward hung his head. "I behaved foolishly. What must I do?"

"D-do you love each other?" Mrs. Longdale asked.

Edward, his clothes a bit in disarray, put his arm around Janie, who looked a bit like a rag doll in her messy, floral day dress. The lovebirds regarded each other and answered in unison. "Yes."

"Edward, make this right. For your mother, for me, and all the people involved," Mr. Longdale said.

"Janie and I will apologize to Sheriff Baxter and everyone else." Edward took a deep breath. "I will work to pay you back for the damages from the fire and for Sheriff Baxter's time." Edward glanced at Janie. "Father, what else can we offer in the way of making restitution?"

Thinking, Allie leaned her chin on her fist. "Janie may want to volunteer to help Marla and Dr. Mitchell at their hospital."

"I p-promise I will be there every day." Janie took a hesitant step toward her mother-in-law. "I-I am truly sorry, Mrs. Longdale, please don't hate me. I couldn't bear that."

Mrs. Longdale embraced the girl. "Why would I hate you? You are my son's wife, and now you are my daughter. Promise me from now on that you will be honest. No secrets."

"Yes, ma'am."

"Mama," Mrs. Longdale corrected. "Call me Mama."

"Mama," Janie repeated, smiling.

"We'll invite your aunt for a visit."

"Th-thank you. I owe my aunt an apology."

"Are you going to write about this in your newspaper?" Edward asked in a shaky voice.

"No, I'll write about how truth prevailed."

Edward thanked Allie and Mia. He turned to Peter and offered his hand.

"Sheriff Baxter needs to know you and Janie are here and safe. How about you and your father go over there now to give him the details," Peter said.

"Yes, sir."

Captyn padded up to Edward and lifted his paw. Edward shook it and laughed. Captyn gave a soft ruff. "What a smart dog."

Allie beamed. "He is, indeed."

"Sorry to be the bearer of bad news, but we must break up this wedding celebration and leave." Peter expelled a breath. "Thank you for your hospitality." He nodded to the Longdales.

When Peter, Mia, and Allie set out on the path leaving the farmhouse, Allie squealed, "Hooray!" her arms raised in a victory formation. "Another of our mysteries solved." She looped her arm into Peter's, sharply poked his ribs with her elbow, and turned to him. "*Listen to me*," she said, emphasizing the words. "Let's find out how much probing your so-called friend scientist Robert has done. By now, he *must* have information leading to my mystery."

CHAPTER 30

*A*fter a jostling ride in the carriage, they arrived at the inn, standing prominent and proud in its nighttime cloak. A bit of moonlight squeezed between the trees, casting dark shadows on the portico. The sconces inside held flickering candles lighting the palatial lobby's edges, the evening quiet from the gentry.

Allie crisscrossed her arms, closed her eyes, and rubbed her shoulders. A hot bath could not happen soon enough.

"Ma'am, a package arrived for you today." The clerk handed Allie her room key and the package. The smoky glow emanating from the central chandelier gave Allie's skin a ghostly color.

Mia stood at the reception desk, fingers double-tapping impatiently, waiting for her sister. "What's in the package? Maybe Mama sent you something?"

Allie shrugged. "I'll open it upstairs. I can't wait for a bath."

Peter put a hand on her arm. "Open it now, Allie."

Allie pointed at Peter in case he wasn't sure to whom she directed her remark. "You're too bossy." She unwrapped the package, revealing another music box. Allie lost her breath. She put her hand to her throat and stood mesmerized. When she lifted the lid, the ballerina with flowers in her hair whirled in a circle to Tchaikovsky's "Waltz of the Flowers." Oddly, the box smelled like daffodils and orange blossoms on a spring morning after the rain.

The note included read:

> You flit and flutter from flower to flower. You think you hold all the power. Words are just words, and you will not win. All that you do is a terrible sin.

Allie met Peter's eyes over Mia's shoulder.

"I'm sorry, my sweet sister."

Holding the open package in one hand and the ribbon in the other, Allie tried to smile. This latest message left her empty and close to tears.

Once in their sanctuary, Mia sat on the settee. Peter and Allie stood across from her at the fireplace.

"I'm not finding humor in this any longer. These music boxes and notes are a threat, aren't they?" Finally, her eyes flooded with tears. She laid her head on Peter's chest. He embraced her and brushed the hair off her forehead.

Allie moved back and gazed into Peter's eyes. "I can't stand this distress. Who is victimizing me? Why in the world would . . ." Allie jumped at the knock on the door, her tongue dry as toast.

"Don't worry. Before we came to our rooms, I sent a runner for Baxter," Peter said.

With a sigh, Allie plopped down on the settee with Mia. As she ran her hand over the soft velvet, she let out a deep breath. Mia took her sister's hand.

Peter tore open the door. "Ah, my man, you're a splendid fellow." Peter put his hand on Baxter's shoulder. "Thanks for your prompt response." They shook hands. Baxter left his two men in the hallway at the suite's door.

"Bad news. Another threat arrived today." Peter tossed the words at Baxter along with a nod. "Take a seat here on the sofa."

"Let's see what you have." Baxter looked the goods over near the oil lamp on a table close to him. "Let's figure out who made the delivery. Are you in?" he asked Peter.

"Good idea. Before we leave, I need to make sure Allie and Mia are secure. Can your men stay at the door until my men, Davenport and Williams, arrive?"

"Sure, I'll wait in the hall for you," Baxter said from the doorway.

Allie bent down to adjust the laces on her boot, avoiding Peter's eyes. "I would feel better going with you. I'm coming, and Mia too."

Peter didn't appreciate another challenge from Allie. "No," Peter said, waving off her words like they were mosquitoes. "You would only slow down the process."

She peered into his eyes. "You prefer Mia and I stay here in our room and do nothing? Does that make sense?"

Peter looked at Mia for support. "This arguing is counter-productive."

"Allie and I can make a list of suspects while we wait," Mia said with a half smile.

Allie exhaled and agreed. Captyn moaned and sat up to lay his head in her lap.

"Yes, Captyn, this day is turning out to be a real stinker." Allie patted his head.

"I expect I'll be back soon." Peter left with the sheriff.

Downstairs, Peter directed his question to the manager, a short, stocky man with a receding hairline and wire-rimmed spectacles perched on his nose. "Who delivered the package to the Baldwin's suite?"

"A young boy. Not our usual post office deliveryman," the manager said.

Peter glanced at Baxter. "The package didn't have a postmark."

"Which means whoever sent it either was already here or just arrived by train. Did you recognize the boy?" Baxter asked.

"Yes. . ." The manager hesitated.

Baxter twisted his mouth and rubbed his chin. "Speak up, sir. If there's a madman in my town, we need to find him."

"You know the boy?" Peter asked.

The portly manager nodded. "He's the son of one of our cooks, a fine boy who often does odd jobs for us. He developed a bad stutter because of his father's abuse."

Baxter turned to the manager. "Is the boy still here?"

"Yes, his name's Mica. He's helping his mother in the kitchen."

"Mind if we ask him a few questions?"

"No. Follow me."

The manager pushed through the swinging door with Baxter and Peter following behind. The heat of the ovens hit Peter in the face. The familiar smells of pigs recently slaughtered invading the air reminded him of skewered cooked pork, the old cook, and Peter's kitchen duties in his youth.

The manager scratched his head. "Sorry to break in like this," he said to the boy. "This is Sheriff Baxter and Detective Harrison. They have questions about that package you delivered to the inn earlier today."

The red-haired, tall, slim, pimply faced boy, his left arm in a sling, stopped cleaning off the marble worktops and wiped his hands. "Y-Yes, s-sir."

"Mica, pull over that chair and sit," Peter said.

The boy hung his head and said "T-thank y-you" in a shaky, thin voice. He sat stiffly and favored his left arm, holding it with his right hand under the sling to support its weight.

"As a detective, I find the facts of an investigation, and the sheriff here also needs answers. Can you tell us where the package you delivered today came from?" Peter asked.

"M-my paw a-asked me to b-bring the package h-here," the boy said with a pronounced stutter.

"Did your father tell you where he got the package?" Baxter asked.

"N-no, sir," he answered.

"When did your father give it to you? Did he ask you to deliver it promptly?" Peter asked.

The boy's face reddened. He cocked his head. "I-I d-don't re-remember. P-paw pushed m-me. I f-fell, hurt m-my a-a-arm. I-I couldn't wait to g-get rid of the d-darn thing, r-ran all the way here, a-and just gave it to the m-manager."

"Any idea about what time all this happened?"

"N-no, sir."

"Thank you. I hope Doc fixed your arm. Is it broken?" Peter asked.

"N-no, s-sprained is all."

Peter and Baxter shook the boy's hand and patted him on his shoulder. He thanked the manager for his cooperation.

"Nice young man," Peter said to Baxter, pushing through the swinging door and out of the kitchen.

"Damn." Peter shook his head. "If a man beats his kid or his woman, he belongs in jail. Baxter, I say we pay the boy's father a visit," Peter said.

"Can you keep the boy and his mother here for now?" Baxter asked the manager. "We need to shelter them while we deal with the father."

"I'll do better than that," the manager said. "They can live here in the hotel under our protection until they want to leave."

They headed over to the boy's father's place near the edge of town. They found him sprawled out on a cot behind a curtain in the small, one-room cabin, his arm wrapped around a bottle of whiskey.

"C'mon. Wake up, man." Baxter poked him with his boot.

Peter looked around the clean, meager surroundings and knew what Allie would say in a heartbeat. "Disgraceful that a man could do this to his family."

Baxter grabbed the snoring man's shoulder and shook him. He snorted a few times and fell back into a deep sleep.

"This guy is out cold. Let's give him a nice rest in a jail cell." Peter interlaced his fingers and turned his hands outward. "What do you say, Sheriff?"

They hauled him into the sheriff's wagon, and Baxter drove him to the town jail.

"I have to get back to the hotel," Peter said. "Send for me if the creep wakes up."

Baxter hooked his thumbs in his belt loops and relaxed his stance. "I've seen this before. I doubt he'll wake before the morning. Will you be around tomorrow to question the drunkard?"

Peter firmed his lips. "I'll be around late afternoon. Does that work?"

"It does. We'll question him together."

CHAPTER 31

*M*ia sat on her bed and Allie at the writing desk by the window. Allie had drawn the curtains closed to keep out the evening chill. They put a list of suspects together while munching on cinnamon biscuits and sipping their third cup of tea. Allie filled her notebook pages and handed her list to Mia. "Here's a list of those I wrote about who are possibly guilty of this music box folly." They reviewed the list and crossed out each name for one reason or another.

"Perhaps it was not someone you exposed in one of your articles."

Allie took a bite of biscuit. "What do you mean?"

"If you angered a landlord or a business owner, he would attack Papa, not you. Is that not so? After all, he owns the newspaper. Whoever did this purchased two expensive music boxes and wrote two threatening notes. It is someone has a personal connection to you and our family and follows your every move."

"Mia, have I told you lately how brilliant you are?"

Mia laughed. "Well, not lately. It's always nice to hear."

Captyn, snoring in front of the fireplace, lifted his head at the sound of the laughter, gave a muffled woof, and turned his back to them.

"We have disturbed his royal highness." Allie giggled and popped the last bit of the biscuit in her mouth. "But who could it be? How did the news about my trip get around? Who has a grudge and wishes me ill? We can rule out the family, of course."

Allie took a deep breath. "And the staff. Wait a minute. What proves it's not the butler, the cook, or servants?"

Mia's eyes widened. "Hmm, contemplate the possibilities."

Allie shook her head. "It's beyond me. It could not be my friend Frankie, could it?"

"No, but what about her mother?"

Allie turned away from her sister's hard stare.

Mia blinked. "What are you hiding?"

Allie stretched long and hard, she yawned. "I'm not hiding anything."

"You are."

Allie blew out a breath. "Mrs. Waverly keeps a music box on a table in her parlor. She said it was a gift from her late husband."

Mia grinned. "That's not a reason to suspect Mrs. Waverly, and besides, music boxes are popular."

"It's like the one I just received. I'm not Mrs. Waverly's favorite person, but surely she would never do this nasty business."

"Are you going to speak to her about it?"

"No, never." Allie shook her head. "She's my best friend's mother. How can I even imply her involvement? What would Frankie think? That reminds me how much I miss her. I'm used to getting together with her almost every day."

"Doctor McDougall mentioned it could be a woman," Mia said.

"Maybe it's one of those rich matrons that came to the fundraiser. They are revolting. They disagree with what I do and who I am, don't you think? Let's get all the facts and be sure they are clear before we even think about approaching Frankie. She is the last person in the world I would want to hurt."

Mia put two fingers on her lips. "What did you think of Doctor MacDougall?"

"What? Why are you asking that suddenly?" Allie grinned and nudged her sister with her elbow. "What are you not telling me?"

"Nothing."

"It's not *nothing*."

Mia smoothed her hand over the silky pillow on her lap and cocked her head. "He seems to live such a solitary existence."

"That's because he's so disagreeable."

Mia jumped off the bed, ready to strangle her sister. "You are wretched. That's unkind."

"I'm sorry, I didn't mean to be nasty. But you have to admit he's a singular sort of man."

Mia bowed her head. "I think he has suffered a tragedy."

"Should we ask Peter if he knows anything about him?"

"No." Mia shook her head. "Please, not a word to Peter about my inquiry. It will mortify me. He would think me promiscuous."

Allie's eyebrows raised a fraction. "We could ask Peter if he has heard from the doctor regarding any clues to the music box mystery? We don't have to know if the doctor has suffered a tragedy, do we?"

Mia kicked off her slippers, got back on the bed, and tucked her feet under her skirt. "Just one more thing about the doctor. I hate to see anyone in pain, and I glimpsed stark pain in Doctor McDougall's eyes."

Allie gave her sister a sideward glance. "Come now, that's enough. I know that you have intuition and a big heart."

Mia's lips quivered. "All right, but I want to know more about him."

There were male voices in the vestibule. Mia and Allie exchanged glances.

Captyn began barking. He skidded past the girls into the vestibule. Allie ran after him, both stopping dead at the feet of Peter. Mia came in behind them.

"Heavens, I couldn't imagine what startled Captyn. Thank goodness it's only you. He's a good watchdog after all."

"Good boy. He needs a treat for a speedy job checking me out." Peter, sitting on the floor, got his cheek doggie kissed. Peter stood with the grandest grin on his face. "Yup, you are a good boy."

"Captyn's treat will wait. Please, tell us—what did you find out?" Allie asked Peter.

"We don't have any new information," Peter said, "at least until we talk to the man who had his son deliver your parcel."

"What is this world coming to?" Allie said. "I don't understand all this mystery. Why am I even worth the bother?"

Peter grinned. "You are a clever writer, Allie."

Allie sucked in a breath, a lump forming in her throat. "Am I really a clever writer?"

Peter captured her gaze with his. "Listen, Allie, you are in the forefront of the news, the public reads what you write, and your words have influence. You may have angered one of your readers."

"Ridiculous. I don't remember writing anything controversial."

Mia shook her head. "Oh, come on. You don't remember?"

"Not one of my readers has ever threatened me before. So, no, I don't remember. I can't stand this, Peter. What you're talking about? I have no enemies."

Peter's lips turned up at the corners, and he took Allie's arm, then let it go before she could pull it away. "If you believe you've offended no one, you are naïve."

Peter appeared to have a knack for knowing people, whether working with the sheriff or getting the best out of his men.

"Never mind. Let me look at your list. Have you finished?" Peter asked.

"My list is of those I've written about in my column. There's no culprit there."

Grrr. I'm tired of telling him.

"You must know, though, your writing style may be provocative to some," Peter said.

Allie stood, strode over to the window, and pushed the curtains aside. A moonbeam had swooped down on the ancient tree in front of the inn. Darkness blanketed the beach and water, except for the reflections. "Honestly? You've read some of my articles?"

"Yes, and when you point out a subject's faults, it's pretty clear how you could have made an enemy or two.

"Mia mentioned that I might have touched some sore spots and someone is retaliating."

Peter grinned at Mia. "Well, it seems sleuthing runs in the family."

Mia patted her stomach. "If it weren't for my edginess, this would be exciting."

Allie drew the curtains, waved her hand in the air, and faced her sister. "There's no need to be on edge. I refuse to cower. Let's talk with this ne'er-do-well and jail the lout."

"We won't be doing anything of the sort right now, and you're not coming with me to see the boy's father."

Allie glared at Peter and shook a finger at him. "Whatever do you mean? You are neither my father nor my keeper, and we are *not* staying cooped up in this suite until Monday. Don't tell me what to do. You can get your beefy friends away from the door."

Peter tried to console Allie. "We will not coop you up, just keeping you safe until we leave for the Harrison House where my family lives. It's close to town and has gated grounds."

"Well, if that's the case, I'd rather go home."

"I've already sent a detailed telegram to your father and mine. There's no reason to change our plans."

He was right. Going home would solve nothing. Besides, she did not want to put up with her father's negative attitude. He would slap down her involvement and say leave it to Harrison. Meeting Peter's family held appeal, but also some apprehension. She looked forward to getting to know his father and stepmother.

"We never finished our argument about marriage, so maybe I'll believe what you said after I meet them. Still, there's more to learn about relationships. All right, agreed, but Mia and I are going with you when you continue the search."

Peter shook his head and feigned innocence.

Allie lifted her brows. "I mean it, Peter. You will not leave me twiddling my thumbs."

"Let's discuss this later," Mia interrupted. "In the meantime, we can pack our things." Mia tipped her head toward Peter. "I assume we'll be leaving first thing in the morning for your family estate?"

"First thing." He turned to face Allie, took her hand, and kissed it. She blushed at his tender touch.

"Now, if you'll excuse me, I'll pack and return later for dinner. Sheriff Baxter had an emergency and had to take away the two sentinels at your door. For this last night, we still have one guard at the main entrance of the inn. I'll be sleeping here in your suite instead of the guards we lost. We don't have a choice."

"I'm not comfortable with that arrangement. What will people think?"

"Can you think of an alternative?"

"Not at the moment. I just know that you cannot sleep in our suite. Why can't you be at the door in the hall instead?"

"Wouldn't you feel safer with me inside the suite?"

"I'll feel safe with you outside our door if you don't mind."

"Sorry, Allie. I am taking the inside position tonight. My idea was for Captyn to be a backup should anyone break in. I know he's not ferocious, but his size and bark are deterrents. I'll sleep on the sofa in the parlor with Captyn."

Allie blew out a breath and realized arguing would be for naught. When Allie did not get her way, she found taking a couple of deep breaths, walking away, and putting time between her and the task helped settle her emotions. Allie tolerated no one telling her what she could or could not do, like when her bratty brother, Adam, who teased her nonstop, defied her to climb the tree he was in. "You big fraidy-cat," he'd goaded. Allie had spat on her hands, rubbed them together, and made a beeline for the tree. Adam sat on the lowest branch halfway up the tree, watching her and launching insults while she climbed the trunk. She would have made it, too, if Mama and Papa hadn't come upon them. Papa lifted her down, and Mama scolded her. It was a scary and compelling lesson in her defense mechanism and decision-making.

SOMEONE WAS KISSING HIM, LIKE A HOT, SMELLY, WET RAG dragging all over his face. Peter cracked one eye open and found the culprit responsible. Those large brown eyes beamed at him with adoration while the drool from the droopy jowls landed on his chin.

"Captyn has to go out," said an all-too-familiar feminine voice that was trying hard not to laugh.

Peter pushed the noble beast off his chest, stood, and faced Allie.

"I'm sorry," she said. "I knew you were sleeping."

"I wasn't successful." He scratched the back of his neck and gave her a smile that indicated he wasn't sure he should smile.

The small sofa in the sitting room was just too short to fit his oversized frame, even lying on his side. So, he'd pulled the foot-stool close to the couch and stretched out, but that didn't help either.

"Are you able to come with us or not?" Allie asked.

"I'm coming. I'm coming. Can you give up being brash for a minute?"

"Perhaps for a minute. Mia is asleep." Allie glanced back at the bedroom. "I'm concerned about leaving her here."

"The deputy is downstairs at the main entrance. No one can get in without identification."

They made their way down to the lobby with Captyn by their side.

Peter acknowledged the deputy.

"Sheriff Baxter's men must get bored standing around," Allie said.

"The men would rather stand around than be shot at or chase thieves and risk breaking their neck. Besides, they get paid well. You're not afraid, are you?"

She smiled one of those soft, sweet smiles. "No. How would I be able to function if I was fearful?"

Captyn sauntered along the street, sniffing and scratching, and finally found the perfect place to make his mark. Allie gave him a head pat. "Good boy." He stayed close to his mistress. "I thought the first music box was a prank." She looked up at Peter, her voice floating on the night's November wind. "But the second box delivered here . . ." Her voice trailed off. She stopped and turned to him, her eyes reflecting the moonlight.

He wanted to hold her. Instead, he tried to reassure her with words. "You're out of harm's way while in my custody."

"Not even Peter Harrison can be everywhere at once."

"I'm intuitive."

She smiled up at him, and he could not help himself—he leaned down and gave her a soft kiss. Her eyes fluttered closed, her arms wrapped around his neck, and a breathy sigh escaped her, drawing him back to her parted mouth. A second kiss. This time her lips clung to his. His hands moved to her waist as he deepened the kiss.

She gasped and pulled away. Her hand flew to her mouth. "You. Kissed. Me."

He arched a brow. "Yes, but you kissed me back." He grinned at her wide eyes and blushing cheeks.

CHAPTER 32

*P*eter fastened one valise on the top of a carriage that had no crest on the carriage's door to identify its owner. "Ladies, your chariot will be ready to go when I get this last hefty valise tied up."

Standing close to Allie, the pleasantly fresh fragrance of her soap wafted under his nose. Hoping to stop the unfamiliar emotions running through his body, he lifted the valise into place. The unexpected weight of it stopped him. A gust of wind picked up Allie's curls and blew them around her glowing cheeks. Her porcelain hands were a little darker than her face and at least three times smaller than his.

"Do you need help?" Allie asked with more color than usual on her face, most likely from pinching her cheeks, or maybe she was flushed or blushing, but the corner of her lips turned up.

Damn, I don't know what to make of this woman.

"Do I look like I do?" Peter said before lifting the last of the two pieces.

She is a nymph, a devil.

"I'll push," Allie said.

"No, stop, I don't need . . ."

She wound up and gave a sharp shove to the valise—right out of Peter's hold. The suitcase fell open, spilling its contents across the path, and Allie tumbled into his open arms. Both fell backward into the open carriage in a compromising position. She was sitting on his legs, his lap, actually.

He could live without Allie. Of course he could. It was just that she was so . . . so beautiful, and impish, and more than adorable. He would have liked that they remain in that position for at least another twenty minutes, maybe a lifetime.

Allie's clothes, her outerwear, and intimates were on display. Peter held onto her. She was soft, and her giggle amused him. Her voice sounded like music, even when she rebuked him.

Mia jarred him into reality. "You two are a pair of clowns. Here, Allie, take my hand. Come on, it's getting late. Let's pick up the mess."

Allie stood, turned to face Peter, and offered him her hand. "Don't just sit there. You look ridiculous."

He grabbed her hand and thought better of pulling her back down into his lap. Instead, while holding her warm, delicate hand, he pushed himself up, allowing her to believe she helped him. "If you hadn't been so impatient, your belongings would not be all over the place."

"I thought you needed my help," Allie said in a soft voice while quickly gathering her intimates and shoving them into her valise.

Mia helped pick up the corsets and stockings while Peter picked up Allie's outer garments, folding them as best he could.

Allie grabbed them away from him. "Don't bother. You are folding them all wrong anyway."

He stood still with his hands on his hips and a shy smile on his lips, watching the ladies finish the job.

Allie snapped at him. "It's all yours. Please be more careful next time."

"Careful—are you blaming me for this state of affairs?" Peter asked.

"Yes, I am. I just wanted to help. You were wimpy and couldn't hold on to the valise. Next time get someone else to help you."

"Help me? I didn't need you to get involved. This incident was exasperating and a waste of time." Peter spat the words out through gritted teeth. He turned away, climbed up onto the coach, and secured Allie's valise with Mia's.

Peter made his way down and stood in front of Allie and Mia. He clicked his heels and bent at the waist as a perfect gentleman would do. "Are we all set?"

Allie placed both hands on her hips. She grinned at Peter. "We are ready."

He offered his hand to both ladies and helped them into the carriage.

In her fashionable, high-button, silk, green dress, Allie wound the handle of her reticule around her wrist and tried to smooth the creases in her dress without success. Her mother insisted that she be careful sitting and to run both hands under her bottom as she sat. In her sunshine-yellow day dress, Mia sat opposite, with Captyn taking up the center.

"Call if you need anything," Peter said before he joined the driver. "I'll be riding upfront to give you more space in the carriage."

Peter knew the road, a narrow strip of dirt that turned into sucking mud in wet weather. He checked sky conditions before choosing this shorter path that ran alongside a sprawling, forbidding cemetery with benches for folks visiting relatives. He could imagine no one sitting on those cold, hard seats on this bleak, ominous piece of land.

Once past the dirt road, it opened up for a smoother ride. Lined up along the way were homes of slaves that once worked at the Harrison estate. The housing was less than a mile from his house, on the outskirts of the property. When the war was over, the freed slaves of the Harrisons remained in their cabins. The children that lived there always seemed happy, running and playing their games after a day working in the fields. Mothers cooked and tended their needs, their fathers there every night managing their small vegetable gardens to supplement the Harrisons' rations.

Peter was once jealous of a friend who lived in the cabins. He had a dutiful father, someone to talk to, play ball with, care for him, and understand. Peter had expected a similar relationship with his father, but it never happened, at least not when he was a child. He shook off the memory of promises never kept. He didn't understand his father's lack of forethought about responsibilities before he married.

Now, weeds were tall enough to hide an entire cabin, roofing material lay scattered, and entry doors in faded colors dotted old wooden porches. Cedar had long faded to gray, bleached out by the sun, beaten down by the cold weather and the snow.

ANOTHER BRONTË NOVEL ENGROSSED MIA. ALLIE GLANCED AT her sister out of the corner of her eye. She hadn't yet told Mia about the kiss.

She touched her lips, lowered her head, and closed her eyes.

Allie opened her copy of *Great Expectations* by Mr. Dickens, the next book on her reading list with Frankie. Time had gotten away from her, and she was falling behind on her reading. It would take an afternoon to tell Frankie everything that happened in Fairfield. Could she talk to Frankie about her feelings, knowing her friend's heartbreak over Adam?

When had Allie's life become so complicated? Her family,

her friendships, and her work were equally important, but now with Peter around, her life had become muddled.

Allie put her hand on Mia's arm. "You are smart and accomplished. I have a pressing question for you. What do you think of Peter?"

"Honestly, you must know by now that I find him delightful."

Allie rustled the flounces in her most feminine day dress. "Mia, can we talk?"

Distracted from reading, Mia gazed at her sister. "Do you mind? I want to finish this section? Can it wait?"

Allie rolled her eyes. "I guess," she drawled in a squeaky, modulated tone.

Peter differed from other men she knew at home and work. Aside from his rugged, manly face, he was Adonic. He had a perfectly straight nose, a square chin like Michelangelo had sculpted it, and that wasn't all.

"All right." Mia interrupted Allie's deliberations. "I'm all yours. Is this important?"

"It is, and it isn't." She took a deep breath and hurried the words out. "Peter kissed me."

Mia jumped up, almost banging her head on the carriage's low ceiling, and gave Allie the biggest hug ever. "When? How were you able to not tell me immediately?"

"I wanted to keep it a secret, Peter's and mine only, but that did not work. I was bursting."

"I won't tell a soul. What was it like? Are his lips soft?"

"His lips on mine shocked me, so I didn't notice. I felt tingly all over, though."

"Did you kiss him back?"

"I do not know. Peter said that I kissed him back. There did not seem to be time to do anything. What will Peter think of me? Will he see me as a floozy, an immoral woman?"

Mia doubled over in laughter. "You best get reading Bronte

and learn what it's like to be wanton or a kissed, respected woman."

"While I waited for you to finish your section, I thought about Peter. I think I'm falling in love. He has a confident manner, and he's kind and generous, and I want him to kiss me again. Once isn't enough, is it?"

"I'm sure you'll get kissed again."

"Best of all, he makes me laugh, like Mama and Papa when they laugh together."

"I think our parents probably like each other. That's almost more important than love. It's what I see when we're together with them," Mia said. "Could I be wrong?"

"I believe you are right."

Allie considered meeting Peter's family an opportunity. The place where he grew up should reveal much about him.

"That last music box note scared me." Allie's voice was soft and shaky.

Mia squirmed in her seat. "I haven't said too much about the threatening packages, but honestly, all those notes have been unsettling. It'll be a good day when they find out who the nasty culprit is."

Allie tightened her hands around the book in her lap. "How does that senseless person keep finding me?"

CHAPTER 33

*a*fter passing rows of handsome, naked maple trees with good bones arching over the road, the carriage approached the iron-gated entrance and came to a halt.

"I'm excited but nervous about meeting Peter's family," Allie said.

Mia put a reassuring hand on hers. "Worry no more. We shall have a splendid visit and respite from the ordeal in Fairfield."

Peter appeared at the door of the carriage, and Allie commanded Captyn, "Stay."

She gave Peter her hand and stepped down, entranced by the splendor of his home. She breathed in the fresh air and aroma of the tall pines, recalling a country stay with her family last summer. The Harrison House stood proudly in a valley surrounded by gardens and natural woodland plantings.

The adjacent lake's boathouse was easily visible and had a rising island beyond; the banks were in its natural habitat. Allie, a city girl, rarely had seen nature in its natural environment, untouched and left in its simplicity, except for Central Park.

"This is your home?"

Peter gave a slight nod. "My father's home."

"You grew up here?"

"Yes."

"It's like Pemberley in Jane Austen's *Pride and Prejudice*," Mia said.

Before Allie could stop him, Captyn leaped out of the carriage and ran up the steps of the wide front porch, his leash trailing. He barreled into an approaching footman. In his exuberance, Captyn toppled him off the last step. The poor man landed on his rump and was, for a moment, winded from the oversized dog hovering over him. Captyn licked the astonished man's face.

Peter rushed forward to help the sputtering man to his feet.

"Captyn, no." Allie grabbed Captyn by the collar and pulled him off the footman, who was wiping his face of dog drool.

A stunning beauty with a handsome man started down the steps. He had a smirk on his face, and she had her fingers on her lips, most likely holding back laughter. Three young girls trailed behind them, laughing and shouting at each other. They raced to the Great Dane, now seated by Allie's side, his leash firmly in her hand.

The girls kneeled in front of the dog and wrapped their arms around him, gave him tight hugs, and sang to him. "You are too grand." Captyn panted and leaned into his two front paws, bowing to his admirers.

"Papa, can we have a dog like this one?"

The question came from the tallest girl, the image of the stunning, golden-haired woman standing beside the regal gentleman. His similarity to his son astounded Allie. Same height, broad shoulders, and piercing eyes. Thomas laughed and shook his head. "You'll have to ask Mama's permission. Your mother makes final decisions regarding pets."

The three girls turned to their mother. "We'll discuss it at another time. Your brother is here. Aren't you going to greet him?"

Their daughters giggled and remembered themselves. They gathered around Peter, hugging, laughing, and dancing a circle around him. Captyn pranced around with the girls, barking at their feet.

"Peter, we're happy you're here," the more miniature replica of the older girl said in a sweet voice. "Your dog, he's cute, and he likes to dance."

Peter hugged all three girls and said that he completely understood how they could forget themselves in the presence of such a noble beast. "Captyn, I regret to say, is not mine. He belongs to this lovely lady, Miss Baldwin."

"Father, Samantha, allow me to introduce you to Miss Allie Baldwin and her sister Miss Mia Baldwin of the New York City Baldwin family. And ladies, this my father, Thomas Harrison."

Thomas nodded. "A pleasure to welcome you."

"And these three darlings are my sisters. Carol, eleven; Betsy, nine; and Dolly, seven." The older girls executed perfect curt-sies. The youngest one bent too low and toppled over. Peter chuckled and scooped her up into his arms.

Allie and Mia curtsied for the girls. "Delighted to meet you."

Carol clapped, and her sisters joined in. "You are pretty when you curtsy."

"Oh, please curtsy again," Betsy asked.

Allie and Mia complied. They lowered their heads, put their right foot behind the left, held out their dress with their thumb and forefinger, and together bent their knees into a royal curtsy.

Betsy giggled. "Do you practice? Your bow is so perfect." She tried the curtsy. "Like this?"

Allie, with a smile, gave Betsy a hand clap. "Lovely."

Betsy ran her fingers under her hair, pushed it up into the air, held it for a moment and let it drop. "Mama, I want red hair like Miss Allie."

"I want black hair like Miss Mia," said the eldest.

"I want hair too," said Dolly, the youngest.

"You have hair," Peter said, squeezing her into a hug. "You have the prettiest, perfect, golden hair."

"Oh, thank you, Peter." Dolly grinned at him.

"Please follow me," Samantha said. The Harrisons had painted the walls in the front hall a warm, neutral color. Allie caught her breath at the two Grecian columns separating the sitting room. The painted mural on the domed ceiling depicted a lush spring garden.

"Your home is glorious," Allie said.

"Thank you. We love it here."

Allie pulled on Mia's shoulder. "Do you smell the fragrance from the flowers on the middle table, or is it from the painted florals on the ceiling above the crystal chandelier? Am I mistaken, Mr. Harrison?"

Thomas laughed. "I've often wondered myself. We always have fresh flowers in this hall, except during these colder months. Samantha fills the porcelains with her beaded flowers and touches them with a bit of her French perfume."

The housemaid showed Allie and Mia to adjoining suites, where they unpacked and refreshed. A half hour later, Mia opened the door to the most insistent knocking, like many sticks playing on a drum. The three girls stood at the threshold, jumping up and down and chattering away.

"Oh, please come with us. We have a surprise for you." The girls led Allie and Mia downstairs to an all-glass, octagon-shaped sunroom where Samantha waited beside her wicker rocker. "I thought you might enjoy some light refreshments after your trip."

The maid had set out pineapple juice and pastries on a sideboard.

"How thoughtful. Thank you, Mrs. Harrison," Allie said with

her hand in a salute above her eyes, shielding them from the brightness.

"Allie, are you receptive to using first names?"

"Please, let's do. Good with you, Mia?"

"Of course."

Allie's eyes finally adjusted to the light. She took a glass of juice. The windows in the room reflected the morning light so that it seemed brighter inside than outside.

"Glass walls, clever," Mia said.

Samantha, a young, pretty woman, was tall and slim, maybe Peter's age, wearing a long-sleeved yellow dress with a high-buttoned collar. The color mimicked the sunshine pouring into the room and matched the juice in her crystal goblet. "It's my favorite room," she said.

Allie noted men picked younger women when they married a second time. It made sense, after all. Samantha had never married, and she would want a family. She guessed Samantha was around twenty years old when she married Peter's father. The sunlight tempted Allie to shield her eyes again, but she hesitated. She didn't want to embarrass her hostess and give her the idea that the light was annoying.

"It's my favorite room too," Carol said.

"Me too," Betsy said.

Dolly giggled and did a little jig, "Me three."

Allie and Mia laughed at the exuberance on the girls' faces.

"We can see the sunrise *and* the sunset from this room," Samantha said. "I suffered from melancholy after Carol was born in the winter when the days were short. The doctor recommended light to lift my spirits, so Thomas built this room for me. I spent the daylight hours here and felt considerably better."

"I've read about melancholia," Allie said. "It's difficult to explain."

"It is indeed," Samantha said. "Mine came upon me after the

birth of each of my daughters. It eventually passed. I'm very thankful for Thomas. He's a good, nurturing man."

Not according to Peter. Shocking what men did to save their souls—anything at the expense of others. His father left, leaving Peter in charge. Allie couldn't understand how a man could be so unkind to his son and sickly wife and marry again in complete oblivion. The situation was absurd. Thomas was a creepy man. How could she be polite to him? Her stomach lurched into spasms.

"Allie, are you all right? Your face lost all its color," Samantha said.

Allie barely smiled. "I-I'll be fine. I think the light might be too strong for me. Let me drink some of that juice with one of those raisin cookies, and I'll feel better," she lied.

CHAPTER 34

*P*eter stood at the window in his father's library, gazing out on the manicured grounds. He turned to face his father.

"Let me explain. The situation with Allie is critical. I had limited options to keep her safe from harm. I appreciate you helping."

"Your timing couldn't be better. We were home and not traveling. It's a blessing that we could coordinate with you."

"The blessing is all mine, Pop." Peter walked over to his father and embraced him.

Thomas stood stiff, like the starched collar around his neck.

Peter hugged his father tighter. "It's all right. You can hug me back."

His father gave Peter a friendly smile, shook his hand, pulled him in, and gave him a long hug. "Thank you, son."

"The character chasing Allie is unpredictable. It isn't clear what he wants. We fear for her life. Written notes point to her writing for the *Sentinel*, but we don't know why. The girls made lists of people who were possible suspects. None were apparent.

Are you aware that her father owns the *Sentinel,* a syndicated newspaper? The office is in the city."

"I know of that paper. What does Allie write about?"

"She mainly covers society engagements, marriages, and fashions. Her father gave her carte blanche to cover more important topics until she wrote about saving a young girl in danger at a dance hall. Readers complained it was not a place where Allie or a young girl supporting her family should work. They threatened not to buy the paper.

"Her father stopped her from writing anything controversial, vowing not to publish anything she wrote if she didn't listen. She's eager to write about the woman's vote. He refused to post anything on the subject until a few suffrage women met with them at the *Sentinel* offices earlier this week. They convinced him otherwise, but only temporarily. Now this mystery has her trapped with psychopathic insinuating notes threatening to maim her if she keeps writing."

"I take it that Allie's feisty?"

"She is, and hard to convince to listen to anything. Delivery of the last music box and note to the inn came via a boy whose hopeless drunk father asked him to do it. We could not question him. He's sobering up in a jail cell in Fairfield. Hopefully, he'll be sober enough to answer our inquiries."

"That lead sounds good. I hope you are right."

Peter scratched the back of his neck. "Will you please keep watch over Allie and Mia? I fear Allie might put herself in harm's way, even here under your protection."

"She'll be all right here." His father poured two brandies and handed one to his son. "We stationed guards on the perimeter of the grounds and at each entrance."

"You're always one step ahead."

"For family, you can't be too careful. Besides, we make our share of enemies in our line of work. Our motto is secure and protect."

"Indeed."

Thomas eased his tall frame into the leather armchair. "There is more, though, isn't there, Peter?"

Peter held his breath and took a sip of his drink. "What do you mean?"

"You know well what I mean, son. Are you interested in this woman?"

Watching Allie walking and laughing with his sisters, Peter had trouble keeping his mind on the investigation.

"Father, would you mind if we joined the women and children? They're taking a tour of the grounds."

"Changing the subject, are you?"

"You bet. I'm Allie Baldwin's protection. There's no reason to take it any further."

"The man doth protest too much. Allie is more than a client, isn't she?"

"Must you keep digging? I have yet to decide whether I want her."

"Want? That's a strange answer."

"Allie is independent and a working advocate for woman suffrage. I'm not sure that I can keep up with her. Besides, I hesitate to get involved with any woman before I retire."

"Why so, Peter?" Thomas asked in a flippant voice.

"I thought you and I had settled it all, but I suppose not if you're asking. Must we indulge in old memories? You plagued me with a burden. It's finally gone. My head pounds talking to you about an era long ago. You are a different man. Look around you, Pop. Is there anything in your library here that reminds you of your life before Samantha?"

Thomas, from his comfortable chair, gave a furtive glance around his private domain. "That's a ridiculous question, Peter. I wouldn't have anything here to remind me of the poor decisions that lost me a wife and a son."

"Do you have regrets?"

"In my youth, I missed the importance of time, relationships, and how to care for another human being. My driving force was money and success. It was top priority."

"I didn't have a father until you retired and married Samantha."

"You didn't look unhappy when I handed you a successful business. With what I put in place, and if you keep our clients satisfied and bring in new business, you'll have what you need for life."

"The business doesn't make up for the missing years."

His father peered at him over his glasses and lifted a graying brow. "I have no way to give back lost years, and regrets are useless."

"Father, I have a job to do, and you have guests that need protection. There's no satisfaction in discussing a hurtful past. Please reassure their safety."

"Rest assured we will shelter Allie and Mia while you continue your investigation in Fairfield."

Peter's eyes darkened with determination. "We'll find the lunatic who is haunting Allie."

CHAPTER 35

That evening, when Allie and Mia arrived at the dining room, the Harrison daughters headed straight for them. The youngest grabbed Allie's hand. When the other two sisters fought over Mia's hand, Mia took Carol in her left hand and Betsy in her right. The children began pushing and shoving to sit next to their guests.

Dolly's eyes misted over. "Oh please, Papa, I want to sit next to Miss Allie."

Allie put her arm around Dolly. "There, there, you'll see. If you wait, it will be fine."

Thomas waved his arm in the air. "Stop, wait a minute. Before this gets further out of hand, ladies, do you mind if I arrange the seating to make everyone happy?"

Allie found the savoir faire of the host and hostess exemplary. "Not at all."

"Here, Dolly, I think we should give you a place between our guests. Betsy, you sit beside Allie—she's at Mama's right—and Carol, you sit next to Mia. I will take my place opposite Mother at the head of the table."

"Where's Captyn?" Betsy asked.

Allie laughed. "If this is disarray, can you imagine the ruckus if my Great Dane were here?"

"My goodness, that could've been an impossible distraction. Where did you leave Captyn? Did he have his dinner?" Samantha asked.

"Thank you for your concern," Allie said. "He's in my suite. Your servants graciously tended to his needs, his food, and a walk on the grounds. He's most likely sleeping on the comfy dog bed your servants so kindly made for him."

When they all were finally seated, the servants began pouring the lemonade. Allie enjoyed the glittering of the shiny silver pitcher and the sparkle of the crystal. Allie lifted her drink and offered her host and hostess a toast. "May God bless this beautiful home and family and give Peter a jewel in his crown if he gets into heaven for bringing us here."

"Hear, hear." The cheering was loud and melodic like the jingle of a tambourine.

"Speaking of beauty, Samantha, you have exquisite taste," Allie said.

"Thank you. I love to shop, but I must admit that some tableware came with Thomas when we married. Fortunately for me, Ellen was a woman of class."

"Papa, where's brother Peter?" Carol asked.

Thomas took command of the conversation. "I'm sorry, but Peter will not be joining us. He left for town to work with Sheriff Baxter. He hoped to question the drunkard whose son delivered the package to the inn. Peter also mentioned that he planned on sending a wire to Robert MacDougall, his forensics doctor, regarding any clues he might have discovered."

Allie put her hand up to her throat and spoke up, the words running through her head like a screeching, buzzing bell. "Peter said nothing to me about this," she said in a high-pitched voice. "Why did he go without a word?" Allie seethed until her mouth dried up like a waterless riverbed. She shut her eyes tight.

Dolly faced Allie and in a quiet voice said, "Please don't be sad, Miss Allie."

"It's all right. Thank you for caring, my sweet girl," Allie replied with a half smile.

"Mama, can we go out on the lake tomorrow with our new friends?" Dolly asked.

"No, dear. It's too cold this time of year."

Dolly slumped down in her chair at her mother's reply.

Allie hid her smile. Memories of her mother's no's hurt even now. Dolly had chattered on about the rowboat that went almost everywhere anytime and asked her parents, repeatedly, if they could go the next day.

"But Mama, I want to show off the magical island and the cottage that Papa built for Miss Ellen."

"Now, with the foliage off the trees, you can see the cottage and where Papa made the garden. Why not point out the island from here?"

Dolly pouted. "It's not the same. You can't see the giant sunflowers cause they're not out anymore."

"I would love to hear a special story about the island," Allie said.

Mia smiled at Dolly. "Please do tell. I'm curious."

"Thomas built a cottage and greenhouse for his sick wife on the island that he named Ellen's Island. She died before she ever got to enjoy cottage or the island," Samantha said. "We grow strawberries in the greenhouse now. We love having them all winter."

"The strawberries are so big you need two hands to hold them," Carol said.

Allie gave Samantha a meaningful glance. "You hold Ellen in high regard. That's admirable."

"Ellen was Peter's mother. She deserves my respect. Peter is a wonderful man. I believe you would agree, Allie?"

Allie looked down at her hands.

Peter was a good man, but that could change. Perhaps deep down, he would become like the abusive males that made her angry enough to fight even more for the woman's vote. No man should hold women back from what should be rightfully theirs —freedom of choice. And although Allie loved her father, and the kiss she shared with Peter dominated her thoughts, both men tried to control her, which she found unacceptable.

Dolly went on like children do. "And the big, beautiful dahlias that only grow in the summer." She tugged on Allie's dress and asked her: "Do you know my actual name?"

"No, do tell, please."

Dolly beamed. "It's Dahlia." She turned to her mother. "Papa named me after his favorite flower."

Allie's heart melted at the way Dolly looked at her mother. Her observations of this mother and daughter filled her with yearning. Perhaps Allie's mother was right. Maybe marriage didn't have to be the end of her career like it was for her mother and it was a choice on her mother's part. Peter could be a contender as a husband if he would at least consider Allie's opinion and requests. He was bossy and sneaky, but he was also honorable, intelligent, and funny. Not to mention the way he seemed to make her heart race.

"I'll ask Papa. He'll let me go," Dolly pleaded.

"It's too cold to go out to Ellen's Island," Samantha said to her youngest. "We've had rainstorms, and if the temperature drops, it could snow."

Dolly kicked the legs of her chair, and her mother gave her a scolding stare. Allie recognized it all too well. Clara had given her the same look many times, the one that said, "You are dangerously close to pushing me too far." Dolly swallowed and sat up straight. Motherhood was not for the faint of heart, Allie realized. Would she make a wonderful mother? She hoped so. Her mother was an excellent teacher.

Mia tapped Dolly on the nose. "Have you ever painted a picture?"

Dolly's eyes opened wide. "No, I draw lots of pictures of Mama and Papa, our house—Betsy and Carol, and trees and flowers and bunny rabbits, but I haven't ever painted. Would you teach me?"

"It would be my pleasure." Mia told the Harrison girls a story about painting the forest and all the beautiful trees and animals, the sky, the lakes . . .

Dolly interrupted, "Like our lake? Can you paint our lake?" Forgotten were Dolly's sad feelings about not going to Ellen's Island, at least for the moment.

CHAPTER 36

The following day, Allie was up early working on her article for the newspaper. She wrote about the excellent work that Marla Mitchell and her husband were doing in Fairfield, not only for its citizens' health but also for the well-being of the women at the farm. The Longdales generously educated the farmworkers. She opted not to write about the dramatic events that led to the fire. Mary Lynn had learned a valuable lesson about heartache and heartbreak. Janie learned the importance of telling the truth, and Margaret and Anne learned lies could lead to potentially tragic circumstances.

At that age, Allie and her sisters had preferred their studies and their pursuits to pining after young gentlemen. Joseph and Clara had raised independent women, but in doing so, had they ill prepared them for love and marriage?

She glanced at her dog, scratching at the bedroom door and barking sharply. "Hush, Captyn, or you'll wake the entire house."

He stepped on a piece of paper sticking out from under the door. "Excuse me, Captyn." She directed him out of her way and retrieved the note. The paper depicted a smiling girl standing next to a rowboat holding a fish in one hand and a big strawberry in the other, with a cottage behind her. Dolly's behavior reminded Allie of her childhood and her determination to get what she wanted. The note was from Dolly inviting Allie to join her on the island.

Allie peered out the window at the darkness of a coming storm. Her heart leaped into her throat. Dolly had indeed taken out the rowboat. Allie saw her in the boat, struggling against the gales. Dolly's parents were on the other side of the house. There was no time to alert them. Allie donned drawers, wrapped a cloak around her nightgown, rushed to Mia's adjoining room, and shook her sister awake.

"Dolly's taken a boat out on the lake. There's a storm coming. Captyn and I are going to bring her back in before she gets too far. Please alert the household."

"Yes, go! Go! Go! I'm getting up." Mia yawned. "Don't wait for me. I'm right behind you."

Allie bounded out the door. Her heart pounded as she sprinted down the stairs and out to the garden, with Captyn running beside her. Racing across the meadow, the gusty winds bending the grasses slowed their progress.

Despite losing her breath, she talked to Captyn, encouraging herself not to slow down in the nighttime wet and billowy grass. "Come on, boy, we must run faster." Captyn pranced beside his mistress unencumbered.

Allie dropped her cloak on the dock and dove into the water. The hum of commotion behind her faded when she submerged. With long, swift strokes, Allie propelled herself toward the boat with great difficulty. Captyn swam unfettered alongside her. "Dolly!" The turbulence of the wind and the water swallowed her shout.

Dolly waved frantically.

Memories of that stormy night dinner and Captyn's fear of thunder came to mind and Allie prayed, *Please don't start now.*

Allie kept repeating the mantra in her head as she swam with Captyn to the boat. Allie grabbed the side while Captyn dog-paddled.

"Miss Allie, I tried," Dolly cried, tears streaming down her face. "I'm so scared. Mama is so smart. Why didn't I listen? I just wanted to get you some strawberries."

"It's all right. Can you sit still and promise not to stand?"

Dolly's head bobbed. "I promise."

"Good girl." Allie tried to get into the boat. If only Dolly were bigger, she could help pull her in. "I can't get myself into the boat," she hollered above the storm. "I'm going to harness the rope from the front of the boat onto Captyn's body, and I'll push. Together we'll get you back to shore."

"I'm afraid. Am I going to drown? I'll listen to Mama forever."

"It's all right. Captyn's with us, and he's the bravest dog."

Dolly gave her a wobbly smile through her tears.

Allie tried to cover the dog's ears when the dark clouds appeared to tangle. A flash of light and rumble reverberated. Captyn whimpered. She found the soaked rope at the bow, wrapped it around the Great Dane's body, and slipped a knot in his snout. Allie screamed to Dolly, "The paddles, use the paddles, and help to row back to shore. I can't get into the boat. You must help Captyn, and I'll get you back to shore now. I'll push." Captyn spied her with his big, brown eyes, and Allie knew he would do his job. Then buckets of water pelted them, and the wild wind rushed across the water.

"Go, boy, go," Allie hollered.

Dolly paddled, Captyn pulled, and Allie swam to the back of the boat to push. "Be brave and paddle hard, Dolly," Allie shouted over the storm.

It seemed like they were fighting all the elements. Allie had a hard time keeping the boat steady with one hand while pushing with the other and kicking hard using her swimmer's legs.

When they were a few yards from the dock, a dozen people appeared on the shoreline. They ran and jumped into the water. Relief washed over her.

Pain seized Allie's thighs and traveled down to her toes. She froze and hung onto the back of the boat. "Cramps, I have cramps!"

"Miss Allie, take my hand," Dolly cried out."

Allie tried and fell away. She tried to tread water to keep her head above the surface. Her legs were stiff, unmovable, and the deluge from the heavens blurred her eyes. The storm was too strong. The moment before the water closed over her head, she thought she heard Peter shouting her name.

Peter! Please, God, get him here in time.

CHAPTER 37

here was a smidge of light cascading through the
dark and stormy clouds, enough to spill over onto
Dolly just coming ashore with Captyn. She stood and waved to
her brother. "Peter, Peter, please see me. Here I am, and Captyn
too," she yelled. "Here, over here—please." Soaked beneath his
cape, Peter rode his steed to the edge of the lake and jerked him
to a stop. "Miss Allie's drowning there." Dolly pointed. "She
went under the water again. I can see her hair come up. It keeps
floating to the top and sinks again. Hurry, hurry, please hurry."

"Allie," Peter shouted. He ripped off his shoes and jacket and
plunged into the rough, rolling water. His heart beat faster with
each stroke as he swam to where he'd last spied her hair. *There
she is!* Peter dove and grabbed her around her waist. He pushed
hard against the water and surfaced with his hands under her
arms. Keeping her head above water, he swam to shore.

Breathless, he lifted her into his arms, dropped to his knees,
and laid Allie's limp body on the wet grass. Her soaked nightgown clung to her. He grabbed his jacket and covered her,
hiding what her nightgown did not, giving her a measure of

privacy. He put his ear to her mouth. A wisp of breath teased his cheek.

Thank God she's alive.

Her head rolled to one side, she moaned, and a slender hand fluttered to her throat. "Allie, can you hear me?" Her plump lips moved—a silent puff of air. She vomited. Her deathly pale cheeks filled with a rosy tint. Peter had never seen such beauty. "Allie, can you hear me?"

The entire household stood by, most in their nightclothes, holding umbrellas, some blown inside out. The rain had let up.

"Thank God she's alive," Peter's father shouted.

Samantha bent down, removed Peter's soaked jacket, and covered Allie with a dry blanket. "Peter, the fireplace can warm your room. Her room in the guest suite is chilly. Are you agreeable to giving up your room? You can take the guest suite on the east side of the house."

"Good idea. I never would've thought to put her there. She can stay there as long as needed."

"Thank you. I will ask the servants to fill it with fresh cherry wood and start the fire."

Allie stirred.

Peter sat down beside her, wiped the water from her eyes, and smoothed the hair from her face. Her thick lashes lifted. "Peter." She wept.

Peter held her close while she cried. "Losing you scared me. I never want to lose you," Peter said.

Peter stood with her in his arms.

"Wait, I can walk."

"Save your strength."

～

PETER GLANCED ACROSS THE ROOM AT MIA CURLED UP BY THE warm fire in his burgundy wing chair, with her Bronte book resting in her lap. Captyn snored on the floor by her chair.

"Peter, I'm sorry to bother you. Would you like to change places so you can take a nap?"

"This chair is comfortable." Allie's hand was still cold in his. "Besides, I want to be by her side when she wakes up."

Other than his meeting with Baxter, nothing more had come of his trip to Fairfield. He never got the opportunity to question the man who had his son deliver the last music box and note. He died in his sleep, drank himself to death. But there was a telegram from the forensic doctor waiting for him at the sheriff's office. MacDougall identified the last note's scent as a woman's perfume by Guerlain, probably purchased at Lord & Taylor. He'd verify soon.

"I think it's time to take Captyn for a walk anyway. It'll be good for me to take a stroll. All right with you?" Mia asked.

"That's fine. I'm sure Allie would agree."

Peter's father stood in the doorway. He moved aside for Mia and Captyn to leave and walked over to Peter. "The Baldwins will arrive tomorrow."

"I didn't know they were making the trip."

"They want to make sure Allie's all right."

"I have to take the blame for Allie's accident," Peter said.

"I'm sure Allie would do it again if needed."

"That's true. Allie wanted to come with me. It turns out it's a good thing she did not. But if I had not left, I would have been the one to get Dolly out of trouble."

Thomas laid a hand on Peter's shoulder. "How could anyone predict this would happen? You can't feel guilty over what was not in your control."

"You still blame yourself for Mama's death, don't you?"

Thomas heaved a deep sigh. "I blame myself no longer. When we are young, there's much to learn. Your mother was not physically strong, and I was immature, too young to understand responsibility."

"My anger lasted a long time, Father. This situation isn't far from yours. Allie could have drowned. If only I had stayed. I can't understand why she did not come to get you right away."

"She saw Dolly in the boat from her window. There was no time to get to us on the other side of the house. Mia was right next door; she came for Samantha and me. When we got to the lake, Allie and Captyn were already swimming out to Dolly. But why do you think Allie didn't get into the boat?"

Peter wiped his brow. "Dolly isn't strong enough to help an adult into a boat, and Allie probably couldn't gain leverage. Dolly heard Allie say she had a cramp. That must be the reason she got into trouble."

Thomas buttoned his shirt collar. "She will get through this ordeal, and you'll be there when she wakes up."

"I think I'm in love with her."

Thomas squeezed Peter's shoulder. "She is a wonderful woman. Give it time."

CHAPTER 38

*A*fter Thomas left, Samantha and her daughters tiptoed into Peter's room.

Peter let go of Allie's hand and stood. He put his finger to his lips. "Shhh, thank you for coming. Allie has not awakened," he whispered.

Samantha nodded. "If we keep our voices low, we can have a brief visit with your Uncle Peter," she said to the girls.

Samantha placed her hand on his shoulder. "You challenged me when your father and I married. I did not know if I had done the right thing marrying your father. You seemed resentful at first, but you've ended up as my best boy. I thought you a standout," she said, coming around to hug him. "You were my helper with the babies, my flower garden boy. You had a green thumb. Anything you planted flourished and filled the garden with color. You made sure the children were safe. Did you know that?" The girls kissed their uncle on his cheek.

"Thank you, Samantha, and thank you, my little women. I needed that."

He embraced his half sisters as they stood side by side with smiling faces. Peter whispered to the girls, "I'm proud of you.

You are growing into fine young women, thanks to your mother. She encourages you to study your lessons, your music, and to love each other. Perhaps in the future, you will come alongside Allie to work with her for the women's vote."

Samantha gave him a wry smile. "Doc said it would time to recover. Allie almost lost her life."

"I'm impatient. I'd feel better if I saw her sparkling eyes. Her recovery is taking too long. I'm concerned."

"Peter, you look tired. These last few days were hard. Not much sleep?"

He pushed the curl off his forehead. "I sat by Allie's side and held her hand. No, it was tough to catch a wink."

"Wait a minute. I have something to tell the girls." Samantha took them around and whispered.

After a moment, Carol spoke for her sisters. "Uncle Peter, we have to leave now. Mama is staying with you for a while." She took her sisters' hands. They left, throwing kisses to Peter and closing the door behind them.

Peter looked at Samantha, his eyes quizzical. "I'm sure Allie would love to sit up and have a chat, but you can see she's not ready for company," Peter remarked.

Samantha folded her arms. "I wanted time with you to give you a chance to talk about your feelings. What happened these past few days?"

"It's been agonizing. I went from emptiness to tears, blaming myself for what happened. I talked to Dad, but it didn't help. He told me not to worry, Allie will come around, but my stomach burns like there's a fire inside me. Nothing helped. Sleep would not come. I felt no hunger, but I was starving."

Samantha put her arms around Peter held him while he wept. "I know."

"Will I ever find joy again?"

Samantha gave him her handkerchief. "It's not about you finding joy. Let joy find you. Wipe your tears so you can see.

Allie's eyes fluttered. I'll wager she's dreaming. After being saved from a watery death, sleep is not peaceful. Her flutter is a good sign."

∼

It was a perfect day.

Allie wore a bridal dress of white silk with short, puffed sleeves and a scalloped lace neckline. She adjusted the strand of translucent pearls.

Captyn trotted to her side. She reached over and stroked his floppy ears.

"Heel, Captyn." Allie secured the leash to his collar and clasped it in her right hand. She looped her left arm through her father's. "Papa, you are the best in the world."

He grinned and kissed her cheek. Joseph Baldwin escorted his eldest daughter with her Great Dane to the altar—an arbor lush with white ribbons, roses, and hydrangeas.

The three hundred seated guests held their collective breath.

Captyn whined. "It's all right, Captyn. Papa is on my left now. He isn't taking your usual spot." Captyn cocked his head and gave her a soft woof.

Newspapers had proclaimed Central Park an exotic location for weddings.

"My word," Mrs. Templeton said. "I believe the dog is part of the ceremony."

"Well, I never," Mrs. Higgins huffed.

A faceless man stood at the altar with his back to Allie. He had no voice.

A chill ran up her spine like a scorpion.

ALLIE WOKE AND FOUND HERSELF IN A STRANGE ROOM, A STRANGE bed, staring into the stormy gray eyes of Peter Harrison. "Oh, dear heaven . . ." Allie whispered on a fragile breath.

He scrunched his brow. Blinked. Squeezed her hand. "Allie, I worried about you. You were delirious with fever for three days." He offered her a warm smile. His words came out delicate, wrapped in a whisper.

She slid her hand from his palm. "Three days? Where am I?" Her voice was so quiet you could drown it out with a sigh.

"Samantha suggested you stay in my room where there's a fire to keep you warm." After a moment, he said, "Allie, where did you go?"

Samantha smiled. "She fell asleep again. This sleep is restful. Would you like to take a break? I can stay with her. Please go, take the dog for a walk. I think he's in Allie's room. If not, he'll be with Mia in the room next to Allie's. Just go."

Peter gave Samantha a crushing hug. "Thank you, but just a brief break. I can't stand it when I'm away from Allie."

The next time Allie woke, her mother took her hand. Samantha, standing beside Clara, removed the cool rag from Allie's forehead.

"Mama, Samantha," was all she could say before her voice cracked. Her hand went to her throat.

Clara fussed with the pillows, helped Allie to sit up, and held a glass of water to her lips. "There, now, is that better?"

Allie nodded and lay back.

Her mother stroked her head, brushing her hair back. "You had a fever for three days."

"How did you find out?"

Mama pulled a handkerchief from her sleeve and dabbed her eyes. "Peter got word to Papa and sent his driver to accompany us on the train. He had a carriage waiting when we arrived here. Emma and Ava came as well."

"I'm here, Mama, and I'm alive."

"Thank goodness."

"How is Dolly?" Allie asked.

"She's fine. Her parents feared she would fall ill, so they put her to bed. After one day of rest, she snuck in here to ask your forgiveness."

"She did? I don't remember, the poor sweet girl."

"I told her to come back when you were better. Mrs. Harrison sat here a while with Peter's father."

Allie wanted to ask about Peter but thought she would raise eyebrows. *Did he save her?*

"Rather than call for a servant, I'm off to the kitchen for a bowl of broth. We are going to make you well again," her mother said.

"Clara, stay with Allie. I will have my servant take care of it," Samantha said.

"Thank you, but I would prefer to see if there's anything else for her in the kitchen. Let's go together, Samantha."

"Mama, before you go, I have a question. You mentioned Dr. Mitchell said it takes time to heal from exposure. What does that mean? A week, a month?"

"He didn't say. You caught a chill and a fever. He'll be back tomorrow. Perhaps we'll get an answer then."

Clara and Samantha passed Peter coming back to his room with Joseph.

Peter smiled as he approached Allie in his bed. "We all thought you were beautiful when asleep."

Her father cleared his throat, sat down on the bed, and kissed her forehead. "How's my girl?"

"I guess I'm getting better, Papa, even though I'm stuck in Peter's room."

Joseph studied her for a moment and turned to Peter. "Why is Allie in your room?"

"Samantha suggested that Allie recover here because of the warmth from the fireplace."

In a short time, Clara came back carrying a tray with a bowl of steaming broth, stewed apples, and tea, the fragrance filled the air. Allie's sisters and Captyn marched into the room behind their mother.

"A good meal will put you to right in no time. Come now. Let's sit up." Allie's father took the tray from Clara, who puffed up the pillows again. Allie leaned back, and Joseph laid the tray on Allie's lap.

Emma and Ava took the tray, gave it back to Joseph, and showered their sister with adoration. They smothered her with kisses until she giggled.

"Stop it, you two. I cannot catch my breath."

Ava gave Allie another kiss. "Aren't you glad you have a breath to catch?"

Allie gazed up at the ceiling from the corner of her eyes. "You are silly, that's not so clever. Can't you be more original?"

Emma tapped Allie's shoulder. "How clever must we be? We're here, and so are you. You are alive." Ava and Emma plopped down at the foot of the enormous bed. Joseph gave the tray back to Allie. By this time, the broth had cooled to her pref- erence. *How could she be all right sleeping in a man's bed?* She glanced around, taking in the leather embossed wallpaper and mahogany furniture, befitting a man's suite.

"We will let you rest now and come back later. Mia and Peter are staying." Allie held her hands up over her head. "My own room is waiting."

CHAPTER 39

*A*llie rubbed the sleep from her eyes and searched her surroundings. Mia was asleep, curled up with a blanket on the lounging couch near the fireplace. Peter sat on his cushioned chair beside the bed, his head drooping sideways, fast asleep. Allie blinked a few times and stretched. The early morning sun squeezing through the draperies created a tapestry of light on Peter's face, reminding her whose bed she occupied.

Peter jerked his head up at the sound of Allie's rattling cough.

"Sorry, I fell asleep, induced by your charming company." Peter slipped his arm behind Allie's back and helped her to sit up.

Mia, now awake, hurried over. "Gracious, your cough doesn't sound good. Can you lean forward?" She flipped over the pillows and plumped them up.

"Thanks." Allie pointed her chin at her caretakers. "I think I could get used to this pampering." She flattened her hand on her chest. "What in the world is on me?"

"Mama fixed a mustard poultice. She plastered it on your chest to help you breathe easier."

Allie sucked in her cheeks and ran her hand across her chest. "Yuk."

"Your mother is very knowledgeable. I'm so glad she's here," Peter said.

Oh, dear, there are those dimples again.

Allie took a deep breath. "What is that foul smell? Captyn, is that you?"

The dog trotted up beside Peter and wagged his tail. Allie patted the bed. "Come on up, Captyn." The dog dropped his tail, backed away, and shuffled back to his favorite spot in front of the fire.

Peter knitted his brows together and laughed. "Allie, I think *you* are the source of the smell."

Allie glanced at Mia. "Me? Are you sure?" She scowled.

"Mama's poultice has dry mustard, flour, and water. The mustard is pretty stinky. She added lavender to combat the odor. Guess it didn't help. But the treatment should help to clear your chest."

"Can we brighten this room?"

"Certainly." Mia drew back the curtains. Sunshine spilled in and bathed Allie in warmth.

"Perfect." Allie held her chest. The weight of the poultice was disconcerting. "I must get up." She peeled back the blankets and swung her legs over the edge.

"I need a dressing gown."

Peter strode to his wardrobe and pulled out his silky, brocaded, long gown. "Here you go, Princess."

"Thanks. Turn your back if you don't mind, and in case you've forgotten, my name is Allie, not Princess."

Peter rubbed his hands together. "I'll take Captyn for a walk if I can find his leash."

Mia jumped up. "It's in my suite. I'll be right back."

"This gown is too big. Look, I can't walk. It's dragging on the ground, and it can wrap around me twice. But it's warm. I'll pull the belt tight and hold it up to walk to my suite."

"You look gor—" What did you just say?"

"I want to be in my own bed."

Peter held up his hand. "Whoa, Allie, your fever only broke last night."

"That's no reason to keep me here. I'm not a prisoner."

Peter's forehead creased. "My room is warm with this roaring fire—in case you haven't noticed. Yours will be chilly. Let's ask Doc Mitchell tomorrow."

Mia returned with Captyn's leash. "Here, Peter."

"Thanks." He whistled, and Captyn leaped up and loped after him. "Come on, boy, let's go out."

Mia sat on the bed beside Allie and rubbed her back. "You aren't looking so good. What's going on?"

"I know it's better for me if I stay here, but I'm uncomfortable—" Another cough. Allie grabbed her water glass from the bedside table and gulped the liquid down. "This is Peter's bedroom . . ."

Allie leaned her head on Mia's shoulder. "When he's near me, my throat tightens, and my face gets hot. I don't like it."

"You just described your chest infection."

Allie rubbed her eyes. "That's absurd."

"Maybe that's where the saying lovesick comes from?"

"Heaven help me if it does. I can't go through life wearing this foul-smelling plaster."

Mia laughed, and Allie coughed.

Their mother appeared in the doorway, hands on hips. "How in the world are you supposed to get well with all this giggling?"

"Mother, it's my fault. I made Allie laugh."

Clara joined them in their whimsy. "Don't stop. I'm just making another poultice."

Allie glanced at Mia, and then they covered their mouths,

holding back more laughter. "Mama, you aren't serious, are you?"

"No, silly girls, of course not. I'm teasing. I think the plaster can come off tomorrow."

"Listen, I don't want to appear ungrateful for Peter's generosity giving up his suite for me, but I would prefer to recuperate in mine."

"I understand, dear." Clara's lips turned up into a smile. "Don't you worry. Enjoy the warmth of the fire while you can. I'll catch Peter before he gets back and talk to him privately. I'll see you both soon."

Mia returned to her couch beside the hearth. Allie took off Peter's dressing gown, walked over to the couch, and gave Mia a shove. "Move over, hog. There's enough room for both of us."

"All right, don't push. Give me a chance."

Allie curled up on the couch with her, the blanket covering her feet, and stared into the fire.

A knock sounded at the door, followed by Peter and Captyn entering like a whirlwind. Peter held the most giant strawberries Allie ever saw. "Mia, may I talk to your sister for a few minutes, please?"

"Yes, I'll join Mama and Papa in the parlor."

Allie retrieved the dressing gown, covered herself, and sat on the edge of the bed.

"All right, Mia, you can leave now."

Mia wiggled her fingers at Allie and Peter. "I'll see you later. Have fun."

"Are the strawberries for me?" Allie asked.

Peter held them out to her. "They are. I saw them at the grocer's earlier and had them delivered."

She bit into a juicy one. "Um, thanks." The juice dripped into her hand. Peter handed her his handkerchief.

"Thanks again."

"Your mother said you insist on moving back to your suite. I would rather you stayed, but I'll help you move if that's what you want."

～

ALLIE SIGHED, THANKFUL SHE HAD HER PRIVACY AGAIN, BACK IN her suite, decorated more to her liking—light colors, white furnishings, and airy curtains. She felt relieved to get away from Peter's massive dark surroundings. On the other hand, there was an advantage to being in his room. She had his company and enjoyed those adorable dimples a good part of the time. The disadvantage to her room—she would not be having the fun she had with him, even if they argued.

Allie answered a knock on her door and welcomed Samantha and her three daughters. She fiddled with the belt on the dressing gown that Peter insisted she wear and smiled at the entourage. "So good to see you all. Thank you for coming."

"It's our pleasure, Allie. We went first to Peter's. He told us you had returned to your suite. It would be best if you were resting. Would you prefer to get into bed?"

"I'm feeling much better. I would rather be together in the sitting room if that's acceptable."

Dolly shifted from foot to foot and wrung her hands. "Miss Allie, I have to tell you something."

"What is it, my precious?" Allie asked from her place on the edge of the bed.

"I want to say I'm sorry. I just wanted to row out to Miss Ellen's House and pick the biggest strawberries I could, like those on your table. But I didn't listen to Mama, and I didn't think it would rain, and I didn't know you would almost drown. And I didn't know Captyn could swim."

"Darling, remember what else we came here to say."

Dolly beamed. "Thank you. I'm happy you're here, and could I please have a hug?" The child curled her index finger at Allie, who leaned forward. Dolly cupped her hand around Allie's ear and said in a loud whisper, "I hope you can come back to visit in the summer, and we can go to Ellen's Island and eat strawberries for breakfast, lunch, and supper."

Allie opened her arms, and Dolly scampered in for a hug. "You hug like my rubber doll."

"Is that good?"

Dolly nodded. "Uh-huh."

Allie cupped Dolly's ear and answered in a loud whisper, "I can't wait to come back."

Carol said to Dolly, "Mama and Papa wanted you to make it special."

"We mean . . ." Samantha interrupted. "We want to extend a special summer invitation to you and your family."

"Oh, that's the best invitation I've had in a long time. I can't wait to taste those strawberries."

"Hooray." Dolly and her curls jumped up and down. The girls kissed Allie on the cheek before marching out of the room after their mother.

She was alone and missing Peter.

FRANKIE GRIMACED. "MOTHER, HERE'S ALLIE'S LATEST EXPLOIT."

"Can it wait a moment? I must get my tea."

Olivia Waverly passed into the parlor from the kitchen with her tea. She sat, holding a teacup and saucer.

Frankie unfolded the crumpled telegram.

CHILD IN BOAT IN DANGER ALLIE IN WATER NOT ABLE
TO GET INTO BOAT TO ROW MUST PUSH DOG PULL
(STOP)

ALLIE CRAMPED COULD NOT SWIM PETER RESCUED
(STOP)
ALLIE SICK TWO WEEKS, NOW RECOVERING, WILL
EXPLAIN WHEN HOME (STOP)
WARM REGARDS, CLARA BALDWIN (FULL STOP)

Olivia set her teacup down beside her music box. "Heavens, why does that girl always give us such worries?"

"Oh, Mother, don't be a bore."

"Francesca, don't speak to me in that manner."

"The telegram is good news. Allie is a brave heart, don't you think?"

Mrs. Waverly crinkled her brows. "The news is frightening. How in the world did she end up in trouble again?"

Frankie glanced at her mother's pale face and reached for her hand. Olivia dabbed at the tears filling her eyes. "Your friend gets into pickles. She makes risky decisions. Allie's like a daughter to me and like a sister to you, but with her foolish ideas, I get concerned when you are together."

"I'm sorry, Mother. You worry unnecessarily. Since your lady friends are coming for tea this morning and I need some fresh air, do you mind if I go to the cafe?"

"Must you? Wait until later. We'll take a stroll together."

"Thank you for the offer, but I prefer to go now. I'm self-sufficient."

She took her cloak from the hall closet, her reticule from the foyer table, her cane from the hat rack, and stepped out into the sunshine.

Frankie strolled to her favorite café, the Parisian-style coffeehouse in Central Park by the lake. The intermingling aromas of freshly brewed coffee, hot chocolate, and pastries permeated the area.

"Bonjour, Miss Waverly," Fleur St. Laurent, the café proprietor, hailed her.

Frankie greeted the young woman. "Bonjour. How is the chocolate today?"

"Sweet and thick, and oh, so good." Fleur gestured inside the café. "Come, I have your table. The weather is beautiful. You might even catch a few boaters out there. Will your friend Miss Baldwin be joining you?"

"No, Allie had some problems in Fairfield, Connecticut. She almost drowned saving a child. She's recuperating and will come home in a few days."

"I am glad she is going to be fine. Stop by with her, and I'll surprise you with one of my new recipes from the bakery."

"It will thrill her to come."

"Your usual, Miss Frankie?"

"Yes, thank you. And your buttery brioche."

"*Mais oui.* I have a delicious lemon curd I made this morning. I know you love anything tangy."

Frankie's eyes brightened. "I'll have one, please."

"I still have a few minutes to chat," Fleur said.

"Miracle of miracles. Please, sit." Frankie held out her hand, pointing to the chair opposite.

"Good news! I wanted to let you know that your investment has paid you back handsomely. The latest profit figures far exceeded our dreams."

Frankie clapped her hands and gave Fleur a hearty smile. "I'm not surprised. Every morsel in your café is delicious. You should know that I invited Miss Baldwin to invest with me. I know she'll be excited."

"It's wonderful to have two of my favorite ladies be part of our business."

When Frankie met Fleur two years ago, the St. Laurents had a cart in Central Park where Fleur and her father served flaky pastries, coffee, and hot chocolate to the bustling crowds. Frankie became a regular, and the three developed a friendship that blossomed into a business partnership when Frankie realized the potential of the proposed café.

An hour later, Frankie took out her book, *Oliver Twist,* to read Mr. Dickens's tale of the young orphan when Adam Baldwin, Allie's brother, greeted her. He brought a message from Allie that she would be traveling home soon and could not wait to see her.

CHAPTER 40

*P*eter reserved five train compartments. Peter and his men occupied the ones on either side of the family. No one could sneak past.

Merely two weeks prior, Allie almost lost her life. One would never know looking at the beauty, tall and lanky in her latest silky fashions minus the hoops and strangling corsets. She scampered along the corridor with Mia and Captyn, eager to settle into their compartment. Allie closed the door behind her.

Mia frowned as she curled up on the velvet bench. "Gads, there's not a lot of room in here. I hate to say this, but Captyn is a nuisance, taking up most of the floor space as always. The twins are by themselves in their berth and Mama and Papa in theirs. Some people get all the good stuff."

Allie lay down. Pulsing shafts of sunlight came through the train window and bounced around the berth, making her dizzy. "My head is spinning, and I feel a bit queasy."

Mia joined Allie, pulling her up. "If you look out the window, you won't spin. Just focus." They sat together and gazed out the window. "Isn't this fun? Look at the bright side. We'll be home in a few hours."

Allie turned to Mia. "You always see the bright side. That's insufferable." Allie gave her sister a grin. "I'm going for tea. Are you coming?"

"No, thank you. I'll stay here. I am having a lovely time on this train. You probably should not eat if you still feel queasy. The last thing you want is to bring up what you ate."

"The tea will help settle my stomach. I am off."

~

CLARA SLID HER COMPARTMENT DOOR OPEN TO THE SOUND OF A knock.

Peter smiled. "Mrs. Baldwin, I just want to make sure your accommodations are adequate."

"Thank you, Peter. They are quite adequate. My husband went to the men's car to enjoy his vises, indulge in a whiskey, and drone on about business."

Allie met up with Peter at her parents' compartment.

Peter clutched Allie by her shoulders. "Allie, where are you off to?" he asked as if it were an inquisition.

She wanted to fall into him and forget about going anywhere. Her queasiness strangely disappeared. "I'm going to the dining car."

"Where's your sister?" her mother asked.

"She wanted to rest."

"Then you two enjoy yourselves," Clara said, closing her door.

"Honestly, Peter, I'm happy to be alone with my tea," she lied but didn't know why. She enjoyed bantering with Peter.

"I would like to join you. Do you mind?"

She could not help smiling at him. "I guess not." *Allie, girl, why did you say it that way? It's so ridiculous. You love his company.*

Peter's brow furrowed with concern. "Spending time with

you is important to me, but regardless, you remember why your father hired me?"

"Oh, that. No, I have not forgotten, but I'm safe. No music box stalkers here. There's no reason I can't have a cup of tea by myself."

"Allie, my job's protecting you. You can sit alone to enjoy your tea, but I'll be close by."

Peter offered Allie his arm, and they made their way to the dining car, passing his agents standing at attention by the Baldwin compartments like the guards at London's Windsor Castle.

"Your agents all look alike," Allie said, settling down at a table.

"I hire only young, strong, unattached men. Most are former soldiers. They know defense. Protection is their priority. Oh, the server is coming. Do you need a menu?"

Allie shook her head. "No."

Allie ordered tea and a sweet. Her stomach felt fine now.

"Where were we? Oh, yes. Father's newspaper employs women. Do you see any difference between your men and the women at the newspaper?"

"Yes, there is a difference. My men work under dangerous circumstances and must remain clearheaded and focused. If I introduced women into our workplace, they could be a distraction."

Allie felt her face get warm, and she had that awful feeling in the pit of her stomach again. "Am I a distraction?"

Just then, the server appeared with Allie's midday treat. The aromatic smell wafted over her like the scent of a rose petal carried by a gentle breeze.

"Wait a minute. This is too much food. Can you take some back?" she asked the server.

"That comes with the order, madam."

"Peter, please have a scone."

"No, thanks. Bring it back to Mia."

"Good idea, I will."

Peter opened his mouth to speak, then paused. A young woman walking by lost her footing when the train rounded a bend in the track, and she fell into Peter's lap. Allie held her hand against her chest and exclaimed, "Oh my."

Peter's face flushed. The young woman looked quite perplexed for a moment, and then she beamed at Peter.

"Oh, thank you for savin' me, sir," she oozed. "Ya'll a true gentleman."

Peter grinned. "You're welcome. Are you hurt?"

"No, sir. You are comfy and soft."

"Pardon, I hope you do not mind, but it would be good if you stood," Peter said.

She put her heeled boots down and raised herself. She turned to face Peter. "Excuse me. I was just gettin' comfortable."

"Allow me to speak on this true gentleman's behalf when I say you are most welcome, miss. Your name is?" Allie asked.

"My name is Miss Molly McGraw."

"It's a pleasure to meet you, Miss McGraw. I am Miss Allie Baldwin, and this is Mr. Peter Harrison."

The curvaceous young woman nodded and smiled a white-toothed grin. Platinum-blonde curls were pinned high on her head. "My pleasure, I'm sure." The bright red dress and lips to match were like the center of a chocolate-covered strawberry. She had colored a black mole on her mouth with kohl, and she used the same to frame her startling blue eyes.

"Won't you join us for tea?" Allie asked.

"Thank you. It would be a pleasure to join you. I was lookin' for some friends, and here I found some," Molly said, reaching out her hand to Allie.

Peter stood up and offered Miss McGraw his seat. The young woman smiled and scooted into the booth.

Allie waved her hand to the seat. "Do sit, Mr. Harrison, and join us once more."

"Thank you," he said in a soft, feathery voice and sat down on the edge of the booth. He called the server over and ordered tea and pastries.

~

THE PASTRIES WERE FLAKY, THE TEA WAS REFRESHING, AND THE orange blossom fragrance of Miss Molly McGraw filled the train car and all other spaces nearby. "This is mah first trip to New York City," Molly said.

Allie gave the lady a nod. "Your first trip, how wonderful. Are you from the South?"

"I grew up in Richmond, Virginia, originally and made my way to Fairfield a month ago. Now I'm headed to the greatest city in the world. I was so excited about goin' to New York that I decided to leave a day early. I asked the nice man at the Fairfield Station ticket counter if he could exchange my ticket for an earlier one. If I had been on tomorrow's train, we never would have met."

"That was fortuitous. Do you have family or friends in New York City?"

"No one, ma'am. The only person I know is my patron of the arts. He's a kind gentleman going to lots of trouble to bring me to New York. You might know him. He's from Fairfield and left earlier to make arrangements for me. You see, I'm going to become an actress on the Broadway stage."

Allie glanced at Peter with raised eyebrows. Peter suppressed a groan at the young woman's naïveté. Perhaps it was a show for two strangers kind enough to chat with her. Peter could already see that Allie intended to help this woman.

Allie tucked a curl behind her ear. "Isn't that exciting, Mr. Harrison?"

"Indeed." Peter cleared his throat and nodded. "I am curious, Miss McGraw, if I know this patron of yours. What's his name?"

Molly's eyes widened. "Mr. Donald Diamond. Isn't that the most elegant and la-di-da name you've ever heard?"

"Oh, yes." Allie's mouth turned up at the corners. "And where will you be staying while in the city?"

"Well, Mr. Diamond has secured a suite for me at the Devonshire Hotel on Broadway."

The Devonshire Hotel was a luxury hotel that catered to foreign dignitaries and politicians. Peter understood Mr. Donald Diamond's tricks. Donald Diamond must be one of the many procurers who staked out the hotels and provided female companionship for visitors.

"You must come to visit me in the city." Molly laid her hand over Allie's on the table. "I'll ask Mr. Diamond to purchase you front row seats for my first performance, and then we can all go to dinner after the show."

"I think that would be splendid. I look forward to seeing your performance."

"Don't forget to stop by for a visit at the Devonshire. By the time I see you again, I'm certain that I'll know what my starring role will be. Thank you for the delectable treats. I must go to my compartment and make sure I have everything in order."

"I promise you, Molly, we'll see you soon."

"I am looking forward to that. Ta-ta." Molly waved at them.

Peter took Allie's arm as Molly left, her fragrance trailing after her. "We have to help that poor girl," Allie said to him, strolling out of the dining car.

"Girl?" Peter said. "I warrant she's almost thirty."

"Nevertheless, the city destroys the innocent. We must do something. Will you look into this Mr. Diamond fellow? His name sounds fictitious."

"I will," Peter assured her. "But you still need to take it easy. No traipsing about the city. Write your article about the

Mitchells and Longdales and then take some time off until we find the music box culprit."

"That's agreeable."

Peter knew the meeting with Miss Molly McGraw stirred Allie's interest.

CHAPTER 41

Frankie rose from the settee, strode over the Oriental rug to the Baldwin parlor's fireplace, and stoked the crackling flames. "Good Lord, Allie. You outdid yourself this time. A near drowning?"

Allie gave her friend a crooked grin. "It's good to see you too, Frankie."

"Oh, stop being nasty. It was frightening to hear my best friend almost drowned." Frankie sat back down and reached out for Allie. "Give me a hug. I want to be sure you are really sitting beside me, alive."

Allie wrapped her arms around Frankie and kissed her cheek. "I'm sorry, I didn't mean to be horrid. It came out all wrong."

"I forgive you, and that hug felt good. Thanks."

"Did my sisters send you a message about what happened?"

"I bumped into Ava in the hallway a few days ago. I've heard most of it, yes, when your mother sent a wire to my mother."

Captyn padded up to Frankie and nuzzled her hand. She rubbed the spot behind his ears. "I missed you too, Captyn. If you could only talk, what stories you'd tell." She planted a kiss on his head.

He returned the kiss with a lick to her face, then plopped himself at her feet, hoping for more head rubs.

"The best part was the telegram saying you were all right. Are you all right?"

Allie regarded Captyn. "Shall we plot my escape from this cushy Sandanko prison? Captyn can be our decoy."

"Your mother has all-knowing and all-seeing eyes. I think she'd intercept your breakout attempt and sentence you to a bowl of chicken soup and a foot rub."

"I think you're right."

"You bet."

Allie told Frankie about the Fairfield escapade, the Mitchells, the Longdales, and the ongoing music box mystery.

"What an adventure. And you and Penelope finding each other. The best was the fire being an accident. Has Mr. Harrison found any clues about music boxes?"

"Peter has been to every music box maker in the city."

"Peter?"

"Yes, Peter. He's in charge of this investigation."

"You called Mr. Harrison by his first name."

"Oh."

"And now you're blushing . . ."

Allie's hands flew to her face. "It's strange. Mama suggested it, so we all are on a first name basis. I like that, and so does Peter."

"Good for you, Allie. Dropping that formality fits with your fight for the women's vote. It is so liberating. That includes tossing your hated corset."

"I'm not sure Mother will approve of tossing the corset, but I'm working on it. Honestly though, Peter's company is wonderful. His dimples are adorable, and the lock of hair that falls over his forehead is titillating. I admit my feelings are kind of strange after only knowing him a short time."

"Sounds like he's modern in his thinking. Is he? Or am I wrong?"

Allie screwed up her face in doubt. "He's little more than a stranger."

Frankie looked at Allie's solemn expression and laughed. "What you mean is you have fallen in love."

Allie hesitated and then shrugged. "I do not know. Can you imagine? I cannot quite grasp love. for now, I'll do nothing."

"That'll get you nowhere."

"Wise words, and yet you haven't taken your own advice with Adam. You have loved him forever, and you do nothing to let him know."

Frankie smoothed her day dress over her legs. "Adam thinks I'm his little sister's friend, and not only that, no one wants a lame lover. Me with this ugly leg, I'm useless."

"Stop saying such awful things. You are a beautiful person. If Adam were not so blind, he would see you as his alter ego. Forget about him. The woman marrying him for his money has him bamboozled. The man of your dreams is out there somewhere."

Frankie laid her head on Allie's shoulder. "I'm supposed to be helping you feel better, and here you are consoling me."

"We are a pair, aren't we?" Captyn sat up and wagged his tail. "At least we have Captyn's undying devotion."

"So, you won't tell Peter how you feel?"

"I haven't sorted my feelings out myself yet."

"If you want to talk, I'm here."

Allie knew Peter cared, but did that mean love? And did she love him? What changed her heart? Somehow, now she wanted love and marriage, perhaps with Peter. She also wanted to fight for the women's vote and freedom. She wanted choices. Could she have it all?

"You are here for me, thank goodness."

Frankie kissed Allie on her cheek and then stood up. "Mother is expecting me for dinner, so off I go. I'm glad you are home. I missed you too much."

Allie received Peter's wire announcing his visit. She snuggled under her warm blanket, a gift from her quilting club she deserted to go to Vassar. The women now had husbands and scads of offspring. They enjoyed Allie's column—the juicer, the better. The gossipers always looked for more. They praised their husbands' mistresses for saving them from unwanted pregnancies. Allie's column reported all the risqué news that made the *Sentinel* a hot seller. Paperboys stood on every corner in the city hollering, "Read the latest society news." The papers sold out.

Allie perked up at the aroma of Mrs. Bigelow's glazed cinnamon buns. From the scampering in the hall, she expected her family to be in the kitchen any minute to chow down the delicious, fresh-baked goodies. Mrs. Bigelow only made the buns for special occasions like birthdays, funerals, and Allie's homecoming. There probably would not be a one left for Peter.

Barnes ushered Peter into the parlor. He swept his arm around the room. "Is it good to be home finally?"

Allie smiled at the sight of Peter. She picked at the loose threads of the colored quilt, pulling one off and winding it around her index finger, then threw the quilt off. "What a ridiculous question. Of course it is," Allie said, putting her bare feet down on the cold polished floor.

"Please don't get up. Stay under your quilt," Peter said.

She crawled back under the cover. "Thanks. Any news about the music boxes?"

He leaned on the wall next to the hearth. "Nothing to report."

She'd hoped to work up the courage to talk with Peter, but she was uncomfortable approaching him. She worried he would not come around once they solved the mystery. There was no security in this love thing, anyway. No one would want her. She was far too contrary, far too strong-willed, and far too impetuous. She did not know what to think anymore.

Mrs. Bigelow brought in a tray with coffee and sweets. She set the carafe and two cups on the tea table in front of the settee. Thankfully, Allie's family had left a few cinnamon buns. It seemed odd to Allie that the aroma reminded her of mother-daughter relationships like Frankie's broken one and Allie's passion for helping make it better. Peter came over, poured the coffee, and sat beside Allie on the settee.

She turned to him, smiled, and then looked down. Peter put his finger under her chin, lifted her head, and smiled back. She turned away and looked out into the garden, so barren now, and back to him again. "Your face commands attention." She raised her hand and stroked his cheek. Her voice was soft. "You are incredibly handsome." She'd been waiting so long for this moment—this intensity, this passion, this sense of perfectness. What was this? She'd felt nothing like it before.

Peter drew her to him and held her close. "You've stolen my heart, Allie," he whispered in her ear while sliding his fingers down her arm to hold her hand.

She kissed his cheek and took a breath. Taking her hand from his, she put her arms around his neck. They embraced and kissed.

She nibbled his lips and gazed into his eyes. "This is what I want, Peter."

"I want this too, Allie. Since we began our journey to Fairfield, I had to see your face, breathe your scent, and hear your voice, but my needs cannot deter me," he said. "Your safety is my top priority, and we still have work to do."

Allie turned away and fussed with her coffee, stirring in clotted cream and watching it change from a dark brown to a rich, burnished mahogany. "Yesterday, when I met with Frankie, I told her everything about our trip to Fairfield."

Peter bit into one of the glazed buns. "Not that what's happening is secretive, but we must be careful what we say and to whom. What if Frankie inadvertently reveals something to someone that could put you in danger?"

Allie refused to believe Frankie would ever do that. "She's not a gossip, for goodness' sake."

He gulped his coffee and set the cup down on the table. "We can't rule anything out. On another topic, I have some important news to share."

Her eyebrows shot up. "Uh-oh. What's going on?"

"I discovered the identity of Mr. Diamond."

"Molly McGraw's patron?"

"Yes."

"Who is he?"

The parlor pocket door slid open, and Barnes entered. "Miss Frankie and her mother are here to see you, Miss Allie. They say it's urgent."

CHAPTER 42

*A*llie scooted off the couch into the vestibule and greeted Frankie and Mrs. Waverly with hugs. "It's good to see you. What's so urgent?"

"We have important information," Frankie said.

"Peter is visiting. He's in the parlor."

"Will he have an interest?"

"Yes, I am sure he will. Barnes, will you please take Captyn for his walk now?" Allie patted the Great Dane on his head. "Thank you."

"Yes, Miss Allie. Captyn, come."

Peter stood when Allie escorted Frankie and Mrs. Waverly into the parlor.

Allie extended her palm to her visitors. "I believe introductions are in order. Peter Harrison of the Harrison Detective Agency. Peter, meet my friend Frankie and her mother, Mrs. Waverly."

"It is a pleasure to meet you both," Peter said with a slight bow.

Allie pointed to a couch. "Please make yourselves comfortable," she said as she and Peter sat on the settee across from her friends.

"Can I interest you in Mrs. Bigelow's delicious treats?" Allie asked.

"Thanks anyway, Allie," Mrs. Waverly said.

"We have rather strange news to share," Frankie said. "Isn't that so, Mother?"

Mrs. Waverly's nodded. "Indeed."

"After I visited with you today, I came home, and Mother's friends were visiting. I stepped in to say hello. We spoke for a few moments, and then a curious thing happened. One of her friends, Mrs. Drumple, asked about you, Allie, and inquired about your trip to Fairfield." Frankie hesitated. "She asked if it upset you to receive the music boxes."

"How would she know about that?" Allie asked.

"I don't know. Mother knew nothing about your trip to Fairfield or the music boxes until after the ladies left."

Peter strode to the fireplace and leaned against the mantle shelf.

Mrs. Waverly sighed. "After Frankie told me the story, my God, I think the hair on my head stood up. How did Portia know all that? One of my other friends loved to listen to my music box. She would ask to wind it up to see the dancing ballerina. Portia, I mean Mrs. Drumple, then asked me to shut it off. I mentioned my daughter had a similar music box that we kept in the Waverly House, our summer home."

"Mother remembered a few weeks back that Mrs. Drumple changed her tune," Frankie said. "She exclaimed over the music box and said she wanted one."

"She asked me where she could buy it," Mrs. Waverly added. "I told her my husband purchased it in France many years ago. The bottom has *RB* engraved on it. At our daughter's birth, he ordered another. The boxes are the same, except for one difference…"

"What's that?" Allie asked.

"The ballerinas' tutus are different. Mine is white."

"Mine wears pink," Frankie said.

Peter sat again. "Well, what do you know? The music box ballerina sent to Allie in Fairfield wears pink with those initials engraved on the bottom."

A chill gripped Allie's heart.

"I don't keep my box here," Frankie said. "It has always been at Waverly House. I-I don't remember what happened when I fell from the window all those years ago, but I remember the music and dancing around my room."

Frankie's eyelashes glittered with tears. Allie's heart broke for her best friend. How painful to be reminded. No wonder she hated the box that sat on her mother's side table.

Mrs. Waverly squeezed her eyes closed. "I did not know," she said to her daughter, placing her hand on hers. "I wish I had stored mine with yours."

"You cherish that box." Frankie's voice cracked. "This morning, word from Mr. Langley, our butler at Waverly House, said the estate had a theft of jewelry, gold pieces, and the music box."

"My goodness, Frankie."

"What took so long for Mr. Langley to tell you?" Peter asked.

"They did not know it had happened. A month ago, Langley hired a new upstairs maid named Lizzie. She stole items from the house. Mary, our cook, spied her meeting with a strange man at the stables. She saw the exchange of money. Mary spoke with Langley, who questioned Lizzie. Lizzie broke down and told him they had paid her to steal those items."

"Who paid her?" Peter interjected.

"Donald Diamond."

Allie's hands flew to her cheeks, and she looked at Peter. Donald Diamond was Molly's so-called patron.

"Did you alert the authorities?" Peter asked.

Frankie shook her head. "We haven't yet. We wanted to tell Allie first."

"What is the true identity of Donald Diamond?" Allie asked.

"Wilbur Drumple," Peter said, his words brittle like dried leaves in the fall.

Peter nodded at Frankie and Mrs. Waverly. He took Allie's hand. "Let's go, Allie. We must get to the Devonshire."

Allie leaned down to squeeze Frankie's hand. "I'll tell you everything soon. Barnes, please see our guests to their apartment."

Peter escorted Allie out of the parlor. He spoke to his agents at the door. Two would go, one would stay, and one would alert Joseph Baldwin at the *Sentinel* and Mrs. Baldwin visiting patients at the hospital.

It took twenty minutes to arrive at the smoke-filled lobby of the Devonshire. Men indulged in cigars and pipe smoking. No exotic fall fragrances here, but plenty of whiskey and bourbon claiming men in classy clothes. Yellowed gas lamping offered dull ambiance for the wicked.

Peter hoped they hadn't missed Mr. Diamond. He hurried to the front desk. "Do you have a Miss Molly McGraw here?"

"We do. I'll send my messenger upstairs to let her know she has visitors," the desk clerk said.

"Thank you. Rather you didn't. Has a Donald Diamond stopped in to visit Miss McGraw?" Peter asked.

The clerk paled and shook his head.

"Do you expect Mr. Diamond today?" Peter asked, his eyes darkening.

"Y-yes, sir. We expect him to visit Miss McGraw this evening. She arrived a day early. We checked her in for Mr. Diamond."

"Thank you," Allie said. "We want this to be a surprise. She'll like we've come. Please say nothing to Mr. Diamond that we are here. When he arrives, send him up. My friends over there"—

Peter gestured at two burly men—"will stand close by to remind you."

The clerk's head bobbed.

Allie beckoned to Peter and whispered in his ear. "There's an aged, handsome lady sitting at the desk. Her gown is red silk, and oh my goodness, her décolletage is revealing. She is wearing a wig." Allie sucked in a breath. "Heavens, her lips match her gown. Who is she? Maybe she will give me an interview."

"Allie, no. The woman's job is to direct gentlemen to a guest room. She's a high-class madam."

"I've heard the title, but my education didn't include any madams." She lowered her voice. "She earns a living as any working woman. Right?"

"Sounds like you have her figured out."

"Hmm, we could lose readers if the *Sentinel* published an interview with her."

"Forget it, Allie. You can't stick your nose in her business. She will never give you one word."

He looped Allie's arm through his and escorted her to the elevator. "That slimy sneak won't arrive until later," Peter said, his voice gruff. "Let's get Molly out of here. I'll get word to my contacts at the sheriff's office. We'll be ready for him when he arrives."

Allie regarded his eyes. "It'll be hard to break the news to Molly. She's sweet and unassuming. She wants a break to do self-respecting work. Wilbur Drumple won't get away with his miserable plans."

"I'm sure he'd promote her as a lady of the night to further his business. I'll see to it he spends years regretting his life. Wilbur Drumple and his mother could have planned this together," Peter said in a steely voice.

"It's baffling. Other journalists have written negative things about Drumple's campaign. Why try to intimidate me?"

"You may not realize how much power and influence you

have. If Drumple gets you, he will have your family at their knees." Peter bent his head and gave her a soft kiss on her forehead. "I promise you, Allie, all of this will be over tonight."

Allie closed her eyes. All she wanted was to melt into his arms.

CHAPTER 43

"Oh, my gracious," Molly said, opening the door, the pungent scent of her perfume floating under Allie's nose. Molly hugged Allie. "Come in. You folks are sweet sugar for stopping by. I've been on my lonesome since I got here. This is my first time in a swanky hotel. I ran my hands over all the materials—silky taffeta curtains with little gold flecks, wooden floors so polished I could see myself like in a mirror. Look down, Allie. See? There's your face."

Allie's stomach churned, but she smiled regardless. "You're funny, Molly."

Molly giggled. "I took my shoes off and jumped up and down on the soft mattress. It squeaked, then the bedding got messed."

Sheesh. At least she took her shoes off.

Allie's wide eyes filled with the old, familiar disgust as she peered at the Rubenesque painting hanging over the bedhead.

"Isn't that the most gorgeous painting you've ever seen?" Molly asked.

Peter stood, staring at the painting. "I agree. It's beautiful."

Allie stiffened in response to their ogling and love for the demeaning portraiture of a woman. She pressed her lips together and looked around the room at the reflective material on the ceiling over the bed, the crumpled silk sheets.

Allie put her hands on her hips and took in a deep breath. "I don't believe either of you understand this painting. It's a misguided use of the woman, belittling her to entice a man and use her. This depiction of women makes the suffrage movement important. Did you know most women are slaves?"

Peter held out his hand toward the art. "It's a painting, Allie, by a famous artist. I doubt he had a wicked purpose."

Allie's jaw dropped. "Don't you think a painting can be a negative stimulus?"

Peter knotted his brow. "How about we review the painting together and discuss the artist's intentions?"

Allie took his hand and stood beside him.

"Molly, please join us in this little analysis," Peter said.

Allie didn't like this one bit. "The painting is god-awful, and nothing will convince me otherwise."

"All right, but I want you to notice how the artist painted the delicate subject, giving the woman glory. Isn't that what you see too, Molly?"

"Yes, the glory."

Allie sucked in her breath. "The artist has not glorified the woman. He's destroyed her integrity. Why can't the two of you see that? I've had enough. Please stop this nonsense." Allie turned to Molly. "I can straighten the bedding for you if you like," she said in a high-pitched voice.

"No, thank you, that's all right. I didn't know what else to do with myself, so I marched downstairs and visited with everyone comin' and goin'.

"Sounds like you've had fun," Allie said.

Molly giggled. "Folks are nice here."

"I see you've forgotten about the painting. That's fine with me," Peter said.

"I talked with that older lady wearin' a wig and sittin' at a fancy desk. Her gown was my favorite color, like this red blouse. She spoke funny. Her voice was deep like yours, Mister Peter. Oh, the desk clerk said Donald Diamond is coming tonight."

"I should hope Mr. Diamond would be here for you," Allie said.

"Wouldn't it be a kick if you could meet him?"

"Yes, it would be an absolute kick." Allie glanced at Peter. "Since you've been cooped up in the room, how would you like an outing? We can take a quick ride to my house and meet my family."

Molly's smile lit up the entire room more than the candled lamps set about the floral wallpapered room. The writing desk in the room was not fancy like the one in the lobby, but adequate for a man to write letters using the provided quill and inkwell. He could sit in the rolling cushioned chair, lean back, and contemplate writings to his latest lovers.

"Oh, now, that would be grand." Then a frown chased away her smile. "But what about Mr. Diamond? I should be here when he arrives. Will you bring me back in time, Miss Allie?"

"Most likely."

Molly clapped her hands. "Then what are we waitin' for? I'll get my cloak, and we can be off faster than cricket on a bullfrog."

Peter let his men know of his plans and had them stay behind at the hotel. He accompanied Allie and Molly to the Harrison carriage in the hotel's covered archway.

Peter's driver was waiting. "Boss, I'll drive this one. You relax with the ladies. No traffic this way now. It's an easy drive to the Sandanko."

At the Baldwin home, Barnes greeted the threesome. "So good to have you home, Miss Allie." Captyn's greeting was a little more enthusiastic than the butlers. Captyn nuzzled

Allie's hand and would not leave her alone until she tickled his ears.

Allie looped her arm through Peter's, took Molly's hand, and walked with them into the sunlit parlor.

"Molly, you remember Captyn, don't you? You met him the other day when we said our goodbyes at the train station."

"Why, sure, I do." Molly patted the Great Dane on his head. Captyn wagged his tail. "He sure is friendly." Captyn padded over to his bed by the hearth and settled onto the pillow.

Clara pulled her daughter into a hug and kissed her cheek. "It's delightful having your guest, Allie." Clara rang for Mrs. Bigelow and asked for refreshments for their company. She introduced Ava, Emma, and Mia.

"Molly's a pretty name," Emma said. Her parrot, Lord Wilby, squawked from his perch on Emma's shoulder, "*Molly pretty name. Molly pretty name.*"

"Thank you, Lord Wilby," Molly said. "A talkin' bird, imagine that?"

Emma laughed. "Lord Wilby loves the attention. He knows you're fussing over him. He repeats whatever he hears. We're sorry to have to leave, but we have lots of schoolwork." She and her bird left with Ava and Mia.

While Molly and Allie's mother visited, Peter had a word with Joseph by the fireplace. Allie's ears perked up, eavesdropping on the men's conversation, her eyes on Peter asking Joseph when Adam would come in from Chicago.

"Tell us, Miss McGraw, why do you want to be a singer?" Clara asked.

"I was always dreamin' of a way to leave home, so I ended up in Fairfield workin' at a tavern and singin' every night. I love to sing. But it was lonely with no family—"

When she hesitated, Allie laid her hand over hers. "How did you meet Mr. Diamond?"

"After hearing me sing one night, he told me he could make

me a star and invited me to come to New York. I couldn't say no."

"You were brave coming here on your own," Clara said.

Allie met Peter's eyes. He gestured to her with his hands. "I need to head over to the Devonshire."

Allie glared at him. "I'm coming with you. Don't tell me no."

The tension in his face eased. Allie realized her presence mattered, and it left her feeling elated.

"Molly, I must go with Peter. We'll be back soon enough."

CHAPTER 44

The sun was sinking below the tall buildings, leaving behind a pinky-orange strip of color in the sky. Peter's driver waited with the coach on the street outside the Sandanko to take his passengers back downtown to the Hotel Devonshire. Rush hour traffic slowed down their travel.

By the time the carriage stopped in front of the hotel, Peter had convinced himself to go easy on Diamond until they talked about what Diamond's game was with Miss McGraw and what he was doing in Fairfield. Peter alighted from the carriage, gave Allie his hand, and helped her from the coach. He thanked the driver, and they walked into the lobby. The desk clerk nodded a greeting. "The man you're looking for hasn't arrived yet. Would you like to wait here?"

Peter glanced at the tall clock standing near the entrance. "It's six. I expect he'll be coming through the door shortly. We prefer waiting in Miss McGraw's room."

The desk clerk handed Peter a key, which Peter acknowledged with a nod. "Our lady over there at the desk is waving for you. Can you take another minute to talk with her? She mentioned this hotel is no place for a lady. Did the woman who's come here with you have any plans to live here?"

"No. She's here with me and will leave with me when I go," Peter said. "I very much would like to talk to her about her gender-bending disguise, but perhaps another time. Explain that the woman with me is not interested in working here. Please convey my apologies."

The elevator took Peter and Allie to the top floor. They went into the sitting room, high ceilinged and airy, where the open French doors led to the balcony. An icy breeze chilled the room. Allie closed the doors, drew the curtains, and sat on the wing chair flanking the fireplace. An Oriental rug with a geometric pattern, faded and worn, lay on the floor. Allie was sure the once vibrant colors complemented the reds in the wallpaper.

Peter took his place in the armchair opposite Allie, stretching out and leaning back. "Ah, it's good to sit."

Allie straightened herself in the chair. "Heavens. God, help us, another one of those paintings," she said, pointing to the canvas over the mantel. "The three women are homely and fat. And the ornate frame is tasteless. How many more must there be in this hotel?"

"I'll wager that every room in this building has art depicting women, clothed or not, in precarious positions."

"It's disgraceful. Burn the paintings."

"No one here will destroy these works of art. To change the subject, we have a few minutes to ourselves before our visitor arrives-. I want to tell you something."

Allie's face softened. "What is it, Peter?"

"I'm disappointed."

"What do you mean?

"You don't seem to recognize art through the ages. History has shown that women have pervasively modeled for artists. They were always a favorite subject to paint—for centuries, even today."

"Exactly, and it has to stop. I can't believe the women posed."

Peter laughed. "That's what the artist and their clients wanted. He earned his living painting women willing to model for whatever reason. Even women artists painted women, but of course, they clad the models."

"Of course they were wearing something. Women respect each other, but men, well, that's another story, isn't it? Here I am focused on helping fight for a cause, and those pictures send out the wrong message—women for sale. I give up. When is Mister Diamond expected?"

"I thought he might arrive at six. It's now almost seven according to that mantel clock."

"Shhh, someone came into the vestibule," Allie said. "They're taking off their coat—and hanging it on the hall tree."

The footsteps came closer and louder. "Miss McGraw, where are you?" The voice was gravelly, like a mouth filled with sand.

Peter rose from his chair, and with an open palm, he gestured to Allie. "Wait here. I'll be right back."

Peter greeted Diamond in the vestibule. "Mister Diamond, I take it?" Peter extended his hand.

Diamond squinted and shook Peter's hand with hesitation. "What are you doing here, Harrison?"

"I take it you're the infamous Donald Diamond?"

"I am he. You must have already heard about this hotel?"

"No, Mr. Diamond, I have heard nothing in particular. Is there something you want to tell me?" Peter asked in a modulated tone.

"I think you'll figure out the activities here by yourself."

"No problem, I believe I've figured it out. Now, how do you prefer to be addressed, Donald Diamond or Wilbur Drumple?" Peter asked.

Diamond twisted his face into a sneer. "What are you getting at, Harrison? What difference does my name make?"

"Are you suffering from dual personality syndrome?"

"You know I'm running for mayor under Drumple. Diamond is my working name here."

"The hotel is pretty swanky. Are you the proprietor?"

"Yes. Now where are you hiding my lady?"

"She's not hiding. She's out for a visit with someone you know."

"Yeah, who might that be?"

"Do you remember offering your services to two ladies at the inn?"

If anyone sounded like a frog, the groan from Drumple exemplified the small web-footed amphibian. "In Fairfield? You mean at the inn's dining room?"

"That's the place."

"Oh, yes. The Baldwin girls. I kindly offered my services. They foolishly turned me down."

"Well, you have another opportunity now. Miss Allie Baldwin is in the sitting room waiting for us. Shall we?"

"Of all the surprises, this one surpasses anything prior, Miss Baldwin. How have you been? How are your articles for the mayor's race coming along?"

Peter pointed to one of the chairs beside the fireplace. "Have a seat."

"Thanks, I'd rather stand," Drumple said, his hands in his pockets.

Allie shifted in her chair and smoothed the front of her dress. "Funny you should ask. You must know that I write the society column. Only once did I write about the mayoral race. Father had me leave the politics to the other journalists at the paper."

Drumple scratched the back of his neck. "Why would he tell his reporter daughter not to write about the race?" he asked, blinking rapidly, avoiding her eyes.

Allie pointed a finger in Drumple's direction. "Someone is sending me threatening notes."

Drumple's face reddened. He cracked his knuckles. "That's strange. Who would care what you write and send notes to you to watch out?"

"How did you know what the notes said?"

"What are you talking about?"

"We mentioned nothing about their content. You sent Miss Baldwin the notes and music boxes, didn't you?"

"No, not me. Coincidence. Yes, that's what it was."

Peter crossed his arms over his chest. "I don't think so. Where did you get the music boxes?"

"I'm not your culprit. Look somewhere else . . ."

"I don't need to look anywhere. The music box fiend is standing in front of me." Peter slammed his fist on the table.

Drumple's eyebrows squeezed together. "You can't scare me into a confession. I had nothing to do with any music boxes."

"Do you remember meeting a young housemaid at the Waverly's summer home?

"No."

"That's strange. She confessed to stealing items and exchanging them for money with a man who called himself Donald Diamond. That's you, Drumple."

"So what! That proves nothing!"

"No? One of the stolen items was a particular music box that had the initials of the maker on the bottom. The same initials were on the music box you sent to Miss Baldwin."

"Anyone could have bought one of those."

"They are only sold in France by the *maker*. Been to Paris and back in the last few weeks? You sent the one stolen from the Waverly house to Miss Baldwin. You're in big trouble, Drumple. We also know you had an accomplice, a woman."

"How do you know it was a woman?"

Peter bared his teeth in a sly grin. "So you admit you had an accomplice. The notes you sent Miss Baldwin had a specific scent to them. Our forensic doctor determined the scent came from a perfume made in Paris. A perfume sold only at Lord & Taylor. You don't have a wife who would purchase it, but you do have a mother with an account there. And the store confirmed she purchased that specific perfume recently. Mrs. Drumple was the genius behind this fiasco, wasn't she? You'll be better off if you confess, Drumple."

Drumple's face blanched. He slumped down in a chair opposite Allie. "At a fundraiser a few weeks ago, Mother overheard Miss Baldwin tell her sisters about her upcoming trip to Fairfield. Mother told me to go there, pretend to run into her, and introduce myself. She wanted me to show Miss Baldwin my capabilities. No doubt she would write an article advising her readers to vote for me as I would make a fine mayor.

"Fine mayor, indeed," Allie interjected.

"Mother had me pay someone to deliver the box. I met a drunkard at a local tavern one night and paid him with two bottles of whiskey to deliver it to the hotel."

Peter shook his head and glared at Drumple. "You went along with your mother's scheme to terrorize a young woman and cause worry to her family."

Allie put her hand on her chest. "I can't believe what I'm hearing! Why did you go to so much trouble to silence me?"

"I needed the mayoral position. There's no more inheritance. Mine is gone, and so is Mother's. I—"

"You gambled it away," Peter jumped in.

"Yes, and all of that would have changed if I won the election." Drumple thrust his chin up. "Mother and I had it all planned. We bribed maids to steal from their employers to fund my campaign. Still, when Miss Baldwin wrote that article about the candidates, Mother said we needed to stop her from writing anything that might be detrimental to my candidacy. She thought we could scare Miss Baldwin into backing off and that I could implicate the guy that delivered the box. I would be the hero. But when Harrison here and Sheriff Baxter arrested him, I knew it was too late. Then he died in his sleep, drunk himself to death."

"Kidnapping your opponent's his infant son was a distraction," Allie said. "You're pretty dumb, you know. If you wanted to scare Halton out of the race, kidnapping would never work. That would only create sympathetic voters."

"My plan almost worked, but Mickey Boyd couldn't do the job no matter how I set it up. He bungled the whole thing, and his sniveling wife couldn't keep quiet. If you had minded your own business, I would have sent her to California with her husband."

"Where is he? In California?"

"You're smart. Figure it out yourself."

"What were you thinking to do with the innocent Miss McGraw?" Allie asked.

"Please don't tell Mother about Miss McGraw. That wasn't p-part of her plan. Miss McGraw was my idea. Every great politician has a mistress, and I chose her to be mine."

"You're lucky we're taking you to the sheriff and not subjecting you to our brand of justice," Peter sneered.

Drumple covered his face with his hands. "It was all her. M-mother's the real criminal."

"You went along though, didn't you? Your father must wail in his grave. You and your mother have defiled his name."

"My father," Drumple spat. "He donated my inheritance to that damn Baldwin Hospital. Mother could not stop it. He made it official in his will that I had to work to prove myself worthy."

Peter, hands at his side, pulled himself up and squared his shoulders. "Honest work was never your forte, Drumple."

Drumple hung his head. "There's nothing more to say."

"There's plenty more to say. Where's Boyd?" Peter asked.

Drumple sniveled. "Will you go easier on me if I reveal his whereabouts?"

Peter gave him a sly grin. "No promises. But you have nothing to lose. Best to tell me and take your chances."

"He's holed up with his concubine in a utility room in the basement here at the Devonshire."

Allie grimaced, the concern in her eyes deepening. "It's heart-wrenching that you have incriminated yourself and your mother."

It was midnight when Peter sent a messenger to the police to arrest Drumple and haul him to the police station.

Peter then sent another messenger to O'Malley to pick up Boyd at the hotel and take him to the police station.

Peter grabbed his jacket from the hall tree in the vestibule and helped Allie on with hers. His driver and carriage waited for them when they exited the hotel. Peter sat by Allie's side. Memories flooded back to the countless tête-à-têtes and sorrows with his mother. He embraced Allie and brushed his lips lightly over hers.

CHAPTER 45

$\mathcal{C}$ lara shook her head. "I can't say that woman's name without feeling disgusted." She gripped her cup and took a sip. "And she dares to call herself a mother."

Emma slathered strawberry preserves onto her toast. "Here we believed that Wilbur Drumple was the instigator and dragged his mother through the mud. Not so; she commanded him the entire time."

"Talk about paying heed to your mother. Ha, that's a good one," Ava said in her usual blunt tone, removing orange slices from her fresh fruit bowl.

"Mrs. Drumple and Wilbur have confessed. They'll be doing significant time in prison," Joseph added.

Captyn ambled around the table, sniffing for a bit of sausage. Molly slipped a rasher of bacon to him. Allie arrived and sat beside Molly.

"How did you find out about Drumple, Papa?" Ava asked.

Joseph refilled his cup with the rich, dark brew. "I waited up for word from Peter and your sister. It was about two this morning when they got back here. Allie, why don't you fill us in on the details?"

Allie squeezed her tired eyes closed. "Peter received a wire from Doctor MacDougall while we were at the Devonshire. When MacDougall visited Lord & Taylor, the manager told him that Mrs. Drumple was a regular customer and had purchased Fleur d'Italie perfume.

"We confronted Wilbur, and when he confessed, Peter had a messenger from the Devonshire get the police. They arrested him, then his mother at her residence. They are in separate cells awaiting their judgment.

"And may I add—truth wins." Allie glanced at the grandfather clock standing next to the sideboard. It was a quarter to nine. She sipped her creamy coffee. Life was risky. Why not make the most significant risk of all—her heart?

"Miss Allie, are you all right?" Molly patted Allie's hand.

"Yes, Molly, I'm all right, just tired. And relieved this ordeal is over."

Clara took another sip of her coffee. "Last night, while you and Peter were at the Devonshire, I sat with Molly and explained that her Mr. Diamond's intentions were less than honorable and she must find her way. I offered her work at the Baldwin hospital, setting up a playroom for children and then working with them."

"How does that sound to you, Molly?" Allie asked.

Molly jumped up and threw her arms around Allie, then Clara, in a hug. "The best ever. Meeting this family has changed my life. Thank you for the soft bed in such a lovely room last night. Thanking you for everything is not enough."

"Allie, I have a suggestion for Molly's living quarters. Do you remember how your cousin Louise needed help with the baby? Well, if you ask your cousin Frederick to provide a suite in his hotel, Molly could help Louise with the baby in return," Clara said.

"I love the suggestion, Mama. I'll send a note to him right away."

"This is quite the perfect family," Mia said, pouring a spoonful of honey into her tea. "Changing the subject, Allie, how are Frankie and her mother doing?"

"I don't know how they're doing. I'll be stopping by later today to let them know what's happened with the music box fiend. Frankie and her mother are trying to improve their relationship, so I would say they are on the mend."

"Who's on the mend?" Adam strolled into the dining room, straightening his tie.

"Frankie and her mother," Allie said.

"Oh."

"Whatever is wrong with you, Adam?" Emma said, taking a bite of jam-drenched toast.

"Nothing. Any strawberry jam left? Oh, I see it all landed on Emma's toast."

Ava giggled. Emma stuck her tongue out.

"Children!" Clara said.

Adam plopped down beside Allie, gave her a sideways hug, and poured himself a cup of coffee.

"Well, dear Allie Cat, have you thought of your next adventure yet?"

"No, I haven't, but I can hardly wait."

"Room for one more?" said a deep male voice from the doorway.

"Peter," the family said in unison.

Joseph waved him in. "Have a seat and join us, my good man."

"I would love to, but I was hoping to speak with Allie privately."

Silence. How odd that her boisterous family had suddenly lost their voices.

She stood, smoothing down her curls. Rain was on its way if her unruly hair was any sign.

"Would you like to talk in the parlor?" Allie asked.

"How about a walk in the park?"

"All right. Can Captyn come along?"

"I got his leash from Barnes," he said, holding it up.

Allie's eyebrows arched. "Pretty confident that I would go for a walk with you if Captyn came along."

Peter laughed. "I guess so."

Allie glanced around the table. Her family watched the exchange like they were at opening night on Broadway.

Her father's shoulders shook. He coughed and covered his mouth with his hand. Not a cough exactly, more like a suppressed laugh. Allie's eyes narrowed. Clara laid her hand over her husband's and whispered something in his ear. He cleared his throat and nodded. Allie loved their secret language.

"We'll be back soon," Allie said.

"Take your time." Her father smiled, and the chatter resumed around the table. Allie smiled back. How thankful she was for her family. Thanksgiving was just a week away, heralding a month of celebrations. The family planned to spend the holidays at Baldwin Manor for some needed relaxation, but she couldn't leave without talking to Peter.

"Shall we, Peter?"

He took her hand and looped it into his arm. They walked to the vestibule where Barnes handed Peter his hat and coat and helped Allie into hers.

Allie grabbed her umbrella. "Best we take this," she said. "It may rain."

They stepped into the brisk air, held hands, and ran across to the park, beating an oncoming trolley. All the colored leaves, now brown and crumbled, were off their branches and blown around on the ground. They made their way to one of the walking paths at Central Park. "Let's sit on our favorite bench." Peter pulled a handkerchief from his breast pocket and dusted leaves off the seat before they sat.

Peter was holding onto Captyn's leash. "Unleash the hound?"

She patted Captyn on his head and took off his leash. Captyn loped up to the closest tree, sniffed, and marked his territory. Lifting his head, he spotted a squirrel and disappeared into the foliage.

"I have something to tell—"

"I wanted to say—"

Peter took both her hands in his, and they laughed together, speaking at the same time.

He took a deep breath. "Ladies first."

"Thank you for everything you have done for me—us—my family."

"You're welcome. It's good you are well and that all is well . . . I sound like an idiot." Peter stood and paced. "Ah, damn." He sat back down on the bench. Allie gaped at him, her eyes wide.

CHAPTER 46

$\mathcal{P}$eter took out a small, blue, velvet box from his pocket, blew out a breath, and said in a rush, "Allie, will you . . .?"

"No!" She stood and knocked him over, rushing past him.

"What the . . .?" He stood.

"Captyn, stop!"

Allie ran after Captyn, who was chasing after a kitten. "Captyn, leave that kitty alone."

The scruffy, gray kitten scampered up a tree and crouched on a branch. Lifting a tiny paw, it hissed.

Captyn managed a few leaps at the sturdy limb while barking.

"Bad dog," Allie said.

Peter ran to the tree, reached up, and grabbed the kitten by the scruff, earning himself a scratch for his troubles. He handed the kitten to Allie, who cooed and soothed the creature. Peter yanked his handkerchief from a pocket and dabbed at the blood on his hand.

Captyn whined at his mistress's affections turned to his new archenemy.

"C'mon, boy. Let's get you back on your leash."

They walked back to the bench after setting the kitten free again.

Peter reached into his pocket for the little velvet box and realized he'd dropped it. Crouching on his knees, he searched for it. Hearing Captyn chewing on something, he turned and spied the box in his mouth.

"Captyn, no!" He snatched the drool-covered box from Captyn and wiped it on his jacket. Lifting the lid, he sighed in relief. Inside was a single, perfect emerald surrounded by glittering diamonds.

Allie's lip trembled. She inhaled. Her smile crinkled her eyes. "It's beautiful."

"My mother bequeathed her ring to me for my future wife. She would have loved you."

Peter held her gaze. "Allie, you have stolen my heart. I love your warm hand in mine and the brush of your hair against my cheek. Loving you is my path to a fulfilled life. Nothing would please me more than if you considered a betrothal."

"Oh, Peter, that's beautiful. I have a tender place here for you," she said, her hand over her heart. "Love, perhaps. I don't know how that's supposed to feel. Yes, a betrothal is a possibility. I must have your answer to my question first."

"I'm listening."

"For my suffrage work, I may have to travel to spread the word. The possibility of trouble exists. I'm asking if you will permit me the freedom to make my own decisions."

"That's a hard question. The effort will take you away from me, from raising a family, from being available for social events, for my business that I'm not ready to leave. Please, will you give up on a quest for something I think will never happen?"

~

314

Saddened, tears welled up in her eyes, but Allie held on. He would not be privy to her tears.

You won't see my heartbreak.

"Then no. I cannot give up on the work. I'm sorry, Peter."

She rose, grabbed Captyn's leash, and ran out of the park, tears running down her face. They crossed the trolley tracks, forgetting to look both ways, the beating of her heart clanging in her ears like the oncoming trolley's warning bell, and ran into the empty, quiet courtyard at home. She sat on the garden bench for a moment to catch her breath, then took the elevator, unlocked the apartment door, and ran up the stairs to her room. Captyn lay down beside the bed while she cried into her pillow.

The knock on her door was whisper soft, then two heads poked in. "Allie, can we come in? We saw you and Captyn run past the parlor. What happened?"

"Frankie, Mia..." Allie broke down, fell on Frankie's shoulder, and bawled. Mia rubbed Allie's back.

"It's all right, sis. Cry it out," Mia said in a soft voice.

"Thanks for your shoulder, Frankie. You both know I have been falling in love with Peter. I cannot imagine living without him. He proposed, well, sort of. But I need to be independent and strong. That's why leaving him hurts more than I ever expected."

"You said no?" Frankie asked.

"He's not willing to grant me the freedom to work for suffrage. The women's vote is primary, and with that comes freedom of choice and citizenship. Women deserve the same rights as men."

Mia shook her head. "Allie, come on, stop lecturing and be serious."

"I am serious. Listen to me, both of you, and think about the importance of this fight. How can I walk away from pushing for that dream? I want the vote to happen in my lifetime. Each day brings it closer to fruition. This battle is not only for me but for our daughters, your daughters, and all future daughters."

Frankie shook Allie's shoulders. "But at the moment, please reconsider. You best give this man some consideration. Peter's genuine, a prince, a gentleman. At least talk to him again."

CHAPTER 47

*H*aving overslept, Peter grabbed his morning wakeup, climbed aboard a Hackney on the corner, and asked the driver to hasten to the Sandanko. His watch read ten. He shoved it back into his vest pocket. Damn woman, the day was half over for Allie. She'd never be home at this hour.

"Hello, Mister Harrison. I presume you are here for Miss Baldwin?"

"You are correct, Barnes. I assume she's not available?"

"Miss Baldwin is indisposed at the moment. Is there anything I can do for you?"

Indisposed? Why that excuse?

"I'm returning the umbrella she left behind yesterday. But I would like to walk her dog if that's possible."

"Captyn would be pleased, I'm sure. He's in the breakfast room sniffing for goodies. Shall I give him a shout?"

"By all means."

One call and Captyn came prancing into the vestibule and sidled up to Peter. Peter slip-knotted the leash onto the dog's collar and off they went into the park. Peter strolled to the bench where he and Allie had their last encounter. Peter sat and played with Captyn's ear. Children playing nearby stopped.

"Can we pet him?"

"Sure, he's friendly, and he loves to play."

A small hand petted his head. Captyn turned and licked the hand.

The child giggled and skipped off, squealing into the wooded area with her friends.

Peter smiled, and he breathed in the fall's floral fragrances, the crispness of the air reminding him that winter was on the cusp. The Baldwin family treated him as though he was a family member, and yesterday they smiled and laughed watching Allie and Peter arrange a simple walk in the park with the Great Dane. How joyful it would be to take part in their family gatherings. He was pleased that Allie would come to him if he agreed to her terms, but sad with so much at stake. Could one be glad and sad at the same time? It was all so confusing. Could you love and hate the same person? This situation was an enigma. He must find Allie and tell her how much he wanted her. Perhaps she would change her mind. But then again, maybe she wouldn't.

"Captyn, come. Let's go for a walk."

BARNES KNOCKED ON ALLIE'S BEDROOM DOOR. "YES, WHAT IS IT?"

"Mister Harrison was here to see you. In place of your presence, he took Captyn for a walk in the park, of course."

"Thank you, Barnes." She stood on her tippy-toes and kissed his cheek. "You have no idea how wonderful you are."

Allie stopped in Mia's room, explained, and hugged her. "Please tell Frankie where I went and pray for me. I'll see you later." She got her wrap from the hall tree in the vestibule, took the elevator down, and ran out into the sunshine. She looked both ways and was about to race across the tracks. The trolley was so close she could almost see the conductor's mouth moving as he clanged his bell, and the screeching of the trolley's brakes was deafening.

She stopped. The trolley stopped, and she waved to the man who was shaking his finger at her. She mouthed "I'm sorry" and carried on running into the park like the clock had struck twelve at Cinderella's ball. She crashed into Peter— "Oomph" catching her breath and falling on her derriere.

"Oh, no!" she managed to pant out.

Captyn, dragging his leash along, sat beside Allie, giving her his paw. She picked up his leash and held on. Tears trickled down her face. Peter kneeled on one knee in front of her and wiped her tears away with his thumb. "Allie, please, I'm yours."

Allie placed her hand on Peter's cheek and gazed into his eyes. "I'm falling in love with you, you big oaf." She raised a finger. "Not because of your military training, but because you are a man of virtue," she said in a lyrical voice.

"Do not make sacrifices. Your goals are noble. Don't change them. Stay your lovely self. I do not want to live without you, Allie. Not only will I stand by your side and support you in your work, but I will also share in the upbringing of our children."

Allie looked around, surrounded by the crumbled leaves that cushioned her fall.

"We are making a habit of this," she said with a grin.

Peter laughed, on both knees now on the ground beside Allie. He gathered her in his arms and kissed her. She pushed Captyn away when he tried to nuzzle between them.

"Stop it, Captyn. Go chase a squirrel." She dropped his leash, and off he went following the first squirrel he saw, only to return shortly, hanging his head, holding the leash in his mouth.

The air smelled fresh and crisp, like it only could in New York, the weather in November changing minute to minute. In the distance they could hear the dull sounds of traffic, the bells of the trolleys, and the horns of tugboats on the Hudson River not far from the park.

Peter closed his eyes for a moment, held out his hand for hers, and together they stood. He took the box from his pocket —again. Allie held out her hand, her finger ready for his gift of betrothal. Peter slipped the ring on. It fit perfect perfectly. She gazed into his eyes. He bent and kissed her.

"You are truly unforgettable, Miss Baldwin!"

They took Captyn's leash from his mouth, and the three walked home.

EPILOGUE

Two years later

The morning sun filtered through the trees at the Harrison Estate on a hot and hazy July day. The intermingling aromas from the lake's mist and weeping white pines permeated Allie's senses. She had hoped the swaying carriage would lull the babies to sleep, but the three-month-old twins wailed like a chorus of baby seals. Allie reached the beach with the infants' cries vibrating in her ears.

A squirrel darted by the carriage, stirring Captyn up. Away he went after his favorite mammal. Captyn barked, left the pursuit, and leapt into the water. Allie lost track of him while calming the babies.

Peter caught up with Allie. She stood on tippy-toes and kissed him. They headed to a wrought iron bench sheltered by the canopy of an old tree. Allie and Peter sat on the bench waiting for their wayward dog to return from his frolicking.

Samantha, out for a walk with her three daughters, came upon Allie and Peter.

"Well, good morning. You are up early. Sleep is not easy anymore, is it?"

"Morning, Samantha," Allie said, sighing. She patted Amy and Noah's blanket in the double pram. "Take a peek at two sleeping infants. A miracle!"

Peter stood, smiled, and hugged his stepmother. "The quiet is so noisy," he laughed.

"We'll catch a nap later. We are just waiting for our wayward dog. He went for a swim."

Dolly peeked in the carriage. Puzzled, she looked up at her aunt and uncle. "Do you mix them up?"

"We do sometimes. Amy's hat is pink, Noah's blue," Peter said.

Dolly put her fingers in her mouth and smiled. "Oh, that's so smart."

"Hello there," Thomas said. "A party's going on here. What am I missing?"

"Look, Miss Allie." Betsy pointed. "Here comes Captyn. He's dripping wet." She giggled along with Carol and Dolly.

Captyn plopped down by Allie's feet. She patted his head, and he licked her hand.

Thomas looked at his son. "I'm curious. How are you at changing diapers?"

Peter chuckled. "Pretty expert. Tough folding the darn things, but once I caught on, Allie put me in charge."

"He's terrific at it, but he prefers changing Amy," Allie offered.

Thomas nodded as if in agreement. "Oh, why's that?"

Peter laughed. "That question is for me, and I'd rather not say."

Looking at his son, Thomas prodded. "Come on, old man. What's the scoop?"

Peter looked down, then lifted his head. "Oh, all right. I cannot tell when a boy has to pee. Allie is faster than me, so she diapers Noah. Does that make me a coward?"

Thomas chuckled, and everyone laughed. "Thanks for the snigger," Peter said.

Peter rubbed his chin and grinned. "It's big news I can change a diaper. Do you know men with that talent?"

He slapped his son on the back. "Confession—I never changed a diaper."

"Pop, you don't know what you're missing. You can change Amy's anytime."

"Humph, I can hardly wait." He smiled and put his arm around his son. "What's happening at the office?"

"I partnered with Johnny, who still works at the newspaper. My man O'Malley runs the agency."

"How is the business doing with Johnny at the helm?" his father asked.

"Excellent. I retired soon after the babies were born."

"Congratulations." He slapped Peter's back.

"Allie received accolades for her weekly Woman's Suffrage column and recently won an award from the National American Woman Suffrage Association. She's a leading suffragist."

Amy fussed. Peter rocked the carriage. "Uh-oh, Noah will fuss too. Forgive us. We're off to get some sleep. See you later."

Samantha nodded. "I remember those days."

The nursemaid had finally arrived to relieve the tired parents. The babies usually slept through the night, but if one hollered, the chorus began—when Allie and Peter were in their deep sleep. They already hired a nursemaid for their New York residence.

Their future might include house renovations with Mama heading up the project with Mia, Emma, and Ava as her assistants, along with opinions from Allie and Peter.

During her pregnancy, Allie partnered with Annette to write

her column and stay on as her assistant. They became known across the states as the *Sentinel* dynamo duo.

Allie never dreamed marrying Peter would change her view of love and marriage. According to the ladies of the New York Society, women needed to marry to find happiness. Marrying gave her more than happiness. Peter was her partner, her soulmate.

The End

THANK YOU

Dear Reader,
Thank you for reading *The Unforgettable Miss Baldwin*.
I'd be eternally grateful if you took a moment to
<u>Leave a review (or rating) on Amazon.</u>
When you leave a review, it helps other readers find my books.
Your review would make my day. Thank you!
All the best,
Gail Ingis

ABOUT THE AUTHOR

 Gail Ingis is the author of two historical romance novels, *The Memorable Mrs. Dempsey* (formerly *Indigo Sky*) and *The Unforgettable Miss Baldwin*. Brooklyn born, look for her forthcoming memoir. She is a retired member of the American Society of Interior Designers (ASID). Gail founded the Interior Design Institute (IDI) in 1981 and later merged it with Berkeley College. Besides her design work, she served the academic community as a professor in the arts, interior design, and history of architecture and design. She taught at IDI, the New York School of Interior Design, and several universities in the New York tri-state area. Her award-winning art has appeared in the New York Times and other publications. Gail is a noted art juror, primarily for Lockwood Mathews Mansion Museum, a USA Today award-winning museum in Norwalk, Connecticut, where she serves as trustee and art curator. She lives in Connecticut with her handsome husband. Together their favorite activities are tennis, gardening, Masterpiece Theatre, and Costco. Between them, the happy parents have five remarkably well-bred grown children, fifteen grandchildren and two perfectly gorgeous great-grandchildren (and counting).

Check out Gail's website at <u>gailingis.com</u>, where you'll find Gail's blog featuring a cornucopia of more than 500 articles about books, writing, art, food, family, humor, life, and more.

You can follow Gail on: